Praise for *Dry Bones* and the Longmire series

"The [Longmire] series continues to be fresh and innovative. In *Dry Bones*, Johnson accomplishes this through a 'sixty-five-million-year-old cold case' with current social and political implications, as well as via vibrantly complex characters. Devoted series fans won't feel a sense of déjà vu in *Dry Bones*, but they will easily identify Johnson's tendency toward innovative imagery ('my brain felt like it was bouncing around like a sneaker inside a washing machine'), crack dialogue, humor, and a strong sense of place. Absaroka's maker brings dem bones to life, and readers are sure to rejoice."   —*Shelf Awareness*

"Yet another classic Craig Johnson mystery."   —*Deseret News*

"[Walt Longmire] remains tough, smart, honest, and capable of entertaining fans with another difficult, dangerous case."   —*Kirkus Reviews*

"It's the scenery—and the big guy standing in front of the scenery—that keeps us coming back to Craig Johnson's lean and leathery mysteries."   —*The New York Times Book Review*

"Like the greatest crime novelists, Johnson is a student of human nature. Walt Longmire is strong but fallible, a man whose devil-may-care stoicism masks a heightened sensitivity to the horrors he's witnessed."   —*Los Angeles Times*

"Johnson's hero only gets better—both at solving cases and at hooking readers—with age."   —*Publishers Weekly*

"Johnson's trademarks [are] great characters, witty banter, serious sleuthing, and a love of Wyoming bigger than a stack of derelict cars."   —*The Boston Globe*

"Johnson's pacing is tight and his dialogue snaps."   —*Entertainment Weekly*

"Stepping into Walt's world is like slipping on a favorite pair of slippers, and it's where those slippers lead that provides a thrill. Johnson pens a series that should become a 'must' read, so curl up, get comfortable, and enjoy the ride."   —*The Denver Post*

PENGUIN BOOKS

DRY BONES

Craig Johnson is the *New York Times* bestselling author of the Longmire mysteries, the basis for the hit Netflix original series *Longmire*. He is the recipient of the Western Writers of America Spur Award for fiction, and his novella, *Spirit of Steamboat*, was the first One Book Wyoming selection. He lives in Ucross, Wyoming, population twenty-five.

By Craig Johnson

CRAIG JOHNSON

DRY BONES

PENGUIN BOOKS

PENGUIN BOOKS

An imprint of Penguin Random House LLC

375 Hudson Street

New York, New York 10014

penguin.com

First published in the United States of America by Viking,
an imprint of Penguin Random House LLC, 2015
Published in Penguin Books 2016

THE LIBRARY OF CONGRESS HAS CATALOGED THE HARDCOVER EDITION AS FOLLOWS:

Johnson, Craig, 1961–

Dry bones : a Walt Longmire mystery / Craig Johnson.

pages ; cm

ISBN 9780525426936 (hc.)

ISBN 9780143108184 (pbk.)

1. Longmire, Walt (Fictitious character)—Fiction. 2. Sheriffs—Fiction. 3. Wyoming—Fiction. I. Title.

PS3610.O325D79 2015

813'.6—dc23   2015001102

Printed in the United States of America
11th Printing

Set in Dante MT Std
Designed by Cassandra Garruzzo

For Joe Tuck,
because Heaven needs drivers,
and the Lord likes to keep his blacksmiths close . . .

Them bones, them bones gonna walk around
Them bones, them bones gonna walk around
Them bones, them bones gonna walk around
Now hear the word of the Lord

Disconnect them bones, them dry bones
Disconnect them bones, them dry bones
Disconnect them bones, them dry bones
Now hear the word of the Lord

ACKNOWLEDGMENTS

I was wandering through the Natural History Museum in London with my granddaughter when we stumbled onto a *T. rex*—from all places, Wyoming. I asked my friend paleontologist Bill Matteson and he informed me that the majority of *Tyrannosauri* populating the museums of the world were from around our area, here in the Northern Rockies.

I vaguely remembered a situation in the '80s that had escalated among the Black Hills Institute of Geological Research, an Indian rancher, his tribe, and the FBI over the largest, most intact *T. rex* fossil that had ever been found—all of which seemed rife for a Walt Longmire mystery.

Attacking the subject with half-remembered scenarios and forty-year-old public school science would've been a mistake, so I jumped into the dig with both feet, reading as much as I could about the creature itself, the history of the dinosaur wars here in Wyoming, and finally the titanic cluster that took place right across the border in South Dakota. Many books, including Peter Larson and Kristin Donnan's *Rex Appeal* and Steve Fiffer's *Tyrannosaurus SUE* were essential to understanding what had happened in the tiny town of Hill City, South Dakota, along with the marvelous documentary, *Dinosaur 13*.

Two more fabulous sources, which convinced me how little I knew about dinosaurs, were Robert T. Bakker's *The Dinosaur Heresies* and Peter Larson and Kenneth Carpenter's *Tyrannosaurus rex: The Tyrant King*.

To dig up a good story you need a team and mine starts with Gail "Hylaeosaurus" Hochman, and Marianne "Mosasaur" Merola at the office in Times Square, one of the most unpredictable hunting grounds in the world. Down island in the West Village epoch reside the fiercely loyal Kathryn "Carnotaurus" Court and her hunting partner Lindsey "Stegosaurus" Schwoeri. Barbara "Compsognathus" Campo reads the fossil imprints and Victoria "Spinosaurus" Savanh handles the details, both large and small. Carolyn "Conchoraptor" Coleburn keeps an eye to the horizon while Ben "Parasaurolophus" Petrone and Angie "Megalodon" Messina keep the herd moving in the right direction and away from extinction.

There's always a big thanks to Marcus "Rhabdodon" Red Thunder.

Then there's Judy "Tyrannosaurus rex" Johnson, who makes my cold blood run warm.

DRY BONES

1

She was close to thirty years old when she was killed.

A big girl, she liked to carouse with the boys at the local watering holes, which of course led to a lot of illegitimate children, but by all accounts, she was a pretty good single parent and could take care of herself and her brood. One night, though, a gang must have jumped her; they were all younger than she was, they had numbers, they might've even been family, and after they broke her leg and she was on the ground, it was pretty much over.

There was no funeral. They killed her and left what remained there by the water, where the sediment from the forgotten creek built up around her, layer after layer, compressing and compacting her to the point where the bones leeched away and were replaced by minerals.

It was as if she'd turned to stone just to keep from being forgotten.

It's interesting how her remains were found; her namesake, Jennifer Watt, was traveling with Dave Baumann, the director of the High Plains Dinosaur Museum, when they got a flat—not an unusual occurrence on the red roads the ranchers used for the more inaccessible areas of their ranches where the larger chunks of shale attacked sidewalls like tomahawks. The bigger rock is cheaper, but it's also the size of bricks and has lots of sharp edges, edges that like to make meals of anything less than ten-ply.

Dave had been trying to squeak another season out of the tires on the '67 Land Rover, but there they stood, staring at a right rear with a distinct lack of round, in the middle of the Lone Elk Ranch. While he fished the jack and spare from the hood and began the arduous task of replacing the tire, Jennifer unloaded Brody, her Tibetan mastiff, and went for a walk. Hoping to meet a friend on the place, she followed a ridge around a cornice, but the dog, who was 150 pounds with a heavy coat, began panting. Before long Jen decided that it might be a pretty good idea for the two of them to try and get to some shade, not an easy proposition out on the Powder River country; luckily, there was a rock overhang along the ridge with plenty enough room for her and the dog to get out of the late afternoon sun.

She wore her blonde hair in a ponytail that stuck through the adjustment strap of her Hole-in-the-Wall Bar ball cap, and, pulling the collapsible dog bowl from her pack, she slipped out a Nalgene bottle, took a swig, and then poured the mastiff a drink.

Jennifer looked out onto the grass that undulated like a gigantic, rolling sea. It was easy to imagine the Western Interior (Cretaceous) Seaway or the Niobraran Sea that had once covered this land, splitting the continent of North America into two landmasses, Laramidia to the west and Appalachia to the east. The great sea had stretched from Mexico to the Arctic and had been over two thousand feet deep. Jen settled under the rock and petted the dog, her green eyes scanning the landscape.

She pulled her video camera from her pack and panned the distance, seeing things out there on the high plains, things that didn't exist, at least not anymore—predatory marine reptiles like long-necked plesiosaurs and more alligator-like mosasaurs almost eighty feet long. Sharks such as Squalicorax swam through her imagination along with giant, shellfish-eating Ptychodus mortoni.

When she'd been six, her father had brought her to this country from Tucson, Arizona, and had dragged her along on his private excavations that helped support his rock shop on the old highway out near Lake DeSmet between Durant and Sheridan. She still remembered what she'd said one day as they'd gotten out of his battered pickup, her fingers climbing up his pant leg until she found the reassuring hand with gloves worn like saddle leather, the adjustment straps with the transparent red beads. "There's nothing out here, Daddy."

He surveyed the rolling hills that led from the Bighorn Mountains to the endless Powder River country, smiled as he pushed back his straw hat, and spoke gently to her. "There's everything here; you just have to know where to look."

Jennifer had learned to look and had never stopped; Dave Baumann's hands and hers were in the excavations that had led to the displays that crowded the High Plains Dinosaur Museum in Durant, and at twenty-six, she was still searching.

Truth be told, Jen liked dead things better than live ones—they were less trouble, the conversations being one-sided. A lot of investigators and paleontologists are more comfortable that way, able to accept the consensus of truth, disregarding the absolute as something that always carries the danger of being overturned by some new and extraordinary piece of evidence.

She lowered the camera, took another sip of water, and poured her dog more. Brody sighed and shook his massive head, and Jen leaned back under the rock overhang to try to decide what she was going to do with the old man's rock shop, a ramshackle affair near the lake that had started out as a trailer but through the years had evolved into a labyrinth of wooden fences lined with geodes, gems, quartz, and rock samples, most of them worthless.

He had died the year before, and she knew the land was more valuable than the structure itself, but she'd grown up there and loved the old place, as cluttered and tacky as it might be. She pulled the cap over her eyes and dozed until she became aware of a protracted growl in her dog's throat. She swatted at him, but he continued to rumble a warning until she finally lifted the bill of her cap to look at him. He was looking directly up. Jen's eyes followed to where a two-fingered talon stretched out of the rock ceiling down toward her, almost as if it were imploring. She grabbed the camera and began to film what would become one of the greatest paleontological discoveries in modern times.

Victoria Moretti sipped the coffee from the chrome lid of my thermos, leaned forward, and, peering through the windshield, watched the man with an intensity that only her tarnished gold eyes could command. "Is that some weird-ass Wyoming fishing technique I don't know about?"

I could see that Omar was tossing something into the water from the banks of the man-made reservoir.

"What the hell is he doing?"

Ruby, my dispatcher, had received a call from him early in the morning and had bushwhacked Dog and me with it when we came in the door. I had filled up my thermos and in turn bushwhacked Vic before heading out to the ten-thousand-acre Lone Elk place to find out what was up.

Outdoor adventurer, outfitter, and big-game bon vivant, Omar Rhoades had contracts with all the big ranchers and sometimes used their property for extended hunting and fishing junkets. Usually he kept his spots secret, but this time he'd told Ruby where he was and that I might want to come out and meet him.

Most everything was in bloom in late May, and I breathed in the scents from the open windows of my truck. As I stared at the aspens and cottonwood, they all began stretching to the sky like those cypresses in Italy that looked like thumb smudges.

My undersheriff turned and looked at me some more. "I thought he was in China."

"Mongolia."

The Custer look-alike was dressed in a state-of-the-art fishing vest, waders, and his ever-present black cowboy hat with more flies stuck in it than Orvis has in its catalog. All in all, I estimated the total worth of his outfit at somewhere close to two thousand dollars, and he wasn't even carrying the fly rod, which was sticking out the rear of his custom-made SUV that dwarfed my three-quarter-ton.

I leaned forward and stared through the windshield. We watched as he drew something from one hand, carefully took aim, and tossed whatever it was onto the smooth surface of the water, black like an oil slick.

Vic turned to look at me as she reached back and scratched the fur behind Dog's ear. "Do you think he's finally lost it?"

I pulled the handle and climbed out of the truck, careful to keep the Saint Bernard/German shepherd/plains grizzly inside. "Let's go find out."

The beauty of Italian descent followed with my thermos as we glided our way through the morning dew in the buffalo grass. "You know, the landed gentry get like this when they spend too much time alone."

I whispered over my shoulder, "Like what?"

"Fucking nuts." She increased her pace and caught up with me. "He's not armed, is he?"

"If he were, I don't think he'd be throwing rocks." I stopped at the worn path surrounding the reservoir, curious, but still attempting to abide by the protocol of the high plains angler so as to not upset the fishing—if, in fact, that was what he was doing.

"Hey, Omar."

He started, just visibly, and spoke to us over his shoulder as he continued throwing pebbles into the water. "Walt. Vic."

"What are you doing?"

He glanced at us but then tossed another stone. "Trying to keep those snapping turtles off that body out there."

We tiptoed to the edge of the bank in an attempt to keep the water from seeping into our boots, and Vic and I joined Omar in his target practice, Vic showing her acumen by bouncing a flat stone off the shell of a small turtle that skittered and swam into the depths. "Any idea who it is?"

Omar leaned forward and lifted his Oakley Radarlock yellow-tinted shooting glasses to peer into the reflective surface of the water at the half-submerged body. "I'm thinking it's Danny."

I stared at the corpse, which was a good forty feet from the bank, and tried to figure out how we were going to retrieve it, in that we had no boat. "Himself?"

My undersheriff squinted. "How can you tell?"

"Not everybody has hair like that." Omar nailed a big turtle that had risen beside the body like a surfacing submarine and had gotten caught in the mass of silver locks that had fanned out from the body. "Danny always had nice hair."

Omar reached behind him and, pulling out a fancy, stainless steel thermos of his own, poured the tomato-red contents into a cut-glass double-old-fashioned tumbler. "Libation?"

She stared at him, one hand on her hip. "It's eight o'clock in the morning."

He shrugged and sipped. "Sun's over the yardarm somewhere."

Omar and I watched as Vic expertly skipped a pebble across the glossy surface of the water, the pellet deflecting off another turtle. "How many turtles are there in this damn thing, anyway?"

Omar grunted. "Danny and his brother Enic protect them; nobody is allowed to hurt them—they're sacred to the Crow and the Northern Cheyenne."

Vic shook her head and nailed another. "Is there any living thing that isn't sacred to the Crow and the Northern Cheyenne?"

I tossed a stone but missed. "Nope."

Omar sipped from his Bloody Mary. "They're a totem for fertility, protection, and patience." He turned to look at me. "How are your daughter and granddaughter?"

There was a silence as I formulated an answer, but before I could speak, Vic chimed in. "Excuse me, but did I miss a transition in the conversation here?"

I tapped my shoulder. "Cady's got a tattoo of a turtle—reminiscent of her willful youth at Berkeley." I glanced back at him. "Should be here the day after tomorrow."

He nodded. "Lookin' forward to meeting Lola."

I smiled and picked up my thermos. "Any ideas on how we get him out of there?" I glanced at the big-game hunter. "You've got your waders on."

He shook his head. "Oh, no. The bank drops off ten feet out, and the reservoir is about sixty feet deep—used to be a shale pit."

I nodded and drank some coffee as Omar refilled his glass and Vic tossed a rock, this time missing her shelled target but causing it to duck its head and silently retreat into the depths. "Can I assume that nine-thousand-dollar Oyster fly rod of yours will do the trick?"

Vic crouched at an inlet on the other side of the pond. "I'm trying to resist saying something about the ironic aspect of a guy who protects the turtles but then falls in his own pond and becomes snapper chow."

"We don't know it's him."

"Sure we do." She held up a paper bag. "I found his lunch, and it's got his name on it." She read, "Daddy-O."

"Topflight detecting, that's what that is." I watched as Omar flipped the fly rod back and forth, trailing the line in cyclical patterns, reflecting in the morning sunshine. "Think you can get him on the first try?"

He ignored my crass remark and flipped the fly forward, yanking it back to set the hook in what appeared to be the sleeve of a green canvas shirt. The outdoorsman carefully walked the banks and reeled in the body as we watched who we assumed was Danny Lone Elk spin slowly with his one arm extended like a superhero in flight, a trail of disappointed turtles in his wake.

As the body came alongside the bank, I reached in, grabbed it by the collar, and dragged the upper part of him onto the grass. "He weighs a ton."

"Lungs are probably full of water." Vic leaned over and

grabbed the other side of his collar and we both heaved the deadweight onto the bank, a forty-pound snapping turtle with a carapace the size of a washbasin attached to the dead man's left hand.

Vic dropped her side and backed away from the radially set iridescent eyes, the color not unlike her own. "What the fuck?"

The aquatic monster released the dead man's hand, hissed like a steam train, and extended its neck toward us, evidently not willing to give up its breakfast.

Vic drew her sidearm, but I pushed it away. "Don't. It doesn't mean any harm."

"The hell it doesn't; look at him." She considered. "I've shot people for less than that shit."

I kneeled down, and the beast stretched out its neck even further and struck at me with snakelike speed, the reach surprisingly far. "You know these things are seventy million years old?"

Vic reluctantly holstered her weapon. "This one in particular?"

"They appeared before the dinosaurs died out." I picked up a stick and extended the end toward the animal's open mouth. "See the little wiggly red thing at the end of its tongue?"

Vic raised her eyebrows. "What, that means he's popular with the ladies?"

"That's what he uses to ambush fish—they think it's a worm."

"That's disgusting."

I walked around it and raised its rear end, placing my hand underneath the plastron and lifting the creature, rather awkwardly, from the ground. Its head swiveled back, and it snapped with the sound of a small firecracker.

Both Omar and my undersheriff stepped back. "He's going to bite the shit out of you."

"No, they can't reach if you're holding them from the bottom." A stream of something dribbled down the length of my jeans onto my boot.

They studied me, Vic, of course, the first to speak. "Did that thing just piss on you?"

"I believe it did." I swung the big beast around, lowered it back into the water, and watched as the creature settled in the mud and looked back at me, apparently now in no great hurry to get away.

"I guess he likes you."

I shook the water from my hands and studied the round eyes that watched me warily. "Might be a female."

"Well, anytime you're through turtle diddling, we've got work to do." She approached the cadaver again and rolled the body over, looked at what remained of Danny Lone Elk's face, and immediately turned away. "Oh shit, his eyes are gone."

Omar kneeled by the dead man and turned his chin. "Critters always go for them first." He sighed. "Those turtles sure did a number on him." They both turned to look at me as I stared at the body. "Walt?"

It was a man I'd seen before, in my dreams.

"Walt?"

In the dreams, he also had no eyes.

"Walt."

The man's words came back, and it was almost as if he were standing beside me, repeating the mantra of warning I'd stowed away: *You will stand and see the good, but you will also stand and see the bad—the dead shall rise and the blind will see.*

"Walt."

I took a deep breath. "You're sure it's Danny?"

Omar nodded and looked back at the body. "His belt says Danny." He paused for a moment. "And I recognize what's left of him."

"Does he have a wallet or anything else on him, like a fishing license?"

Checking the pockets of the dead man, Omar shook his head. "Nothing, but he's on his own property. I don't carry my wallet with me when I'm fishing—always afraid I'll dunk it."

I glanced at Vic. "Did you check his lunch?"

"Might as well; I'm about to lose mine." She reached down, picked up the brown paper bag, and, rummaging through the sack, called out the items. "Daddy-O had one can of orange soda, one cheese sandwich, one bag of Lay's potato chips, an assortment of celery and carrot sticks, and . . ." She fumbled in the bag, finally pulling out a withered, handmade billfold. "One wallet."

"Is it Danny's?"

She held it up for us to look at. "Well, seeing as how it has DANNY engraved on the outside, I'd say yes." She opened it and studied the Wyoming driver's license and the face of the elderly Cheyenne man. "He liked putting his name on stuff, didn't he?"

Omar reached out and straightened the collar of the dead man's shirt. "He was a good old guy—let me bring clients out here whenever I wanted and even let me fly my helicopter into this place."

I glanced around. "Where is the ranch house from here?"

He ignored my question. "There's going to be trouble." He pointed. "The eyes—the medicine men will have to do something about this or Danny will wander the earth forever." He looked up, and I could see tears for his old friend. "Lost and blind."

I nodded, fishing my keys from my jeans so that we could load the man into the truck bed and take him to Doc Bloomfield and room 32, the Durant Memorial Hospital's ad hoc morgue. "I'll get in touch with the family, Henry, and the Cheyenne tribal elders." Walking back to my truck, I thought about my vision and what Virgil White Buffalo and the stranger had said—that stranger, the stranger with no eyes, who ended up being Danny Lone Elk.

The last time I'd seen Danny was at the Moose Lodge at the end of town. It had been a few years back, and he had still been drinking. I'd gotten a radio call that there was a disturbance, but by the time I'd gotten there, no one seemed to remember who had been involved in the altercation.

Asking why he was a Moose and not an Elk, I'd grabbed a Rainier for myself and joined him.

"They got a better bar down here."

He looked up at me and smiled. Lined with more wrinkles than a flophouse bed, the old man's face was cragged but still handsome and carried the wisdom of the ages. He reached over to squeeze my shoulder with a hand as large and spidery as a king crab.

Well into his cups, he spoke to me through clinched teeth;

Danny Lone Elk always talked as if what he had to say to you was a very important secret, and maybe it was. "You off duty, Sheriff?"

"End of watch. I came here looking for trouble, but there isn't any."

"Can I buy you a beer?"

I gestured with the full can. "Got one."

He closed one eye and looked at me. "You too good to drink with an Indian?"

"No. I—"

"'Cause you gotta have a reservation." He kept his eye on me like a spotlight, guffawed uproariously at his own joke, and then leaned in close. "You wanna know why they called you?" He gestured down the bar where a small contingency of men did their level best to ignore us. "You see that sharp-faced man with the ball cap? That fella in the cowboy hat beside him asked him what he was gonna do on his vacation and he said he was gonna go to Montana and go fishing. Well, cowboy hat told sharp-face he couldn't understand why he was going fishing in Montana 'cause there was nothing but a bunch of damned Indians up there." Danny sipped his beer and looked past me toward the men. "Then sharp-face asked cowboy hat what he was gonna do on his vacation and cowboy hat said he's goin' hunting down in Arizona and sharp-face said he couldn't understand why he was going hunting down in Arizona 'cause there was nothing but a bunch of damned Indians down there."

I nodded. "Was that all there was to it?"

"No." He grinned the secret smile again. "That was when I told them both to go to hell, 'cause there sure wasn't any Indians there."

His voice rose. "Bartender." He looked back at me, again smiling through the ill-fitting dentures. "I think that's when this guy called you."

The man approached somewhat warily. "Can I help you?"

He lip-pointed at sharp-face and cowboy hat. "Yeah; I think I better buy those guys down there a beer; I'm afraid I might've spooked 'em."

As the barkeep went about distributing the conciliatory beverages, Danny leaned in again. "I knew your daddy."

"Really?"

"Yeah, made the mistake of tryin' to get him to go to Indian church one time."

"Uh-oh."

"Yeah." He grinned again and nodded. "I was working down at Fort Keogh and lived out your way—had this wife that thought since your family lived so close we should go and invite them to go to church with us." He leaned in again. "Well, just my luck, your father answered the door, and boy did he give me an earful."

"I'm sorry; my mother was the religious one."

"He said he figured I was just tradin' one superstition for another."

I took a sip of my beer. "He wasn't a big one for churches."

"They still have that place out near Buffalo Creek?"

"I have it now—they've both passed."

He nodded. "I am sorry to hear that—they were good people." He was silent for a moment and looked down at his lap. "Do you ever see them?"

I turned and looked at him, thinking that I hadn't made myself clear. "They're dead."

He nodded again and then stared at the can in his hands. "Yeah, but do you ever see them?"

"Umm, I don't . . ."

"When I am alone, hunting or fishing . . ." He breathed a laugh. ". . . And that is the only time I'm alone, by the way . . ." He looked at me. ". . . I see my ancestors, the ones who have walked the Hanging Road to the Camp of the Dead. When I see them, they are far away but watching me like the eyes of the stars."

Not quite sure what to say to that, I nodded. "That's nice . . . that they're looking out for you."

"I don't know if that's what it is." He took out some antacids, shook a few of the chunky tablets into his hand, and washed them down with some beer. "Mmm, peppermint, my favorite." He started humming the theme to *Dragnet*, which was also the jingle for the pills. "Tum, tum, tum, tum . . ." Then he opened a prescription bottle that he took from the pocket of his shirt, shook out a few pills, and swallowed them, too. He looked at me blankly. "What was I talking about?"

"Family."

"Oh, right . . . I am old, and I know I am standing on the brink of the life nobody knows about, and I am anxious to go to my Father, *Ma-h ay oh*. To live again as men were intended to live, even on this world, but I fear for the remains of my family."

I knew that his ranch was vast and there had been talk of gas, oil, and fossil deposits, but I still couldn't understand Lone Elk's concerns. "You've got children, right? I'm sure your family will look after those things after you're gone, Danny."

It was a long time before he spoke again. "Maybe that's true, but I would take some things back if I could."

———

"I said . . ." My undersheriff raised an eyebrow and sighed, still holding her end of the now blanket-wrapped body. "Did you hear that?"

With Danny Lone Elk's voice still resonating in my head, I turned and looked around, fully expecting to see the man and his ancestors. "Hear what?"

She glanced at Omar, and then they both looked at me. "A gunshot."

I took a deep breath to clear my head and my ears. "Close?"

"What, you were having some kind of out-of-body experience?"

"No, I was just remembering when I had seen Danny last." I thought about adding more, but I hadn't shared my experiences in Custer Park with anyone. "Probably the hands who worked for Lone Elk, chasing off coyotes or plinking prairie dogs." I looked around. "Where was the shot?"

Vic looked toward the ridge. "Not far."

We hurried to get Danny loaded as quickly as we could, having decided to use Omar's massive SUV since it had better cover for the body than the open bed of the Bullet and, of all things, a slide-out game rack.

He gestured toward the passenger side. "Get in."

I glanced at my truck. "Maybe we'd better leave Danny in yours and take mine."

He shook his head. "This thing's faster—besides, it's bullet-proof."

Ushering Vic into the front, I climbed in the back and

gaped at the leather and burl-wood interior. "Omar, what the heck is this thing?"

He fired up the engine, slapped the transmission in gear, and tore up the two-track toward the ridge, the three of us thrown back into the butter-soft bucket seats. "A Conquest, Knight XV—it's handcrafted out of Toronto."

As we flew across the prairie, I glanced up through the skylight. "What does something like this set you back?"

He shrugged. "Couple hundred thousand, I don't know—the accountant said I needed to spend some money fast, so I did."

When we made the top of the ridge, Omar wheeled the glossy black fortress to the left and stopped; we rolled down the windows to listen but didn't hear anything. Vic leaned forward in the passenger seat and pointed down the valley. "There are some vehicles parked at the fence down there through a few cattle guards—you want to go check it out?"

Spinning the wheel, Omar drove down the slope to a better-maintained road and started off toward the area Vic had indicated.

She turned to look at me. "So, you know the deceased?"

Thinking it best to keep the visions to myself, I told her about the Moose Lodge encounter. "I had a couple of beers with him one time a few years ago." I could feel her looking at the side of my face as I looked out the tinted windows. "There was a disturbance at the bar and when I got there it had settled down, so I had a beer with him. He was worried about some things, so we talked. It took a while for me to remember him."

She nodded, not buying a word of it. "What was he worried about?"

"Nothing, getting old, the land, family, the usual stuff."

"He should've worried about learning to swim."

I recognized Dave Baumann's weathered, light-blue Land Rover, emblazoned with the logo of the High Plains Dinosaur Museum, driving at high speed toward us. He slid to a stop alongside Omar's rolling fortress. A quarter of a mile away, I could see another gate where two flatbeds were parked nose to nose blocking the entrance, with some people milling about; beyond that was a working backhoe.

I rolled down the window and was about to speak when the paleontologist began yelling to the young blonde-haired woman in the passenger seat. "They're using a backhoe!"

I stared at Dave, an athletic-looking fellow with glasses, curly light-brown hair and beard, blue eyes, and an easy smile that made him popular with the young female scientists who sometimes came to intern at the private museum—they called him Dino-Dave.

"Excuse me?"

He took a deep breath to calm himself and continued. "They're digging up one of the most valuable sites in recent history with a backhoe."

"I'm no expert." I sighed and glanced at both Vic and Omar. "But that's probably not good."

"No."

"Who's in charge here?"

"I am." He studied me and revised his statement. "What do you mean?"

I had been involved in these kinds of conflicts where the university, the colleges, the museums, and the landowners quibbled about the exact location of digs, and I liked to get the full story before mobilizing the troops. "Is this official or something more loosely structured?"

"It's a straight-ahead deal; I paid thirty-seven thousand dollars last year for the fossil remains."

I opened the door. "I guess we'd better go over and take a look. Why don't the two of you jump in here with us, Dave?" They did as I requested, and I thrust a hand toward the blonde. "Walt Longmire."

She didn't take my hand or return my smile. "Jennifer Watt." She raised her small video camera and began filming through Omar's windshield.

I shrugged and sat opposite the two of them—the behemoth vehicle had limousine-style rear seating—feeling like I was in some sort of executive conference room. "Tell me about the deal."

Dave leaned forward as Omar drove south. "It was the standard arrangement with the landowner and the HPDM— that we would search for fossils, and anything we found, we would share the profits."

Vic turned and looked at him. "I thought the museum was a nonprofit?"

He nodded. "It is at the end of the fiscal year, but when we first unearthed the jawbone last August and we needed more time, I thought we'd better cement a deal with the landowner." He pointed toward the backhoe. "Just to make sure that exactly this type of thing didn't happen." He paused for a moment and pointedly sniffed the air. "What's that smell?"

Vic threw a chin toward me. "Oh, the sheriff here got pissed on."

It was about then that a round from some sort of small

arms fire caromed off the cab, leaving a narrow but nasty gash on the windshield, and Dave ducked. "My God, they're shooting at us again!"

I stared at the groove as Omar yelled back over his shoulder, "Ballistic armor glass."

He hit the gas and barreled down the makeshift two-track toward the roadblock as I turned back to Dave. "They shot at you before?"

"You're damn right they did!"

Another ricochet and Omar fishtailed to the side and gunned it again, in hopes that if we made it closer to the parked vehicles the shooter might be less inclined to fire. We stopped in front of the two flatbeds.

Vic drew her Glock, but I held out a hand, rose up, and got out the other side, just as an Indian cowboy charged up the hillside to slap what looked to be a bolt-action .22 from the hands of a teenage boy.

I walked around both trucks with my hands raised, quickly covering the twenty yards between us. "All right, I'm not sure whose property we're on, but we need to stop the shooting right now."

With one last, hard look toward the kid, the Indian cowboy turned as another, older man in a black flat-brim hat joined him. "Sorry about that, Sheriff . . ."

The teenager interrupted. "You told me to stand guard and not let anybody in!"

The Indian cowboy picked up the rifle and threw it to the older man with the black hat as Vic and Dave joined us. "I didn't mean for you to shoot the sheriff."

"What's going on here?"

He smiled a wide grin. "Protecting our investments." He slapped the teen in the back of the head, knocking off his straw hat, and gestured toward Dave. "You can shoot Dave if you want to . . ." The kid actually reached for the rifle on the older man's shoulder. "Leave your uncle alone; I was kidding." He then threw the bearded paleontologist a glance. "Kind of."

I looked at where the bucket of the big CASE backhoe was scraping away the side of the hill. "You need to stop excavating. Dave here says that you're going to do irreparable damage to the dig."

The Indian cowboy lifted a hand and whipped off his own hat, raising it in a wide wave, his dark hair swooping around his head like a flight of crows. The sound of the heavy equipment halted almost immediately. He turned back to look at us, his perfect teeth contrasting with the tan skin of his handsome face as he extended his hand. "Randy Lone Elk, Sheriff. I don't think we've met." He gestured toward the older man holding the rifle. "This is my Uncle Enic." He lip-pointed toward the teenager. "And the All-American sniper here is Taylor, my nephew."

I shook the hand and gestured toward Baumann. "Dave here is concerned about the integrity of his site."

"*His* site, huh?" He continued grinning. "Then he doesn't know exactly where *his* site is." He spread his arms and half turned, exemplifying the open country. "We are trying to draw some attention, and I guess it worked." He gestured toward Dave. "These guys are attempting to get this fossil out of here before anybody could find out, but we're renegotiating the deal." He looked at me and then at Omar's vehicle. "What the hell is that thing, anyway?"

I ignored the question. "Dave here tells me that you've been compensated to the tune of thirty-seven thousand dollars on this dig."

Randy Lone Elk pointed a finger at Baumann's chest. "That's bullshit, and even if it wasn't, thirty-seven thousand dollars is a joke, if not an insult."

The paleontologist spoke up. "It's a fair price for what we've uncovered so far, more than anyone has ever been compensated . . . And there's the profit sharing."

Randy laughed and returned his hat to his head with a tug, settling it hard on his forehead. "Sheriff, do you know what she's worth? One smaller than this in the Black Hills went for over eight million dollars twenty years ago."

I shook my head. "I don't even know what we're talking about."

Baumann looked a little embarrassed but then provided the much-needed information. "A Saurischia, suborder Theropoda, genus . . ."

"A *T. rex.*" The rancher began yelling again. "Maybe the largest and most complete ever found."

Baumann shook his head. "We don't know that until we get the rest of her."

Unable to contain his enthusiasm, Randy yelped, "We measured the exposed fossil bones, and Jen's a lot bigger than the one at the Field Museum in Chicago—probably the biggest in the world!"

I couldn't help but ask, "She?"

Baumann answered, "We can't tell what sex it is, but generally the larger ones are female."

Vic laughed. "Why Jen?"

Dave gestured toward the young woman still filming while leaning against the front of the SUV. "Jennifer was the one who found her, and usually you use either the Latin, or a place name, or the name of the person who discovered the specimen for its name." He continued to shake his head as he glanced back at Randy. "Anyway, it really doesn't matter. I already paid for the find, and I'm not paying again."

Randy approached him, sticking his nose inches from Dave's face. "Well, who the hell did you pay, 'cause it sure wasn't me."

"Your father—I paid Danny."

He took a deep breath and swung around to look at all of us, his fists planted at his hips. "Then I guess we'll have to wait for the old man to get back from fishing to find out about that."

2

"It's the type of asphyxia that is the direct result of liquid entering the breathing passages and preventing air from going into the lungs—in other words, all you need to do is submerge the mouth and nose."

A full twenty-four hours later, I leaned against the wall of room 32 and watched as Isaac Bloomfield continued examining the body we'd found. "So, he did drown?"

"Not necessarily." Peering at me through thick lenses, the doc adjusted his glasses. "The sequence of events pertaining to drowning are breath holding, involuntary inspiration and gasping for air at the breaking point, loss of consciousness, and finally, death."

Vic folded her arms. "And then feeding the turtles."

Isaac moved some of the hair away from Danny Lone Elk's face, revealing the missing eyes and other assorted mutilations. "And feeding the turtles, yes." The doc was approaching ninety and so sat on a stool he'd wheeled over to the examination table, a habit he'd picked up in his dotage.

"Randy says his father went fishing the other morning and that he didn't come home last night."

"That would coincide with my findings." Isaac reached out

and lifted the dead man's hand, damaged where the turtle had attempted to make a meal of it. "I'd say he went into the water at around seven p.m. the day before yesterday."

Vic leaned forward and looked at the devastation. "So the turtles took their time, huh?"

"I'm no expert on herpetology, but there seems to be a great deal of flesh removed from the fingers." Isaac examined the bite marks on Danny's hand, the ring finger having been almost severed. "But they probably wouldn't have begun feeding on him until his body began to cool." He looked back up at me, annoyance writ on his face. "Weren't they worried that he'd disappeared overnight?"

I shrugged. "I guess he did it a lot; they said there are seven different fishing spots on the ranch and nobody ever knew where he went until he got back."

"Seems irresponsible for a man his age."

I sighed and restated my question. "So, he drowned?"

He lowered the hand and sighed. "From the initial examination, I would say reversible cerebral anoxia. Note the frothy substance emitting from the mouth and nostrils?"

"Yep."

"Hemorrhagic edema fluid, the result of mucus in the body mixing with the water; the presence of this contributes to the prevention of air intake and the final asphyxia."

I glanced at Vic and then back at Isaac. "So, he drowned."

He stared at the marred features. "The only thing, Walter, was that Danny was a very good swimmer."

"How do you know that?"

"He, like myself at one time, was a member of the Polar Bear Club."

Vic glanced at me with an eyebrow arched like a fly rod at full strike, and I figured I'd better explain. "It's where these crazy people get together and jump into freezing cold water in the middle of winter, usually to support a charity."

She looked at me, incredulous. "You mean like a frozen lake?"

"Exactly." Doc Bloomfield stood and redirected an examination light over Danny's face. "Our chapter used to hold events out at Lake DeSmet on New Year's Day. There was an instance where one of the younger members jumped in the hole in the ice and became disoriented. The channels are dangerous near the cliffs, but Danny here dove in and brought him back up to safety—as I said, he was an excellent swimmer." He focused the light, the contrast making the damage to the man's face that much more horrid. "So, how is it that he could've drowned in one of his own reservoirs on a beautiful day in May?"

Vic glanced at me and stepped forward to study Danny's face. "Why did he stop doing the jump-in-and-freeze-your-ass-off party?"

Isaac carefully brushed more of the hair back. "He was getting older, and he was having drinking problems."

"So, maybe he got plastered and then fell in the water?"

"He took pills."

They both turned and looked at me.

Remembering the night I'd met the man, I pushed off the wall and stood over the body, reached toward the rolling table that held the dead man's clothing, and unbuttoned the breast pocket of the same sort of green canvas shirt where I'd seen him get his pills all those years before. Fishing inside, I pulled out a prescription container and rattled the contents. Handing the waterproof bottle to the doc, I watched as he adjusted his glasses and read, "Omeprazole." He looked up at me. "Nothing surprising here; it's a proton pump inhibitor that blocks the enzyme lining of the stomach and decreases acid."

"He was also chewing Tums when I first met him."

"Danny suffered from stomach trouble his whole life."

I gestured toward the bottle. "So this stuff is just prescription Tums?"

"Pretty much."

"Who gave them to him?"

He read from the plastic container and handed it back to me. "A doctor in Hardin named, of all things, Free Bird."

"You're kidding." I shook my head as I read the name. "Not Cheyenne or Crow, for that matter."

Vic piped up. "Maybe he's a Lynyrd Skynyrd fan."

Isaac continued to study the body. "There's something else that bothers me, Walter." He reached out and turned Danny's face. "The reddish coloring in the cheeks, fingers, and toes." He examined the damaged hand again. "And there is some exfoliation on the digits, but it's possible that that was the work of the turtles."

I studied the pill container. "Can you get in touch with this Free Bird? In my experience, doctors tend to be a little more open with their own kind."

"Certainly." He suddenly noticed something in Danny's other breast pocket, and he unbuttoned it, producing a large flask with a beaded leather sleeve. "Hmm . . ."

"Was he supposed to be drinking with his condition and taking those prescriptions?"

"No; as far as I know, he was a recovering alcoholic." He turned the cap and sniffed the contents. "I'm not so discerning, since I don't drink, but it's certainly alcohol."

I took it from him and inhaled the sweet/sour fragrance. "Whiskey, and I'm no expert but I'd say the good stuff." I pocketed the flask in my jacket as I snagged it from the hook on the back of the door. "But I know an individual . . ."

Vic followed me as I headed out, Doc Bloomfield calling after us, "What about the autopsy?"

I caught the door as she breezed under my arm into the hallway. "Let's hold off until we get permission."

Vic handed her menu to Dorothy. "I'll have what he's having."

The Busy Bee Café's chief cook and bottle washer looked at me as I made a show of reading my own menu. "Why do you even bother?"

I glanced up at her. "What?"

"You always order the same thing."

"Maybe I'm finally changing my ways."

"It's a little late for that, isn't it?"

"Hey, did you hear I'm a grandfather?"

She smiled. "Months ago . . . I also heard they're coming for a visit." She peered at me through the salt-and-pepper bangs. "You ever traveled with a five-month-old? It's like maneuvers of the Eighth Army."

I handed her the menu, and we said it together: "The usual."

Vic watched her go and yelled after her, "And a couple of iced teas, if you would be so kind?" She turned to look at me.

"So, dead bodies in the morning and the usual for lunch—just another day in Absaroka County, Wyoming."

"I just hope it's not turtle soup."

She smiled and nodded. "So, how is the little family?"

"I guess everything's fine. I'm not quite sure why Cady is wanting to bring Lola out here as young as she is, but I'm not arguing."

Vic sipped one of the iced teas that Dorothy had brought over and then put it on the counter. "Maybe they need a change of scenery."

Lena Moretti, Vic's mother and Cady's mother-in-law, had been in close contact with my daughter and had been helping out a great deal over the past months, and I was beginning to wonder if something was up. "What do your spies tell you?"

She sighed and studied Dorothy's back as the owner/operator labored to fix our two usuals. "Ma says that they're kind of overwhelmed." She fiddled with her straw. "Personally, I think your daughter is getting tired of being just a mom and is looking forward to getting back to work on a more full-time basis." She shook her head and continued, "I know my brother, and I figure he's only so much help with the baby." I'd noticed that Vic rarely said Lola's name, continually referring to her as "the baby." She turned and smiled at me. "I mean, as soon as she's old enough to drink, play cards, and go to Phillies games, the dynamic may change."

Vic lifted her iced tea in a toast, and I was relieved when she finally said my granddaughter's and her niece's name: "To Lola."

I lifted my own, having finally accepted the fact that my

granddaughter was named after a Baltic-blue T-bird convertible. "To Lola."

She set her glass down and studied me. "So, why didn't you order an autopsy?"

"The Cheyenne are touchy about that." I sipped my tea. "And Danny was a big deal, a friend of Lonnie Little Bird and a tribal elder who held the medicine for the Northern Cheyenne Sun Dance."

She nodded and looked out the window. "So, what are we going to do about the dino wars out at the Lone Elk place?"

I smiled. "You know, this is not the first time this type of thing has happened in this part of the country. Just about every tyrannosaurus skeleton in the world comes from this area." I twirled my glass in the ring of condensation it had made, turned toward her, and tipped my hat back. "As a matter of fact, there was a big fight between two of the first paleontologists in the country, Othniel Charles Marsh and Edward Drinker Cope, right here in Wyoming."

"Jeez, with those names, didn't they have enough to worry about?"

"Marsh's Uncle Peabody bought him a museum at Yale so the young man could start the study of dinosaurs in this country. Up until 1866 there really hadn't been all that much scientific study on the subject, although there are some who believe that fossil remains might have been responsible for formulating some of the Native American mythologies."

"We have to call Henry."

Ignoring her sarcasm, I continued with my Wyoming dinosaur history. "Marsh and Cope started out as friends, but I guess the friendship evolved into a colossal pissing contest."

She thought about it. "Was one of them from Philadelphia?"

"I believe Cope was."

"Figures."

"Anyway, I guess the competition got to be too much for them. Back in 1872 down in the Bridger Basin where the two had competing digs on the same site, Cope used to go up on a ridge and spy on the Marsh group. Well, Marsh got together with his diggers and fabricated a fake dinosaur from a bunch of parts and buried it; they actually have a term for this bit of skullduggery—it's what they call *salting*. Then the Marsh group made a big fuss, talking about this incredible find; Cope couldn't stand Marsh getting credit, and later that night Cope and his group snuck over and dug the fake dinosaur up and then published papers about this significant find."

"These were grown men? I thought scientists were supposed to be above that kind of thing."

I shrugged. "Cope had recurring nightmares where he dreamed that the creatures he was uncovering came back to life to attack him." I rested my elbows on the counter. "There are rumors that when Cope died, Marsh attempted to buy his bones from the Museum of Anthropology and Archeology at the University of Pennsylvania, but they said no. I guess they finally loaned his skull out to some scientist down in Boulder, and he had it sitting on his desk."

"Oh, gross."

"When Penn decided they wanted Cope's head back, the guy in Colorado said he'd be happy to accompany the skull, but the museum told him to just send it FedEx."

She rested a marvelous cheekbone on a fist and stared at me. "Are you trying to ruin my lunch?"

I smiled down at her. "Nope, I just thought you were interested."

"I was; the operative word here is *was*."

Our two open-face meat loaf sandwiches arrived, and I looked at my plate. "Since when is this the usual?"

Dorothy glanced up at the vintage BEST OUT WEST clock advertising "Enriched Flour Tomahawk Feeds for Livestock & Poultry" that had been up there since I'd been a kid. "About thirty seconds now." The phone beside the cash register rang and she answered it as we dug in, but a moment later she was holding the receiver in my face.

I swallowed. "What?"

"It's for you."

I took it, fully expecting to hear the voice of my daughter, but, keeping it professional for propriety's sake, I finally croaked, "Longmire."

Ruby's voice sounded more than a little concerned. "Walter, the FBI is here in the office."

I thought of our sobriquet for big Indians. "Which FBI?"

"No, the real FBI as in Federal Bureau of Investigation, a.k.a. the Department of Justice."

I sighed. "What do they want?"

"I am just the lowly dispatcher, and they have not deigned to tell me."

I stared at my food. "Do you think they can wait until I eat my lunch?"

There was a pause as Ruby cupped the receiver and spoke with whom I assumed was the federal government, then came back on the line. "They say they're hungry, too."

"Send 'em on down." I started to hand Dorothy the receiver but then pulled it back and asked Ruby, "It's not Cliff Cly, is it?"

It turns out it wasn't, but that doesn't mean I didn't recognize the suited individual with the crew cut who walked into the Busy Bee, cased the café, and then strolled over to the counter to extend a hand.

We shook. "Agent in Charge McGroder."

He removed his sunglasses and smiled a broad smile. "I wasn't sure if you'd remember me, Sheriff."

I returned the smile. "You're looking better than the last time I saw you."

He shrugged. "You mean almost bleeding to death?" He leaned past me and extended his hand to Vic. "Mike Mc-Groder, out of Denver."

I interrupted, "I thought you were Salt Lake City."

"Transferred—more work in Colorado." He turned and swept a hand back to introduce the two suited, sunglass-wearing individuals at the door, one male and one female. "But my staff is out of the field office in Salt Lake."

Vic nodded and looked past him. "They on a mission?"

He shook his head. "No, but they are vegetarians and one's a vegan."

I glanced down at the meat loaf on my plate. "I'm betting that they're about to go into red-meat protein arrest?"

"Something like that; you know of any place where they can eat?"

Vic barked a laugh. "Boulder."

"Not exactly what we're known for here in Wyoming." I

thought about it. "I guess they could go up to the deli at the IGA and put something together."

He nodded. "Back up Main and then a left on Fort toward the mountain?"

"Yep." As he sent his team off to graze, I scooted down one so that he'd have a place beside us and looked at Vic. "McGroder was the AIC on the prisoner exchange up the mountain last year."

"I remember." She mock-saluted him. "The cluster fuck."

The agent sat. "Yeah, the cluster . . ." He looked at our plates as Dorothy brought over a menu. "I'll have what they're having." Mike smiled. "I've learned never to argue with my Indian scouts in this part of the country."

I forked off a section, steered it into my mouth, and chewed, giving him time to tell me why he was here, but he only sipped his water and made small talk with Vic about her connections with the Department of Justice in Philadelphia, her old stomping ground.

He finally turned on his stool and placed his back against the counter, crossing his arms and looking at Main Street. "It was a nice little town you had here, Sheriff."

"Why are you saying that in past tense?"

"Because it's about to turn into a circus."

I placed my fork on my plate and turned toward him. "And why is that?"

He sighed. "You ever hear of Skip Trost?"

"Nope."

"You know, you need to get out more. Skip Trost is the acting deputy U.S. attorney for, among other states, Wyoming, and was sworn in about five months ago with little or no federal trial experience, but he had served as a legislative aid—"

"I get the picture."

"Well, Trost here is suddenly in the catbird seat and decides that he's going to make a name for himself with the American people by instituting an investigation into nationwide fossil collection and even going so far as initiating a sting to expose illegal collections and sales of state property."

I was glad I'd just about finished my meal, because I was rapidly losing my appetite. "Oh, no."

"Oh, yes."

"A dinosaur by the name of Jen?"

He pulled a piece of paper from his breast pocket and examined a Post-it attached. " 'The Hope Diamond of fossils with unlimited scientific value in research, exhibition, and education and a specimen with a quality of preservation and completeness of structure unlike any ever before seen.' " He shrugged and looked out the window. "As soon as they get all of it out of the ground."

I set my fork on my plate. "Jen."

"It's going to make the Scopes monkey trial look like a lemonade stand." He swiveled back around. "The High Plains Dinosaur Museum came to the attention of the DOJ when a graduate student in vertebrate paleontology who worked as a part-time ranger over in Yellowstone was approached by a private collector who told him he could supplement his income by selling fossils from the park to the HPDM."

"What happened with that?"

Mike smiled as his usual arrived. "A seventy-five-dollar fine. As it turned out, the old guy had sold stuff to the museum and had lied about where he'd gotten it."

Vic laughed. "May J. Edgar Hoover's soul rest in peace."

"Not exactly a priority for the bureau?" I sipped my iced tea. "Okay, so the acting deputy U.S. attorney Trost has it in for the HPDM, and the wheels of justice are going to grind exceedingly fine until—"

"Oh, it's way better than that." McGroder cleaved off a piece of his meat loaf and started it for his mouth before pausing. "It's not enough of a political powder keg for Trost to want to save the poor people of Wyoming from the rapacious clutches of the High Plains Dinosaur Museum." He pointed his loaded fork at me. "This rinky-dink state really has two senators?"

"Yep, same as Utah and Colorado and the other forty-seven. You need to get out more, Mike."

"Well, the networks and large-circulation newspapers really don't give a crap if you cowfolk are getting ripped off, but you throw a few First People/Native American/Indian types into the mix and voila, you've got yourself a national platform from which you can draw the attention of the potential electorate to yourself." He raised a fist in mock support. "Save Jen."

"What Indians are you talking about?"

"The Cheyenne Conservancy, a land trust organization, has filed an order to desist, citing the federal Antiquities Act of 1906 prohibiting the removal of fossils from any land owned or controlled by the United States without permission from the Cultural Committee or the Tribal Historical Preservation Office."

"The site where that fossil is being excavated isn't the Cheyenne Reservation or federal land."

He chewed, and it was almost as if he was enjoying my

discomfort. "Actually, it's both. That portion of the ranch is on Cheyenne Conservancy land and you have to have a permit to dig there, and guess who doesn't have a permit."

"The High Plains Dinosaur Museum."

He continued smiling. "It's all right, Walt, you've still got a hole card; if the possession holds up with the Native American rancher, then the tribe and the federal government are going to be left out in the cold. You see, the rancher bought that particular land from a white homesteader in 2000 and exercised his right to have it held in trust for twenty-five years by the U.S. Department of the Interior under the Indian Reorganization Act of 1934, which allowed him to not have to pay taxes on it. The problem is that putting your land in trust, either federal or Cheyenne, limits the options of selling it or anything on it."

Vic and I looked at each other for a moment, and then I turned to look at McGroder. "Then all our hopes of avoiding this are pinned to Danny Lone Elk?"

He chewed and swallowed, wiping his mouth with a knuckle. "Yeah, I think that's the guy we need to talk to."

Vic shook her head. "Well then, you'd better talk loud."

"This is going to introduce an unwelcome criminal facet to the proceedings."

We'd finished our meal, and I was explaining the eccentricities of the Lone Elk situation to Agent McGroder as we made our way back toward my office at a brisk pace. "Probably not going to calm things down, huh?"

He laughed as we climbed the steps to the courthouse. "All

we need now is a bearded lady and a guy who bites the heads off chickens."

Vic's cell rang, and she answered, talking with whom I assumed was my dispatcher, and then tucked the thing back in her jacket. "Ruby says the FBI is at the office."

I glanced at McGroder. "No, they're not—they're right here."

She glanced at me. "No, our kind of FBI."

"Oh." I began walking again. "So, what happens now?"

He folded his overcoat over his arm and patted the inside breast pocket of his suit. "I'm going to the museum to deliver a warrant and was wondering if you'd like to tag along."

"What are your intentions?"

"Just a look-see. The only fossil I'm interested in is Jen, but I thought I'd get here early and try and nip some of these shenanigans in the bud, so to speak."

"They've barely gotten any of her out of the ground."

He held up his hands. "So much the better. I'm just going to meet my guys at your office and then head over to the museum for a tour, probably with the director—what's his name?"

"Dave Baumann."

"With Dave, and see if any of the fossils have stickers on them that read PROPERTY OF THE UNITED STATES GOVERNMENT, and then make a phone call to Trost, so without any further ado he can start warming up his dulcet tones for the interviews tomorrow."

"Interviews . . . Plural, huh?" I glanced around at the cottonwoods, flower boxes, and the idyllic environs of our small-town courthouse. "Did I fail to mention that I'm going on vacation this week?"

"Yes, you did, and as of now it would appear that you're not."

As we rounded the back of the courthouse, I could see a very large Indian reclined on the steps of the old Carnegie Library that served as my office; he was eyeing the two bureau people who were eating what looked to be lettuce wraps and drinking bottled water. "Uh oh . . . Looks like a standoff."

Vic chimed in. "Wounded Knee III."

By the time that we got there, Brandon White Buffalo, possibly the largest Indian on both the Cheyenne and Crow Reservations, had crushed his cigarette out and, standing his full seven feet two inches, pushed off from the steps to greet us. "Ha-ho, Lawman."

I gestured toward the giant. "The real FBI."

Vic added, "Fuckin-Big-Indian."

I watched as Brandon pocketed the butt.

"Don't you know those things stunt your growth?"

The operator of the White Buffalo Sinclair Station held out a hand with fingers that looked like a collection of Polish sausages, and enveloped my own. "It's a nasty habit, but it is easy to quit; I have done it many times."

I tried not to grimace as he applied his legendary grip. "How are you, Brandon?"

"My heart is heavy, Lawman. The Cheyenne have lost a great leader, and it's not a time when we can spare such men." He sparked an eye at my undersheriff. "Miss Moretti."

She put her hand on her sidearm. "Do not try and pick me up."

Brandon made a habit of lifting people from the ground as a greeting, but a well-placed kick had preempted the tradition with Vic a few months back.

He nodded and glanced at McGroder, who extended his

hands and spoke up quickly. "I'd rather not be picked up either."

Throwing a thumb over his shoulder, Brandon smiled and turned back to me. "The ones who don't smoke are inside—including both the chiefs."

As far as I knew, the Cheyenne were an autarchy, so I was interested to see who the other chief might be. "Henry with you?"

"No, the Bear isn't a part of the party—he prefers to work outside official channels, but you know that." The Buffalo studied me. "You are disappointed?"

I shrugged. "I haven't seen Henry in a couple of weeks, and my granddaughter is going to be in town . . ."

"The little brother is back to seeing the divorcée up at Rocky Boy."

I glanced around and dropped my voice. "Are we ever going to get to meet her?"

"Who knows." The three-hundred-and-seventy-five-pound Crow/Cheyenne hybrid turned and shook hands with the special agent as he introduced himself and then shot a look at the herbivores on the bench. "Those are yours?"

McGroder nodded and studied the giant, probably making the connection between him and his uncle, the man who had saved me on the mountain. "Yeah, I made 'em leave their trench coats at home."

"We did not call you."

I had to smile as McGroder flexed his fingers, attempting to get the circulation back in them. "No."

"Then why are you here, if you don't mind my asking?"

Mike adjusted his sunglasses and looked up at the big man. "At the behest of the American people."

Brandon gestured toward himself. "Are we not the American people?"

"Certainly you are." He looked at me for help, but I was going to let him tread water on his own. The agent licked his lip, smiled, and breathed deep. "We're just here to make sure that everybody plays fair."

Brandon White Buffalo's head tilted to one side as he considered the AIC before laughing. He turned and mounted the steps to my office, his gigantic legs carrying him up like the dinosaurs that had held my imagination recently. "You are about two hundred years too late, Agent in Charge."

McGroder turned to look at me as the glass door swung closed, the gold and black letters of my department shuddering with the soft impact. "I have a feeling that the next week is going to be interesting around here."

"I hope you're wrong."

He smiled, waved good-bye to Vic, and then collected his people from the bench. "Hey, where is the High Plains Dinosaur Museum, anyway?"

I pointed. "South end of town, across from the high school. It used to be the Moose Lodge and before that a carpet outlet."

He thought about it. "The tin building that I saw on the way in?"

I shrugged as Vic and I started up the steps to our defunct library offices. "We take our institutions where we find them."

He pulled out his phone as the trio started toward the black Tahoe with government plates parked at the curb. "I don't suppose it would do any good to ask for your cell number?"

"You can ask."

He shook his head, and they loaded up and started off,

catching the light on Main and disappearing around the cor-
ner.

Vic finally turned. "I've got a question."

I gave her my full attention, the way I always did.

"Skip?" She pulled the door open and entered. "A deputy
U.S. attorney by the name of Skip?"

"I told Brandon that he couldn't smoke in here." My dispatcher
answered a phone and asked the caller to please wait, then hit
the hold button.

I looked around. "Where is everybody?"

Ruby nodded her head toward the hallway behind her
desk. "Your office."

I walked past Saizarbitoria's door and could see that Double Tough, my other deputy, who had just come back from
medical leave, was standing next to Sancho's desk. The skin
on the side of his face was mottled from having been burned,
and I was still getting used to the eye patch. "How you doin',
troop?"

He did his best Blackbeard imitation as Vic and I crowded
in the doorway. "Argh . . ."

The Basquo urged me in. "Boss, we need an opinion here."

"I've got people in my office."

"It'll just take a second."

I entered Saizarbitoria's immaculate but tiny room and
stood there with the other two men, Vic holding at the doorway. "What's up?"

Sancho gestured toward Double Tough. "DT's got a new
eye."

What with Danny Lone Elk, like we didn't have enough ocular problems as of late?

I turned and looked at him. "Well, let's see it."

He glanced around the room, his one-eyed gaze on Vic, and then peeled the patch back, leaving it on his forehead. "It's a fourteen millimeter . . ."

We all leaned in and looked at the artificial orb, Double Tough staring straight ahead and as nonchalant as you can be with three people peering into your fake eye.

"It looks great."

He seemed doubtful. "Really?"

"Yep; if I didn't know any better I'd say it was real." I glanced at Sancho for a little backup. "Right?"

"Yeah, it looks great."

"It's the wrong color."

We all looked at Vic. "What are you talking about?"

She stepped in closer and stared at Double Tough. "What color did you order?"

"I didn't order it, they did . . . It's hazel-blue."

She studied him some more. "Your real eye is more green." She straightened and looked at Saizarbitoria, me, and finally back to DT. "Take it back and have them order up another one."

Double Tough cleared his throat. "Oh, I think it's close enough—"

"Go back and have them order up one that matches." She glanced at us again. "I can't believe you assholes were going to let him wander around here looking like a fucked-up husky because you two were afraid of hurting his delicate feelings—shame on the both of you."

As she stalked out, we all stood there in the uncomfortable silence, and then I leaned in and studied the eye again. "Maybe a little greener, but it looks good, troop."

Sancho nodded. "Really good. A little greener, maybe . . . I mean, you might as well get it right—the insurance is paying for it."

The tribal delegation was waiting for me in my office, sitting in my guest chairs and reading from the plaques and studying the photos on my walls. Brandon thumped a finger on one. "What are all these sheriffs doing in front of this train?"

I turned the corner and sat at my desk across from Cheyenne chief Lonnie Little Bird and Tribal Police chief Lolo Long as Vic lingered near the doorway. "The old sheriff, Lucian— that was the last run of the Western Star back in '72."

Lolo was the first to ask, "The Western Star?"

"The Wyoming Sheriff's Association had this yearly junket that they used to do, a train by the name of the Western Star that ran from Cheyenne to Evanston and back—twenty-four drunk sheriffs shooting sporting clays off a flatbed."

Chief Long pulled a handful of blue-black hair back from her face, revealing the sickle-shaped scar at her temple and the dark, dark eyes. Out of uniform, she was wearing jeans, a black T-shirt, and a weathered leather jacket—all of which seemed to fit in remarkable ways. "Sounds like fun."

She wanted to continue the interrogation, but I cut her off and gestured around the room. "The few plaques are his, but he didn't want them, and I never got around to taking them down."

"What do you have time for these days?"

I smiled at my reservation comrade in arms. "The job, Chief Long, the job." I took my hat off and set it on my desk, crown down, and introduced Vic to the group.

"We've met."

Lolo's head lifted, and she spoke. "Undersheriff."

Vic's voice carried just a little edge to it. "Chief."

I addressed the rest of the war party. "Chief Little Bird."

Lonnie laughed. "Too many chiefs and not enough Indians. Mm, hmm. Yes, it is so."

I glanced at Brandon, who was still standing, and then back at Lonnie. "Is this a formal call?"

"I am afraid so."

"Danny Lone Elk?"

He nodded and leaned back in his wheelchair. "Just so you are aware, we did not do this."

"Do what?"

"Call the FBI."

"Since Wounded Knee II, when the Department of Justice shows up I rarely think that it's the tribe that has called them."

Lolo played with the woven horsehair zipper slide on her jacket. "Danny had made commitments with the tribe that upon his death his ranch was to be signed over to the Cheyenne Conservancy, and that is our only concern at this time. I am not sure if the fossil in question is part of that land or an antiquity that is dealt with differently. Danny mentioned that a home for the dinosaur might be made on the reservation in Lame Deer at the Chief Dull Knife College or that there might be a sale of a limited number of replicas of the skeleton or the donation of some of the bones to the tribal headquarters, but that above all, the proceeds from such a sale should go exclusively to his children and grandson."

"What's your involvement?"

She leaned forward and smiled a dazzling smile that made my toes tingle. "I'm the director of the Cheyenne Conservancy."

"So you were in a sort of partnership with Danny."

"Yes."

"Has anybody talked to Dave Baumann about this?"

"I don't know."

I glanced up at Vic, who rolled her eyes. "Well, it's going to start getting complicated now that the feds are involved."

Lolo studied me. "Did you call them?"

"No."

"Then who did?"

Vic smiled. "Skip."

3

"What do you mean you can't pick us up in Billings?"

Glancing around the reception area at my assembled staff as we took on our greatest challenge at the end-of-the-day coffee klatch, I sighed through the telephone line in an attempt to get out of trouble with the Greatest Legal Mind of Our Time. "There's a big mess going on among the Cheyenne, the High Plains Dinosaur Museum, and the federal government, and I'm betting I won't be able to get free tomorrow. The acting deputy U.S. attorney is going to be here, and then I'll know more."

"*Acting* deputy U.S. attorney—what the hell does that mean?"

"I don't know; I guess it means he *acts* like a deputy attorney or something." I hugged the phone in for a little privacy. "Can't you fly into Sheridan?"

"I'm traveling with a five-month-old, and they don't have a leather helmet and goggles to fit her." There was a pause. "Have you ever traveled with a five-month-old?"

The second time I'd been asked that today—I tried to remember if I ever had. "I think your mother did; I was just ground support."

"Did you get the Pack 'n Play and the car seat?"

I lied. "Yep."

"You're lying."

Uncanny. "As fast as Dog can trot."

"If you can't borrow them, then get them over in Sheridan when you come to pick us up."

"So, you are flying into Sheridan. Why don't you rent a car?" The phone went dead in my hand as I handed it back to my dispatcher and my guideline for all things domestic. "What's a Pack 'n Play?"

Ruby looked at Saizarbitoria, who seemed to have an innate ability to describe child-rearing accoutrements in terms I could understand. "Portable solitary confinement."

"Ahh . . ." I smiled, pressing the joke. "And the car seat?"

"It's a seat. That goes in your car," the Basquo grunted. "I've got all that stuff."

Ruby hung up the phone. "Walt, you can borrow them, but I'm thinking you should buy; this is not the only time they're going to be here—that is, if you don't keep royally messing things up."

I glanced at Lucian, who sometimes showed up at these unofficial end-of-the-day meets, and then the rest of my staff. "Everybody seems to think that, huh?"

They all nodded, but Lucian was the first to speak. "You're not off to a good start, troop."

Vic laughed. "Like you're a knowledgeable source."

I cupped my chin in my palm and postulated as I looked at the previous sheriff of Absaroka County. "I'm trying to remember what five-month-olds are like; what they can do."

Lucian mumbled. "They shit a lot."

Vic bumped him with her shoulder. "When was the last time you even held a baby—the Eisenhower administration?"

Ruby agreed. "You're going to need diapers."

"Is there a service in town?"

"They don't do that anymore; they're disposable." She glanced at Saizarbitoria again. "But I'm betting Sancho is our go-to guy on all of this."

He rolled his shoulders. "Like I said, we've got all that stuff and you're welcome to it, but you might be better off to buy all new. Anthony's over a year old and escapes from everything like a miniature Houdini, but we still use some of it." He smiled. "You've got a long road ahead of you, Grandpa." He thought about it. "At five months they can sit up, scoot, roll, and maybe crawl a little."

"Can they talk?"

"Babble, mostly—kind of like a bad drunk."

Ruby smiled. "As I recall, Cady talked early."

"Yep, and she's never stopped."

Double Tough ventured an opinion. "You're going to need a high chair."

We all turned to look at him.

He adjusted his eye patch, having put it back on. "What? I got nephews and nieces."

I pushed off Ruby's counter and stretched, glancing up at the Seth Thomas on the wall and wondering why all these people were still here, other than to antagonize me. "This grandfather stuff is complicated."

Ruby laughed. "You haven't seen the half of it."

I turned back to Saizarbitoria. "So, I don't suppose I could impose on you to help me buy all these things?"

He nodded. "And put it together?"

"What?"

"You have to assemble the stuff, and I'm thinking it would be best if you had everything done."

I nodded some more, getting used to taking orders again. "At my place?"

Vic stared at me. "Where were you thinking they were going to stay?"

"I hadn't really thought about it, but wouldn't it be easier if they were in town?"

She shook her head. "Oh, no."

"You've got a brand-new house."

"Nice try."

"And if they need anything, they wouldn't have to drive twenty miles . . ."

"Absolutely not."

I turned back to Saizarbitoria. "If you and Maria will help me out with this, I'll give you the rest of the day off."

He made a face. "The day is over—how 'bout tomorrow?"

He had me over a barrel, and he knew it. I pulled out all the cash I had in my wallet and handed it to him. "Will that cover it?"

He nodded, stuffing the bills in his shirt pocket. "If not, I'll get the rest from petty cash."

"Deal. Leave the receipts, so I can reimburse." I turned to Lucian, suddenly remembering the flask in my coat pocket, the one that I'd taken from the recently deceased. "Hey, old man, I need your opinion on something." I pulled it out and handed it to him.

His eyes brightened at the prospect. "Now you're talkin'

about my kind of baby." He unscrewed the top and sniffed the contents. "Bottled-in-bond."

He started to take a sip, but I caught his arm. "Hold up. I took that off of Danny Lone Elk, and it hasn't been tested." Before I could react further, he changed hands and took a strong, two bubble pull. "Lucian . . ."

"Damn, that's good." He licked his lips. "Straight rye whiskey, a four-year-old, if I'm not mistaken—a little metallic, but that could just be from being in the flask too long."

"You're not concerned that it might be poisoned?"

"Troop, I've been poisoning myself with this stuff for nigh on seventy years and I'm sure in the end it will get me, but it's been an elongated and cheerful terminus."

"Brand?"

"E. H. Taylor." He took another nip, just to be sure. "Hundred proof, I should think."

"Nothing wrong with it?"

"Not that I can tell, but I better have another just to be on the safe side."

"Let's save some for the Department of Criminal Investigation, shall we?" I turned to talk to Double Tough and noticed a group of men standing at the top of the stairs: two highway patrolmen named Bob Delude and Robert Hall, aka the Bobs, and a suited man who looked like a bad smell. "Can I help you?"

"Are you Sheriff Walter Longmire?"

"Maybe."

"I'm Deputy United States Attorney Skip Trost."

I noticed he left off the "acting" portion of his title. "Good to meet you."

"Are we interrupting anything?"

"Oh, no. Just the circling of the wagons here at the end of the day."

He stepped forward. "I was wondering if I could have a private word with you, Sheriff?" He didn't wait for an answer but turned and dismissed the two patrolmen. "Thank you, gentlemen; I believe I'm Sheriff Longmire's responsibility now."

Robert rolled his eyes and Bob shook his head as they turned, noticeably glad to be rid of him, and trooped down the stairs and out the door. I knew the Bobs pretty well from dealing with them over the years and would have to talk to them later to get the dope on the ADA.

I gestured toward the hall and my office, the day obviously not over.

"You know why I'm here."

Easing myself back in my chair, I took off my hat and set it on my desk, thinking the thing spent more time there than on my head. "I believe so."

"This is a serious crime against the American people."

I tapped the brim of my hat and watched it spin on the overturned crown. "The American people, huh?"

He folded his overcoat in his lap and regarded me with a set of very pale blue eyes, the kind that sled dogs have—the kinds of dogs that if not fed enough eat each other. "We have an opportunity here to make a statement to these private collectors that the relics and fossils on public lands are not for private sale."

"I wasn't aware that the High Plains Dinosaur Museum was going to sell Jen."

He watched me, probably trying to get a read on my position in all of this, and that gave me the opportunity to study him in turn. He was fit, and I was guessing he was no stranger to the gymnasiums in Cheyenne. "The point is, Mr. Trost, that we don't know if the fossil is on public land, and besides, if they maintain ownership, then they can do whatever they like with Jen. It's a free market, as near as I can tell."

The shoe stopped bobbing, and he grinned. "They told me you were sharp."

"Who did?"

He dismissed my question with a wave of his hand. "Everybody at Twenty-Fourth and Capitol."

"So, I guess you're looking to establish a partnership with the Northern Cheyenne, the Cheyenne Conservancy, and the Lone Elk family."

"His family is active?"

I gave him my warning voice. "Very."

For the first time, he broke eye contact with me and stared at his coat. "Hmm . . ."

"If you don't mind my asking, why is it that the federal government suddenly has a deep-seated yearning to go after the High Plains Dinosaur Museum?"

"They are stealing government property."

I expulsed a breath of air that substituted for a laugh. "Private collectors and paleontologists have been doing it all over the American West for more than a century."

"All the more reason it should be stopped."

"What's the hurry? I mean the thing isn't even out of the ground."

"The head is."

I stared at him. "What?"

He grinned some more. "You didn't know that."

"No. I'm not really privy to everything the museum does, nor should I be."

"I just received a text . . ." He pulled out his cell phone and showed it to me—maybe he thought I'd never seen one. ". . . that the head is on the premises of the HPDM and has been crated for shipping."

"To where?"

"At this time, parts unknown." He studied me. "So your buddy Dave Baumann doesn't tell you everything."

I wondered what Dave was up to, thought about it, and then leaned back in my chair. "I wouldn't call him my buddy, but he's from my county and that does make him mine to defend."

"Defend."

"A long time ago, the previous sheriff handed his star over to me." I thumbed my badge for him to take notice—maybe he'd never seen one before. "And along with this three-inch piece of metal came the responsibility of looking out for my people, all 2,483 of them."

He cocked his head and barked a short laugh. "So, it's going to be the United States of America versus Absaroka County?"

I sighed deeply and brushed the cuff of my shirt over my badge, wiping off my fingerprints. "Not necessarily. You treat the people of this county with the respect they deserve and I'm yours to command, *Acting* Deputy Attorney."

He let that one settle in for a bit and then stood. "I'm afraid you are mine to command no matter what or how I do it, *Sheriff*." He looked down at me, enjoying the advantage. "I think we should be going to the High Plains Dinosaur Museum, but first off I'm going to need personal protection."

This time I went ahead and laughed. "From what?"

He made the next statement as if it were manifest obvious. "Whoever of the 2,483 citizens of the county must've murdered Danny Lone Elk."

I leaned back in my chair and tried not to display the expression I reserved for people who attempted to tell me how to do my job. "At this time, I have no credible information leading me to believe that Danny's death is anything more than accidental."

He carefully unfolded his trench coat. "You're living in a dream world; that collection of bones that was found on his land is worth way more than the eight million dollars paid for similar finds, and that kind of money tends to get people thinking bad thoughts—even your people." He continued to study me and then changed tack. "You have a very high profile here in the state."

"I wasn't aware I had a profile, high or low."

"Well, I'm pleased to tell you that you do and that kind of thing can be instrumental in getting things like this done." He waited a moment and then leaned on my desk. "And since I've dismissed my cadre of highway patrolmen, I still need a detachment for use as bodyguards."

I picked up my hat, carefully straightened it on my head, and got up. Looking down at him, I enjoyed the advantage and smiled. "I've got just the person."

"And what if I don't want to follow fucking Skip around?"

"I thought about having Double Tough keep an eye on him."

"'That's not funny." She leaned against the counter of the gift shop inside the High Plains Dinosaur Museum. "How 'bout if I just *act* like I'm guarding the *acting* deputy attorney?"

"Fine by me." I watched McGroder and his staff examine and document all the parts of Jen's massive head, roughly the size of a sofa, on an assortment of clipboards and forms under the close observation of Trost. Her namesake stood by with her ever-present video camera, recording the FBI men and the acting deputy attorney. *"Quis custodiet ipsos custodes?"*

"Excuse me?"

I gestured toward Jen and the camera. "'Who watches the watchmen?' From the Roman poet Juvenal, usually associated with the philosophies of Plato and political corruption." I gestured toward Trost. "He seems to think there might be an attempt of violence upon his person."

Vic folded her arms, the portrait of disgruntled. "Well, he's right about that."

"I figured you'd be the best at letting me know what his intentions are."

She watched the ministrations of the Department of Justice. "You don't think they're going to try and pick that thing up, do you?" She looked at the shelves of plastic *T. rexes* and then back to me. "So, as I remember, according to Mrs. Tony, my sixth grade science teacher, these things had a brain the size of a walnut."

Jennifer's voice carried over to us, confirming she could hear what we were saying. "Actually, they were the smartest of all the dinosaurs, with the mature animals having a brain about the size of a coffee can—maybe as smart as modern-day alligators." She pointed at the VistaVision-like murals on the

walls that pictured embattled dinosaurs and exploding volca-
noes. "But they had surprisingly powerful sensory apparatus
with a binocular range of fifty-five degrees, better than hawks,
and a visual acuity ten times greater than an eagle's."

Vic thought about it. "So, she'd see you a long time before
you'd see her?"

"She'd see you almost four miles away, but she'd smell you
long before you saw her or she saw you. Tyrannosaurs had
huge olfactory membranes and probably the greatest sense of
smell of all the dinosaurs." She reached over and picked up one
of the toy *T. rexes* and held it out to my undersheriff. "There's
a lot of argument over whether Jen was a scavenger or a
hunter, but there's evidence that they might've even been can-
nibalistic."

Vic took the plastic dinosaur and flicked a fingernail along
the serrated teeth within the gaping jaw. "What do you think?"

"Jen herself has multiple tooth marks on her remains, evidence that some other tyrannosaurs were feeding on her alive
or dead—for all we know, they may have even been family
members." The young woman's face was remarkably expressionless. "I think they ate whatever they wanted, alive or dead."

She went back to filming the FBI as Vic turned to glance at
me.

"What?"

"I'm just thinking of that turtle that pissed on you yesterday morning." Her eyes followed after Jennifer. "She didn't
seem very forgiving."

"I don't think it was a very forgiving world sixty-seven million years ago."

Vic tossed the toy back into the bin. "Judging by what's

been going on around here lately, it hasn't gotten that much better." She studied me for a few moments, and I knew what she was going to ask. "So, what kind of visions were you having yesterday morning?"

I didn't say anything.

"I've seen you freeze up like that before, so what did you see?"

I shushed her as Baumann approached—he looked a little worse for wear having jousted with the state, the FBI, and the Northern Cheyenne within forty-eight hours. He adjusted his glasses and sighed. "I can't believe they're doing this."

"I can't believe you already had the head excavated and didn't tell me about it."

He emitted a glottal stop and then forced the words from his mouth. "I didn't think it was that important."

"Where were you shipping it, Dave?"

"What are you implying?"

"I'm implying that Jen's head is in a shipping crate with your return address on it but no outgoing address, and I'm interested in where she was headed, no pun intended."

He crossed his arms, evidently trying to discern if I was on his side or theirs. "You wouldn't believe me if I told you."

"Try me."

"NASA."

Wanting to make sure I wasn't missing a high plains acronym, I asked, "The National Aeronautics and Space Administration?"

Vic looked at him. "What the hell—you were going to put Jen in orbit or something?"

"We wanted to do a CAT scan of the skull, and NASA is the

only place with a machine big enough for the job; they use it to look for flaws in space shuttle engines and the like."

I gestured toward the FBI men. "Would I be correct in the assumption that you were trying to get it out of here before these guys showed up?"

Baumann looked a little uncomfortable. "Of course not."

"In hopes that dealing with a more scientifically oriented branch of the federal government might be better than dealing with the FBI or the U.S. Attorney's office?"

His eyes widened as I spoke, but his response was definitive. "No."

I put my arm over his shoulder and steered him further into the gift shop, where images of a toothsome generic *T. rex* adorned shirts, lunch boxes, posters, miniature pith helmets, and other assorted tchotchkes. "Dave, I just got through having an abbreviated pissing contest with Mr. Trost, where I made it clear to him that I was on the side of the people of my county." I released my hold on him, and he turned toward me, primed to interrupt; I held a finger up to his face. "And that is going to prove difficult if the people I'm attempting to protect, and that includes you, are not forthcoming with all the information they have."

"I'm not doing anything illegal."

"Maybe not, but it looks illegal and you better start thinking about that, because this situation is going to end up in federal court, and appearances, though deceiving, can lose you a case and a dinosaur." I held out a hand. "You mind if I have a look at the warrant?"

He pulled it from the back pocket of his khakis and handed it to me.

I read: "As a violation of the Antiquities Act of 1906, all the fossil remains of one *Tyrannosaurus rex* dinosaur skeleton (hereafter referred to as 'Jen') and other fossil specimens taken from the excavation site on the property of one Danny Lone Elk, including all papers, diaries, notes, photographs, and supporting materials relating to the excavation of said 'Jen,' are to be confiscated from the premises." I looked up at him. "Basically it says that you've stolen U.S. Government property, and somehow, at the same time, Northern Cheyenne tribal property." I handed it back to him. "Dave, as much as I ever hate to say this, I think you're going to need a lawyer."

I glanced back at the crate and could see Vic and Jennifer engaged in a heated conversation.

"Because I fucking said turn it off, that's why."

I stepped next to my undersheriff, and Jennifer turned the camera to film us. "Miss, do you mind turning that thing off for a minute?"

She ignored me and continued filming. "According to the law in thirty-eight states, including Wyoming, I am allowed to film law enforcement personnel as long as I am not interfering with your duties."

"Yep, but . . ."

She refocused the lens to get a close-up of me, and I turned and looked at the museum director. "Dave?"

He stepped toward her. "Jennifer, really . . . They're on our side."

"We don't know who's on what side, Dave. I just want to make sure we have plenty of evidence so that we cover our collective ass here."

He leaned in to her and spoke in a low voice. "There's no need . . ."

"The hell there's not; you saw what happened to the negotiations with Danny Lone Elk. If I hadn't videoed it . . ."

I turned and looked at her. "You have film of the negotiations with Danny?"

"I do."

I glanced at Baumann, who seemed as surprised as I did, and then back at her. "Film of him accepting the thirty-seven thousand dollars for the fossil remains?"

"It's in the video files on my computer, which, by the way, I'm not giving to you."

I turned back to Dave. "How did you pay Danny?"

"In cash—it was all he would take."

"I don't suppose you got a receipt?"

"Well, he was going to write me one, but you know how Danny was; he just hadn't gotten around to it."

I reached out and tapped the camera in Jennifer's hands. "You realize that recording, then, might be the only evidence you have of having paid Danny."

He turned to her. "We need that footage."

She shrugged and continued filming. "I can get it."

I reached out for the camera again, but she stepped back and kept it on us. "Look, Jennifer, I'm trying to help here, but I'm not going to do it on the Sid Caesar *Show of Shows*, okay?"

"The what?"

I turned back and looked at Dave, and he stepped between us. "Jen . . ."

As he began speaking to her in hushed tones, McGroder came over with his clipboard, stuffed it under one arm, and gestured toward the scientists. "Trouble with little Miss Zapruder? We have a lot of interaction with people carrying phones and stuff; you know you can ask them to step back to a reasonable distance for their own protection, right?"

"And how far away is that?"

"Officer's discretion; I'm thinking a quarter mile, county line . . ."

"Did you guys get what you needed?"

"We have, but now we need a safe place to store the fossils, including the thousand-pound head." He looked at me. "A secure place."

On an epoch-like scale, what he was proposing dawned on me like the beginning of time. "You're kidding."

"No, I'm not." He tapped the clipboard with the end of his pen. "I don't suppose you've got a loading dock at the jail?"

"No." I thought about how I wanted to play this, thinking that keeping Jen's head close at hand might be one of the best ways to establish someone's ownership. "But we do have one of those extrawide utility doors leading into the holding area from the street in the back."

"You think this crate will fit through it?"

"I don't know—is it wider than forty-eight inches?"

"With my luck, probably." He gestured for one of the Mormon twins to check the width of the crate and returned to us. "You got somebody at the jail 24/7?"

"Not generally."

"Well, you're going to need one or I'll have to assign one of mine—I guess I'm going to need more agents anyway." He glanced around at all the crates and started asking questions that he already knew the answers to. "Where is the field office in Wyoming?"

"Colorado."

He grinned. "And who is in charge there?"

I played along. "That would be you."

One of the field agents called out. "Forty-seven."

He pulled his cell from his pocket and began dialing. "I'll get another half-dozen guys up here by tomorrow; rust never sleeps, and neither do we." He was distracted by a voice on the phone. "Kim? I need bodies . . ." He glanced at me. "Know where I can get a forklift?"

"Jay over at UPS might do a freelance, but we aren't going to get him until tomorrow morning."

"Anybody else?"

"That I would trust with a crate containing the head of a fossil worth over eight million dollars?"

He nodded. "Call Jay in the morning, please." He finished his requisition for another half-dozen agents and then turned back to me. "Somebody's going to have to guard the head till then."

I gestured toward Vic. "We're already babysitting the ADA."

"The what?"

"Acting deputy attorney."

"Oh, right . . . him." He thought about it as he glanced over his shoulder at the man, who was writing in his own black leather notebook, the foot bobbing again. "Skip Trost, ADA—sounds like a character on that shitty television show, what's it called?"

"*Steadfast Resolution.*"

"That's it." He sighed deeply. "He really thinks he needs a bodyguard?"

"He fears for his life . . . or so he tells me."

McGroder spared a glance at my undersheriff, who was

giving the finger to Jennifer and the recorder. "I hope you gave him Moretti."

"I did."

"She can guard my body anytime." He tilted his head. "All right, I'll make you a deal. We're staying at the same hotel as Trost—the Virginian. I'll just have one of my Utah guys stand outside his door, knock every hour on the hour, and ask him if he's heard God's good news."

I smiled, pulled a hand from the pocket of my jacket, and stuck it out to him. "Vic will be relieved, and the ADA will be safer."

We shook hands. "Deal."

I handed the crust of my previous piece of pizza to Dog, who, awaiting his due, stood dutifully beside the crate.

"Thanks for getting dinner and the beer."

Vic plucked an anchovy off her piece and deposited it back in the box. "Fish on a pizza; I will never get used to that." She bit in with her elongated canine tooth and chewed, smiling and watching me. "It seemed like you were having a long day."

"What, your uncle never put anchovies on his pizzas back in Philadelphia?"

"I was working at his pizzeria on weekends when I was a teenager and a guy ordered up a pie with anchovies, and when he picked it up he opened the box and complained that there weren't enough." She looked up at me. "Alphonse just looked at the guy and said, "Most people don't like anchovies, asshole.""

"That's an interesting take you guys in Philly have on customer service."

"Fuck 'em if they can't take a joke." She glanced around. "So, you're sleeping in the dinosaur graveyard tonight?"

I sipped my beer and took another slice from the open box that rested on Jen's crated skull. "Yep."

"Seems fitting; you're the biggest dinosaur I know." She waited a while before asking the question I knew was still on her mind. "Okay, so what about that frozen moment you had the other morning?"

I ate more pizza and looked at the box to avoid her eyes, but when I looked back up, she was still watching me. "What?"

"There was one of those visions or whatever you want to call them with the Old Cheyenne, right?"

I reluctantly agreed. "Kind of."

She finished hers and tossed the crust across the crate to Dog, who hit it like a great white shark hits seals off the coast of South Africa. "So, give."

I closed the top on the last piece, rested an elbow on the crate, and thought about what had happened that night and a couple of times before. "I saw Virgil again." She didn't say anything but just watched me. "When I was in the lodge over in South Dakota in the snowstorm a few months ago, and he wasn't alone."

"Who was with him?"

I thought about the woman, who was Grace Coolidge, of all people, and the mystery man with the stars in his eyes. "You're not going to believe me if I tell you."

"I don't believe in your make-believe friend Virgil, so why should I buy any of the Old Cheyenne friends he had tagging along from the Camp of the Dead?"

"That's the third time I've seen him."

She held up two fingers and licked them, then wiped them

off on a paper napkin. "Twice—the first time you met him he was alive, now two times dead."

"I'm worried that I might be losing it a little bit each time."

"What do you mean?"

I said the next words very carefully. "That I'm losing my mind."

She laughed but then noticed I wasn't joining her. She tilted her head sideways and leaned in, searching my eyes. "You're serious."

"I've never had anything happen to me like I have in the last few years—seeing things, hearing things, people that aren't there . . . I'm not exactly given to this stuff, you know?"

"Shit, you are serious."

"I am." I reopened the box, tore up the slice, and fed the pizza to Dog, my appetite having totally retreated. "Normally, I'd just forget it, mark it off as some kind of hallucination or something, but every time Virgil or whoever or whatever it is has prophesized something, it's come true."

She stretched a hand across the crate and rested it on my arm as we both stood there. "Look, maybe you need to talk to somebody."

"I thought that was what I was doing."

She paused for a long time before continuing. "I mean somebody who knows something about this stuff. I'm no expert on the subject, but it's always when you're by yourself; have you ever thought that it might just be you? Maybe your subconscious is trying to tell you something, huh?"

"No, it's dissociative—things I choose not to think about."

"Well, there's your answer right there." She shook my arm, anxious that I not get too serious, and then let go and sipped her beer. "Walt, as near as I can tell, you think too damn much."

"Uh huh."

She set the empty can on the crate. "What did Virgil say?"

"It wasn't just Virgil; this time it was also a man in the snow."

"Okay."

"I was following someone in this dream, and when I got closer I could see it was a buffalo, but when it turned it changed shape into a man, a man with no eyes, just spaces where you could see the stars shining in the darkness—like his head contained the universe."

"And you get all this stuff without the benefit of controlled substances or alcohol?"

"Pretty much."

"And the guy without eyes, you're not going to tell me . . ."

"Danny Lone Elk."

Her mouth made a perfect *O* before she spoke. "That's some trippy shit." She came around and sidled her hip and shoulder against me, forcing Dog out of the way. "So, what'd Blind Danny Lone Elk have to say?"

I took a deep breath—she smelled really good—and then recited: *"You will stand and see the good, but you will also stand and see the bad—the dead shall rise and the blind will see."*

She gave a shudder and then slipped her arm around my waist. "So, why do they always say creepy stuff like that, huh? Why can't they just say you're going to win the lottery or that you're going to get laid?"

"I don't think they occupy themselves with those kinds of thoughts."

"Well, fuck them, I do." She pulled me in closer. "Maybe if the Old Cheyenne got laid every once in a while they wouldn't have to haunt the only single, smart, sexy guy I know." She studied me. "What did he say again?"

"*You will stand and see the good, but you will also stand and see the bad—the dead shall rise and the blind will see.*" I looked down at her. "Does the fact that I'm haunted like an old house turn you off?"

"Just the opposite." She tugged on my gun belt, pulling me in even closer. "I told you, you think too much." She pushed me away, sat on the crate, and began unbuttoning her uniform shirt, only to pause halfway through the operation to bend one knee over the other in a provocative manner. Then she arched her back, spread her arms, causing her shirt to gape even more, as she assumed a pinup pose. "This is a big crate."

I was suddenly having a hard time thinking.

4

I was at the top of a ridge alongside a man who was standing with his back to me, a tall man, broad, with silver hair to his waist. In his shirtsleeves, despite the weather, he stood there singing a Cheyenne song.

It was a clear night, the kind that freezes the air in your lungs with nothing standing between your upturned face and the glittering cold of those pinpricks in the endless darkness, the wash of stars constructing the Hanging Road as it arced toward the Camp of the Dead.

The man next to me had stopped singing and spoke from the side of his mouth. It was a voice I'd heard before, even though I couldn't exactly place it. I heard me call out to him. "Virgil?"

He half-turned toward me, his profile sharp, and I could see that it was not Virgil White Buffalo as he studied me from the corner of one eye. "You're bleeding?"

I watched myself looking down at the blood soaking through my sheepskin coat and the ground around me. "Um, yep . . . I think I am."

He walked effortlessly toward me, his face only a few inches from my own, the empty sockets shooting through his head like twin telescopes magnifying the black, infinite space with only a few aberrant *sparks of warmth from dying stars. Slowly he reached up and wiped the tear from my face. "Good—we can use the humidity."*

I awoke with a start.

"What?"

I turned my head and looked at Vic, covered in the blanket I'd brought in from my truck. "What?"

She yawned and stretched an arm out, then hid her mouth with her hand. "You were talking in your sleep."

I rolled over on one shoulder, closer to her. "I know."

"It was about the blind guy." She studied me, the sparks in her eyes still visible even in the dim confines of the High Plains Dinosaur Museum. "Danny Lone Elk."

I rested my head on my forearm. "Yep."

She waited before finally speaking again. "I mean, you weren't sure, the last time."

"It was him."

She put a hand out and rested her cool fingers on my arm, near a small scar that was a leftover from an altercation with two kids out of Casper who had robbed a liquor store and had been on their way to Canada when I had the fortune or misfortune of pulling them over for a burnt-out taillight.

"Same dream?"

Drawn back from wounds past, I looked at her. "What?"

"The same dream?"

"Yep, pretty much." I lay there looking at her, and our lives seemed to be swirling just then, circling with orbits that were becoming smaller and smaller. "I know."

She looked puzzled. "Know what?"

She'd been shot defending me a few months back, and while she'd been in the ICU, Doc Bloomfield had made the mistake of telling me she'd been pregnant. She'd lost the child, and up to this moment we'd kept our separate peace about that—something I could no longer withstand. "You were pregnant."

She stared at me.

"Isaac told me. He didn't mean to, but it slipped out when I first got to the hospital." Her expression didn't change, and I continued. "I didn't know if you knew that I knew, but I didn't want this to become something between us, something bad."

There was a sudden banging somewhere in the building, and as Dog vaulted from the floor beside the crate and began barking, we both looked around; I found my voice first. "Did something fall over in here?"

The banging started again, and this time I could tell that someone was hammering on the front door of the museum. It was just after midnight, and I'd locked the door, which was a good thing in that it gave me time to climb off the crate and get my clothes on.

"Walt!" It was a man's voice, muffled by the heavy glass.

"Who the hell is it?" Vic pulled the blanket over her shoulders as I hurriedly tried to straighten my hat and my back and started after Dog for the door.

"It sounds like Saizarbitoria."

Dodging through the gift shop, I made my way past the front desk and wrapped my fingers around the keys dangling from the lock on the inside. I yanked the door open and caught Dog by his collar so that he wouldn't mistake the Basquo for an intruder. "What's the matter, Sancho?"

He looked as panicked as I'd ever seen him. "It's Lucian—I think he's having a stroke or something."

"What?" I stood there looking at him and realized I was asking the wrong question. "Where?"

"The home for assisted living; he won't go to the hospital."

I yelled over my shoulder. "Vic, stay with the dinosaur!" I looked down and shoved Dog back inside. "And Dog!"

I ran with Sancho and dove into the passenger side of his sedan. "Give me the lowdown."

"Classic, non-movie-style stroke." Sancho backed the cruiser out, spun the wheel, and flew through the abandoned town with its blinking yellow lights. "The housekeeper found him sitting in his chair complaining of pain and discomfort." He turned to look at me as we flat tracked it onto Fort Street and hit the afterburners again. "He had his leg shot off, for Christ's sake—you would think they would've taken that kind of thing seriously coming from him."

I immediately remembered Danny Lone Elk's flask. "Yep, you would."

"Anyway, somebody else came in a few hours later—he was still in that chair, but he'd thrown up on himself and was saying he was fine, but this time he was having a migraine-like headache, tremors, and slurred speech. Well, they dialed 911, and we got there at the same time. The EMTs got him cleaned up, and he told Cathi and Chris that he was feeling better and they should beat it. Well, he *was* the sheriff, so they did." Santiago made the next turn, and we were almost there. "I didn't think that was the right decision, so I bullshitted with him, but then he started messing up his words and said he was feeling sick again." He slid to a stop at the entrance of the center behind the EMT van, and we leapt out, running for the door, me trying to keep up. "I tried to sit him in his chair, but one of his arms wouldn't work and I knew right then that I had to get the EMTs back there quick."

We blew past the empty registration desk and down the hall. "And then?"

"He was still arguing with them, and you know how he is— he can argue with a stump. So that's when I came after you."

When we got close to room 32, I could see a small crowd of attendees, including the director, Mary Jo Johnson, standing in the hall. "Oh, thank God, Walt . . . He won't listen to any of us, and now he's got a gun."

Sancho and I slid through the group, Cathi and Chris sitting impatiently on the sofa with their equipment, and looked at the man in the high-back, steer-hide-covered chair with the .38 Smith & Wesson service revolver resting on his knee.

"Lucian?"

He didn't look at me, but when I kneeled down in front of him, he raised the pistol up and pointed it in my general direction as his breath came in pants.

"Lucian."

His eyes wobbled toward me, along with the Smith. "I think . . . I think I . . . I done my forty and found."

"What's the gun for?"

"What?" He mumbled something, but I had trouble following him as he gestured with the barrel toward the terrified two on the sofa. "Keep 'em from doin' anything stupid."

"Like keeping you alive?"

He smiled a horrible, death's head grin. "Must be my time; everybody has one, ya know."

"Yep, well, this one's not yours." I glanced around, looking for the culprit. "Did you drink the rest of the rye in that flask you stole from me?"

He took a deeper breath and shuddered. "What?"

"The flask, Lucian. The one I took off of Danny Lone Elk, the Cheyenne fellow who died?"

He didn't say anything, his eyes continuing to wobble along with his breath, as Saizarbitoria circled around into the kitchenette.

"Did you drink the rest of that stuff, because if you did, I think you've been poisoned."

The pistol wavered a bit, and I started to reach for it when he pulled back the hammer. "Somebody." He aimed the pistol at me, dead center. "Somebody . . . poisoned me?"

"Whoever poisoned Danny Lone Elk put something in that whiskey, so if you drank it we've got to get you taken care of." I looked behind him and could see Sancho holding the flask that he must've gotten from the counter and shaking it near his ear. After a second, he looked at me and held it upside down with the cap disconnected—empty.

"The liquor in the flask was poisoned, Lucian." I gestured toward the two highly interested EMTs. "And that's why they're here."

His eyes widened a little, and I was thinking that the idea must've gotten through when the pupils rolled back in his head and his back arched, slamming him into the recesses of his ancestral chair, the pistol jerking up and away.

I grabbed his wrist as the .38 went off and shattered the sliding glass doors, the cracks spidering to the frames like a lightning strike.

The crowd suddenly disappeared, but Chris and Cathi scrambled off the couch as the Basquo caught the back of Lucian's chair and sat it upright.

Tossing the revolver to the side, I lowered the old sheriff to the carpeted floor, the EMTs waiting anxiously.

One of Lucian's hands came up. "Damn, now my head really hurts."

"You just relax."

His eyes raced around. "Where's my pistol?"

I wanted to punch him. "You don't need your sidearm—just lie there and be still."

I punched Saizarbitoria in the arm. "C'mon, let's go get the gurney from the van." As we exited the room, I pointed back at the old sheriff. "You. Do as you're told."

We hurried down the hall. "There's nothing left in the flask?"

"Not a drop."

"Hmm . . . I guess that's what you get when a high-functioning alcoholic steals evidence." We yanked the EMT van doors open and unloaded the gurney, me offering the Basquo my hard-earned advice. "Drop the wheels; it's easier to roll the thing than carry it."

As we rounded the corner and started down the hall, a thought occurred to me. "Was there a glass?"

Backing into the room, Sancho glanced into the kitchenette past the people who had reassembled around the doorway. "No, not that I noticed."

"He always drinks out of one of those Waterford tumblers."

We placed the gurney next to Lucian and collapsed the legs, bringing the mountain to Mohammed. I stepped back out of the way and started for the kitchen just as Mary Jo lifted one of the glasses I'd asked Saizarbitoria about and began to pour the contents down the sink.

"Stop!"

The sound of my voice shocked her so much that she dropped the glass, but by then I was close enough to get my hand underneath to catch it.

I held the glistening Lismore crystal up to the light fixture in the ceiling; sure enough, a bit of the amber liquid was captured in the corner. "Good thing he was drinking it neat."

We sipped our coffee and watched as Jay, the UPS and all-purpose driver, drove the forklift and carefully negotiated it into the back door of the holding cell.

Vic glanced at the Colonel E. H. Taylor Straight Rye Whiskey under my arm. "Starting a little early, aren't you?"

"Scientific specimen I liberated from Lucian's bar." I patted the bottle I'd taken from the corner cabinet in the old sheriff's rooms. "The control alcohol I'm taking over to Isaac."

She raised an eyebrow, and we watched as Jay reloaded the forklift onto his truck and came over, taking off his gloves and handing me a clipboard and pen. "Compliments of the Jayco Corporation."

I looked at the bill. "Two hundred and forty-six dollars?"

He shrugged, his mustache kicking to the side. "Equipment and labor."

I waved him off. "Go find a G-man to give that bill to."

"I did it as a favor to you." I stood there and then signed the manifest as he admired Dave Baumann's workmanship. "It's a nice crate."

Vic ran a hand over the wood. "Yeah, it looks like it can take a lot of punishment."

I handed him back the pen. "Get Ruby to write you a check, and you can save yourself a stamp."

Knowing where the true seat of power resided and not wanting to press his luck confronting her, he ripped the yellow receipt sheet off the pad and handed it to me. "At her convenience."

He raised a fist. "Save Jen."

Then he turned and walked away briskly; I wouldn't want to face Ruby this early in the morning either. I closed the door and looked at the assorted boxes, file folders, and the enormous crate that all but filled the room. "The good news is that it's not our responsibility to go through all this stuff."

"Amen to that." She took another sip of her coffee, slid around the far corner of the enormous box, and leaned against the wall as I set the bottle of rye on the crate's flat wooden surface. "So, how's the old fart doing?"

"Fine." I thought about it. "Well, as fine as somebody who almost met his maker can be." I took a sip of the coffee Vic had gotten for me. "Isaac saw him this morning and said there seemed to be no lingering symptoms other than a pretty good headache, which seems to indicate that he was poisoned by whatever was in the flask, and which leads us to the question of who filled the flask and from what."

"You're going out to Danny's?"

I nodded. "The ranch is huge, and I'm not sure which house Danny was living in, but I suppose I'll find it eventually."

"Is there a Mrs. Lone Elk?"

"Not for some time now."

She held her coffee in both hands. "So, you wanna talk?"

I waited a long time before answering. "I wanted to last night before Sancho started beating on the doors."

She eyed me over the rim of her cup. "You had something you wanted to say?"

I waited a moment, crafting my words carefully. "Nothing specific—it's just that it didn't seem fair to know and not tell you."

She nodded. "You're a big one for the truth, huh?"

"I try to be."

Of all the things she could've said, nothing would've surprised me as much as her next words. "Well, what if I told you it wasn't yours?"

It's a fact that the planet rotates at approximately 1,040 miles per hour, but there are those moments when the world just stops, magnetic poles be damned; you just stop the world with the weight of your own solitary gravitas. "What?"

She smiled, the kind of smile cats reserve for their dealings with mice, and didn't move for what seemed like a long time. Her head dropped and her fingers threaded into her thick hair, her voice echoing off the sixty-seven-million-year-old female skull. "I'm joking, you asshole. Who else would I want to fuck around here, anyway; it's not like the bench is deep."

I stood there, attempting to reacquire the power of speech.

Her face rose, and she shook her head at me. "What in the world makes you think that Isaac didn't tell me that he told you?"

I stumbled over the words. "He swore me to silence."

She laughed, but it was a nice laugh and she looked at me with nothing but pity in her tarnished eyes. "Yeah, but it isn't like you swore him, right?" She leaned her elbows on the crate we'd used most exclusively the previous night. "Isaac is always going to be on the lady's side, Walt."

"When did he tell you?"

"As soon as I woke up." She propped an elbow and rested her chin in her palm, attempting to look pixyish and succeeding in spades. "Besides, he's Jewish; along with the Irish and us Italians, they pretty much corner the market in guilt. There was no way he was going to let something like that slip to you and then not tell me about it."

"So, how long were you going to let me tread water?"

She stood up straight and sipped her coffee again. "I knew you wouldn't last; deception is not one of your strong suits."

"Are you okay?"

She looked at the floor and wouldn't make eye contact with me.

I took a deep breath and asked, unsure if I wanted to know the answer, "Was it a boy or a girl?"

She stared at the crate. "I didn't ask; it just would've made it harder, you know?" Her eyes were wet with tears and reflected the light in the room. "I have to admit that I've never wanted anything in my life as much as I want that Bidarte character's head on a plate."

I took a deep breath and slowly let it out. "Yep."

"I shot him close to a dozen times, and I would like to think that his remains are scattered all over the southern part of the county." She pushed off, wiped her eyes with the butt of her palm, and looked at me again. "But right now I've got a job to do, and life goes on. You know?"

"I know." Grabbing the bottle of whiskey, I squeezed

around Jen and steered Vic toward the hallway by her shoulders. "You know something else?"

"Hmm?"

I turned her around and hugged her in close. "You are the toughest person I know."

She pushed her face into my chest, her voice muffled. "Tougher than you?"

"You bet."

"Tougher than Henry?"

"Yep."

"Tougher than Dog?"

I paused. "Maybe not tougher than Dog—nobody's tougher than Dog."

She punched me and smiled. "So, what's on the agenda for today?"

I pulled out my pocket watch. "Well, I've got an appointment with Isaac to see what else he might've learned from the whiskey sample. Then the acting deputy attorney is making his big speech in front of the courthouse, where I am supposed to be part of the set dressing as third spear holder from the right."

She pulled back and looked up at me. "And then you're driving out to the Lone Elk place?"

I sighed. "Yep, to talk to whomever it was that packed Danny's lunch and flask for him the other morning."

"Aw, hell . . . Let's just talk to everyone, shall we?"

"Then, sometime later today I'd like to go get my daughter and your niece at the airport."

"I thought Sancho was going to do that."

"He's on standby, and besides, he has to assemble the Pack 'n Play."

"What the hell is a Pack 'n Play again?"

I slipped an arm over her shoulder and steered her down the hallway. "See the kinds of things you don't have to cloud your mind with when you don't have children?"

As we passed Saizarbitoria's office, the Basquo called out to us, "Hey guys, we need another aesthetic opinion."

We looked in and could see that Double Tough was leaning on Sancho's desk again. Vic shook her head. "Is it another eyeball?"

DT smiled and nodded. "I got a collection, and I'm trying one out each day."

Always an audience for the macabre, Vic moved into position and stared up in his face, "Too green."

He seemed disappointed. "Too green?"

She pulled back. "Too fucking green. Jesus, Double Tough, it's fucking Lucky Charms green!" She pulled me closer, forcing an opinion. "Well?"

I leaned in and could see that it was, indeed, kelly green. "Um, it's a little on the bright side."

"It looks like the Phillies' uniforms on St. Patrick's Day!" She whirled on the Basquo. "What'd you tell him?"

Sancho raised both hands. "I said we needed a second and likely a third opinion."

She turned back to Double Tough. "Not green greener— hazel greener."

He mumbled. "Yeah, okay, got it."

She stormed out as I glanced after her and leaned in to look at his replacement orb. "She's had a rough night . . ." The thing was the color of a shamrock and a thought traveled lightly across my mind. "Hey, DT . . . No offense, but . . . um, are you color-blind?"

He smiled and then came clean. "Half."

I glanced at Saizarbitoria. "Help him out with this, will you?"

The Basquo nodded, and I glanced back at Double Tough. "Less green green, more hazel."

As I turned the corner into the main reception area, I became aware of a lot more noise than I was used to and was treated to a mob of television news people from all over the region—K2TV and KCWY out of Casper, KGWN from Cheyenne, KOTA Territory News from over in Rapid City, and KULR and KTVQ from up in Billings.

In the frenzy of arguing with Ruby, they didn't notice me or the bottle of rye in my hand. The only one who did was Dog, who crept away from the melee with all the dignity of a lion from hyenas and joined me as I backed down the hallway before the fourth estate could catch us.

Pushing open the back door, I held it for Dog and then turned the corner to find Ernie "Man About Town" Brown of *Durant Courant* fame sitting on the tailgate of my truck. Busted. "Hi, Ernie. How come you're not inside with all the other riff-raff?"

"I'm afraid it's too crowded in there." He patted the bed of the truck and Dog jumped in, sitting at Ernie's side as the newsman produced a biscuit from his shirt pocket.

"How can I help you, Ernie?"

He fed Dog the treat and glanced at the bottle of rye, still hanging from my hand. "Where are you off to?"

"Going to see Isaac Bloomfield, give him this bottle, and find out about the preliminary autopsy on—"

"Danny Lone Elk." He nodded and pulled out a small spiral

notebook with a stubby golf pencil shoved in the wire. "I've got his obituary in the paper this morning. You know, his wife died about ten years ago, but he is survived by one son and one daughter." He smiled and adjusted his trifocal glasses. "You should read the paper, Walter. You'd discover all kinds of things."

Figuring there was no way out of talking to him, I leaned against my truck. "Yep, well, I figure my copy is lying in there at the reception desk, and I'm not going anywhere near that place."

He gestured around him. "Just as I figured." He licked the point of his pencil. "Now, about this announcement that the acting deputy attorney will be making . . ."

"Do you know anything about him?"

"Skip Trost?" He nodded. "Colorado Springs kid, born and bred; worked on a number of elections down that way and was picked up by Tom Wheeler to head his campaign when he ran for the senate here in Wyoming."

"I've heard Trost doesn't have any trial experience."

He fed Dog another cookie. "He doesn't."

I edged a half seat on the tailgate and folded my arms around the bottle so as to not drop it. "A lot of interaction with the media, though?"

He paused over the pad, the tip of his pencil like a wasp's stinger. "I just need an official statement from you, Walter."

All the while thinking that this whole shit storm of a witch hunt was being manufactured by some unconfirmed peon trying to make a name for himself, I switched into publicspeak. "The theft of artifacts is an extremely sensitive issue, and we're just glad to have the cooperation of the U.S. Attorney's office and the Justice Department in this complex situation."

"Anything to say about the High Plains Dinosaur Museum?"

"The HPDM is a fixture within the community, and I'm sure that anything that might be construed as an illegal act will be scrutinized to the fullest and everyone within the organization will assist us in any way possible."

"Anything to say about the Cheyenne tribe's involvement or the passing of Danny Lone Elk?"

Given the fact that I had one dead man and another half-dead one, both of whom had sampled whiskey out of the same flask, I dissembled: "That's an ongoing investigation and unavailable for comment at this time."

He lowered his pencil, and it was not the first time I'd felt he might be reading my mind.

"How's Lucian?"

The more formal portion of the interview over, I packed up my publicspeak and deposited it. "He's okay. I'm on my way over there now to check on him and talk to Isaac."

"Not to change the subject, but do you have any photographs of the *T. rex*'s head?"

"No, but I'm sure Dave Baumann does. I'm sure the FBI does, too, but I'd ask Dave."

"Thank you, Walter."

"You bet."

He nodded, placed his notebook and pencil in the inside pocket of his suit jacket, and raised a fist. "Save Jen."

"You look fit—for a guy who died last night."

His hands frittered over the sheets on the hospital bed. "Well, that's good, because I feel like living hell."

"I guess whatever you drank gave you a pretty good hangover."

He ironed a hand across his wrinkled face and discovered an IV connected to his arm. "How did I get here?"

"Saizarbitoria and I loaded you onto a gurney." I placed the bottle of whiskey on the floor beside my chair and got up, walking over and putting his arm back down before he got the idea of pulling the needle from his vein. I stood back with my hands on my hips, satisfied the hospital equipment was safe for the moment. "What do you remember about yesterday?"

"Got sick." He thought about it. "Had a ham sandwich for lunch and figured it might've been that, but then I started thinking it was the flu."

"Did you drink all the whiskey that was in Danny Lone Elk's flask?"

He smirked his defiance at me. "What if I did."

It was about then that Isaac and David Nickerson, who had just been appointed the head of Durant Memorial Hospital's newly renovated ER, came in the room, both of them holding overloaded clipboards.

I walked back to my chair, reached down, and offered the bottle to the docs, which did not go unnoticed by the old sheriff in the bed.

"What the hell are you doin' with my whiskey?"

"I pulled it from your bar; don't worry, it's not your best stuff." Isaac took the bottle, and I turned back to Lucian. "They need to test it against the stuff you drank from the flask."

"Be careful with that bottle; that straight rye is mighty dear."

David quieted him. "It's all right; all we need is a test-tube full—I'm a light drinker."

The doc gestured toward his younger associate. "He's been able to use our lab to examine the contents of the tumbler, and even though the results aren't going to be as conclusive as those from DCI, we think we've discovered something."

"What?"

The ER doctor cleared his throat. "Mercury."

I glanced at the old sheriff. "You said it tasted metallic."

Nickerson came around the bed and looked across at me. "I'm betting that if we did an autopsy on Danny Lone Elk, we would find he died of mercury poisoning."

"Why didn't it kill Lucian?"

"Because this particular form of mercury absorbs into the victim's system more in an acidic environment, and with Danny's ulcers, his stomach was chronically acidic."

"So, both Danny and Lucian were most likely poisoned?"

Isaac put his clipboard at Lucian's blanketed feet and then came over and took his wrist and checked his pulse. "Possibly, but it could be that the mercury was absorbed from the flask. We have no idea of its age or how long the whiskey had been in there."

5

"Can a press conference be considered impromptu if you're wearing pancake makeup?"

Looking at the crowds of people in green and white SAVE JEN T-shirts, who were protesting the perceived jackboot actions of the feds by holding signs that read SAY BYE, FBI!, I leaned against the red brick of the courthouse and sighed. It appeared to me that Skip Trost was facing an uphill battle.

I studied the side of his face. "You're kidding."

Vic smiled. "And just a touch of rouge to give him that ruddy, cross-dresser-of-the-people look."

I glanced at the hundred or so trampling the newly sown grass on the hill leading to my office and spoke out of the side of my mouth: "Hush, this is bad enough without a running commentary."

"Thank you for being here today for this off-the-cuff announcement, and thank you for the pleasure of being here with all of you this morning." The acting deputy attorney continued talking over the shouts of the crowd. "It is a privilege to see my friends, colleagues, and local leaders assembled here today for this momentous event—it is a wonderful opportunity to thank them for their dedication in serving as faithful stewards to the people and the wonderful place we call home, Wyoming."

"Do you think he thinks they don't know what state they live in?"

Trost adjusted the microphone on the podium and studied the onlookers. "From its earliest days, this state has been bound together by a set of laws and values that define it— equality, opportunity, and justice."

"For all."

"Shhhh . . ."

"When is he going to start talking about the dinosaur?"

"Shhhh . . ."

"These traits are codified in our great state, and there are those of us who are called upon to settle disputes but also to hold accountable those who have done wrong. I have long held the opinion that I am a custodian of the law." He turned around and looked at the courthouse to validate his worth.

"How long has he been in office?"

I mumbled under my breath, "He hasn't been confirmed yet."

He gained momentum. "I hope to give a clear and focused message to those who would take advantage of our great state's magnificent bounty."

She bounced the back of her head against the wall. "Oh, brother."

"Yes, a treasure trove of state antiquities that should not be allowed to fall into any single individual's hands but should be shared by all the people of Wyoming in a communal dedication to the cause of justice and the common good."

"Coming off kind of William Jennings Bryan, isn't he?"

Feeling he'd captured the throng, Trost decided to get literary. "*Salus populi suprema lex esto.*"

She looked at me. "What the fuck was that?"

"Cicero—the welfare of the people is the ultimate law."

Vic studied the telejournalists, all of them looking a little perplexed. "Think they'll subtitle him?"

Warming to the subject, Trost nodded his head. "It is time; in fact it's well past time to address the persistent needs and unwarranted disparities by considering a fundamentally new approach toward the federal Antiquities Act of 1906, which includes a clear prohibition against removing fossils from any land owned or controlled by the United States." He paused for dramatic effect. "I myself would prefer to see Jen remain, if not here in Absaroka County, then within the confines of the state." He raised a fist. "Save Jen!"

There were cheers on that one.

"This is our solemn obligation as stewards of the land so that these antiquities might be preserved for our children . . ."

Vic mumbled, "And our children's children."

"And our children's children." He glanced at us and gestured toward me, and I thought that he might've overheard Vic. "I'd like to ask a man that's well-known and respected by all of you, Sheriff Walt Longmire, to join me here at the podium."

I pushed off the wall and started forward, speaking under my breath as I passed her, "What, no smart-ass remark on that?"

She smiled and patted my shoulder. "Just waiting till you're out of earshot."

Trost pumped my hand as I joined him; he was, indeed,

wearing makeup. He had stopped me on the top step to try and keep his height opportunity, but even with the six-inch advantage, I was still a couple of inches taller. He smiled brightly for the cameras and held on to my hand. "Are there any questions?"

"Sheriff, have any criminal charges been brought against the High Plains Dinosaur Museum?"

"Um, not at this time. We're hoping that—"

Trost reached over and brought the mic closer to his face. "Actually, our office has been planning an intervention to discourage this type of behavior."

A Billings reporter called out to me, "Sheriff, is it true that the Jen was found on Native American land?"

"Well, it was discovered on the Lone Elk Ranch, and Danny was an enrolled member—"

Trost leapt in again. "The Cheyenne tribe has filed an order to desist under the federal Antiquities Act of 1906 prohibiting the removal of fossils from any land owned or controlled by the United States without permit."

The redhead from the Casper station yelled at me, "Does the museum have a permit, Walt?"

I shrugged again. "My understanding is—"

The deputy attorney spoke into the microphone. "No, they do not." He glanced around. "I'm afraid that the sheriff has other duties to attend to, but I'm glad to stay here and answer anything more you might want to know."

As another flurry of questions exploded, I took my leave and collected Vic, shortcutting to our office through the courthouse. I held the glass door open and ushered her in. "So, how did I do?"

"You were a perfect little meat puppet." She glanced back with mock concern. "You didn't mess up his lipstick, did you?"

There are signs on the Lone Elk place, but you have to find them.

Kicking at the boards lying at the base of a post and trying to figure out if any of them might be pointing the right way, I kneeled down and turned a few over, reading the names of owners long past.

"Are we lost?"

I lifted my face, narrowing my eyes in the wind that had picked up, and looked at the rolling hills of the eastern part of my jurisdiction. "Never lost, just mightily confused."

She stood at the fork of the gravel roads and turned around as Dog took a leak on his forty-third piece of sagebrush. "How big is our county again?"

"In square miles?"

"Yeah."

"Just over nine thousand—about the size of New Hampshire." I glanced around some more, making some calculations. "If I were to guess, I'd say we were near Hakert Draw at the Wallows, maybe near Dead Swede Mine."

She walked past me to the edge of the road, Dog following, and looked at the Powder River country, at the vastness of the high plains that seemed to draw your eyes further than you thought possible. "Question number one." She turned to look at me, scratching behind Dog's ear as he sat on her foot. "What is Hakert Draw?"

"Well, a draw is formed by two parallel ridges or spurs with low ground in between them; the area of low ground, where we happen to be standing, is the actual draw. Hakert is the name of the rancher who used to own the land."

She pushed Dog off her foot, walked over, and leaned against the pole. "The Wallows?"

"A few small lakes out here, fed by a number of creeks."

"Like the killer-turtle pond?"

"Yep."

"Dead Swede Mine?"

"That one is a little complicated."

"What, there's a dead Swede at the bottom of a shaft?"

I picked up one of the boards and stood. "There's a legend . . ."

She laughed. "What is it with you westerners? There's always a legend."

"Supposedly there were three prospectors who snuck into this area after it had been cordoned off by the military as Indian territory. As the tale goes, they found gold, a lot of it, but as is human nature, they then fell in on each other. After the altercation, the only one left was a Swede by the name of Jonus Johanson."

"He would be the dead one?"

I examined the board in my hands, running my thumb across the ridges made by the engraved letters. "Nobody knows what happened to him, but a man traveling alone, supposedly with a lot of gold, surrounded by scoundrels and profiteers of every stripe . . . I wouldn't think his odds were very good, but it's just a story."

She glanced around, I guess half hoping to see a timber-supported opening in the hills. "If those men found the mine, then it must be true."

"Not really—it's probably just an old, shallow-shaft coal

mine, a rarity in these parts; but still, as Dorothy Johnson once said, 'when the legend becomes fact, print the legend.'" Nudging my chin toward the Bighorns, I started back toward the Bullet. "If they found gold, it would've been closer to the mountains, but actually there's really not much geologic evidence of any gold anywhere in the area." I opened the door and looked back at the two of them. "Fool's gold, I'd say."

"Have you seen it?"

"What?"

"The mine."

"Once, when I was a kid out with my father." She opened the passenger-side door and let Dog hop in. "We were fishing and I got bored, so I went for a walk over a few ridges."

She climbed in and stretched the safety belt over her chest. "Through the draws?"

"Yep." I glanced over my shoulder at the endless series of hills. "You get in some of these big draws and you can't see the mountains; I was young, maybe six or seven, and not paying attention, and pretty soon I was lost. I got turned around and thought I was heading back, but then I saw an opening in a hillside with timbers and supports." I climbed into the truck, set the board with the etched names, faded with time and weather, across the center console between us, and fastened my own seat belt. "I was a kid so of course I went over and looked into it, but it was dark." I shook my head. "Threw a few pebbles in the opening but couldn't hear anything. Anyway, I got bored again and kept walking." I closed the door and started the Bullet. "Around dark, my father found me heading down Cook Road in the wrong direction. He was pretty mad, but I distracted him by telling him about the mine. We went back and looked for it a few days later; saw an old lineman's shack, but I never could find the mine opening again."

She glanced through the windshield at the fork in the road. "So, where to?"

I pointed my thumb at the arrow on the board that pointed to the left, next to the worn white letters in the reddish wood that read LONE ELK. "The road less traveled, I suppose."

I pulled out and drove over a few more ridges and then hit a straightaway that seemed to stretch to the horizon.

"But you saw it? I mean, it's out here."

"The mine?" I thought about it, but the memories were vague. "Or maybe I just dreamed it." I smiled at her. "I'm getting like that, you know. I think I know things from my past, but it turns out I just think that I know them; my youth is becoming a mythology to me."

She shook her head. "Just for the record? You say some of the strangest shit sometimes."

I went back to studying the road, because ahead is where the trouble usually is waiting. "Comes from having an overly active imagination."

Vic leaned forward in her seat. "Is that somebody?"

"Yep, I think it is." I began slowing the Bullet in an attempt to not powder whoever it might be—being afoot was a daring feat this far out.

I eased to a stop and rolled my window down; I could tell the young man thought about making a break for it but then realized that he might've waited a little too long—he might outrun two cops, but he wouldn't outrun the Bullet. "Howdy."

He shifted the backpack on his shoulder as if it were the

weight of the world, and maybe it was, at least to him. His voice didn't carry much enthusiasm as he studied the hills, one eye swollen, the skin underneath blackened. "Hey."

"Where are you going?"

He shrugged.

"Just headed out for the territories, huh?"

He turned his head, the long tendrils of black hair whipping across his face. "What's that supposed to mean?"

Vic snickered as I explained. "Oh, just something the old-timers used to say." I watched him some more—one tough cookie, as my father would have said. "Reno's nice; ever been to Reno?"

The eye that wasn't damaged narrowed, and he was unsure if I was poking fun at him. "Where's that?"

"Nevada."

He took his time answering. "Is that where you're headed?"

"No, we're headed for your house."

He sighed and kicked at a chunk of red shale in the road with the toe of a Chuck Taylor sneaker. "That's the one place I don't want to go."

I nodded and glanced at my undersheriff. "Well, we're lost and were hoping you could help us out."

He lip-pointed over his shoulder. "S'that way."

"We might miss it."

He sighed again, bigger this time, and then trudged in front of my truck and around to Vic's side like a condemned prisoner. She opened the door and got out, forcing him to the center. He climbed in, setting his backpack on the transmission hump as Dog swiped a tongue as broad as a dishwashing sponge up the back of his head. "'The fuck?"

Dog sat back and looked at him the way dogs have looked at boys for centuries—half-feral kindred spirits.

"That's Dog; I'm his."

The kid nodded toward Vic. "Are you hers, too?"

"I'm not so sure that's an appropriate question for you to be asking." I pulled out. "Where'd you get the shiner?"

"The what?"

"Black eye."

He touched his face. "What did you call it?"

"A shiner. The term can be traced back to a couple of origins; some say it was an Irish term for the beating you'd get if you didn't keep your equipment shiny, others that it was because the discolored, swelled tissue appears to have a shine to it."

He shrugged. "All I know is that if you make a smart remark to my uncle, you get one free of charge."

I drove, and he continued to study us; then he turned toward Vic, even going so far as to shift in the seat.

She stared back at him. "What?"

"You're hot."

"Um, thanks."

"My uncle Randy and me were talking about you . . . he thinks you're hot, too."

Vic glanced at me. "That's nice."

"We watch TV, and he always says that the TV cops are too pretty, that making them look like that is bullshit, but he said you were an exception."

"Oh." She smiled at him. "So, what are cops supposed to look like?"

He nodded my way. "Like him."

I nodded. "Thanks." I drove and thought it might be prudent to change the subject. "You know, I used to run away a lot when I was a kid."

"I'm seventeen, and I'm not runnin', just goin'."

I nodded. "Does your family know you're going?"

"No."

"Well, then, within the narrow purview of the law, that would be termed as running."

Crossing his arms, he slumped in the seat. "What, and that's against the law?"

"Pretty much." I rested an elbow on the sill. "So, why are you running away?"

"I'm not so sure that's an appropriate question for you to be asking."

Vic snickered some more as we made a small rise; at the base of one of the many draws, where the two ridges met, a large, Dutch-shouldered house sat nestled against one of the hills with a sprawling barn and an assortment of outbuildings, corrals, and chutes, along with a small bridge spanning Wallows Creek.

"Is this it?"

He didn't say anything, slumped, and looked at his lap as if we were taking him back to a gulag. I slowed to look at the mailbox, but there was only a number and no name. "Let's go find out."

As I drove the ranch road, I could see a mob of dogs coming out to meet us, mostly border collie and blue heeler mixes. I slowed my truck, trying not to run over any of them, and carefully rolled toward the house. Finally parked, I looked back at Dog, who seemed anxious to get out. "I don't think so."

I pulled the handle and stepped onto the gravel as Vic and the escapee did the same on the other side. The dogs barked and snapped but gave room when a loud whistle emanated from the back of the house; they disappeared without a sound. A woman appeared behind the screen door, only to disappear again.

"Looks like we're not welcome." I placed a hand on the young man's shoulder as we approached the porch. "Maybe it's the company we're traveling with."

A moment later, an impressive and shirtless Randy appeared at the door, pushing it open and stepping onto the red-wood planks in his bare feet; he leaned a shoulder against the facing, the door open. "*Pévevóona'o*, Sheriff."

"'Morning, Randy. Did we get you up?"

He yawned. "Calving."

The tough cookie shrugged off my hand and traveled under his uncle's arm into the house as Randy ducked his head below his armpit and called after him. "You run away again?" He turned back to look at us, shaking his head. "Kid runs away once after every meal."

"A little late in the season, isn't it?"

"Oh, hell no, he does it all year long."

We pulled up at the steps. "I meant calving."

He gestured toward the sun. "Spring. I never could figure out why these ranchers around here would want to birth calves in knee-deep snow in February."

I nodded. "My father did."

"I bet you ran away a lot, too." He gestured back to the house. "We're out of donuts, but you want some coffee?"

We sat on the front porch swing and nursed the mugs that Randy's sister, Eva, had brought out to us as she hummed a song under her breath; it was a familiar tune, but I couldn't place it. Randy regaled my undersheriff with tales of the romantic ranching life. "As calving days get closer, I move them into the smaller pastures just so I can keep an eye on them. I go out on horseback and ride among them in the morning and usually at night, too."

"Old school?"

He glanced at me, but it was pretty obvious he preferred looking at Vic. "Dad never allowed four-wheelers on the place." He raised a hand, imitating the thumb action of an ATV accelerator. "This ain't the cowboy way . . ." His hands dropped. "'Course, if it's a spring blizzard or something, I'll be out there all night, or at the least every two hours or so."

Vic shook her head. "When do you sleep?"

"Usually in the saddle." Randy laughed and gestured to a white-blazed bay standing by a gate. "One time on Bambino over there, I woke up covered with about three inches of snow and we were standing right here at the porch. I swear, if he could've, he would've climbed up the steps and taken me in the house and put me to bed." He glanced around at the bucolic beauty of the Bighorn foothills. "When Dad was sober, I think that was the thing he loved the best, the animal husbandry of it." He paused. "You just don't hear that word so much anymore, and it means a lot, you know?" His eyes went back to Vic. "Anyway, they get nervous and agitated when they're about to give birth and start looking for a secluded place to drop their calves. They walk and walk with their tails spinning like windmills until they find that place, and then when they do—boom."

My undersheriff sipped her coffee. "Just like that, huh?"

I laughed. "Oh no, not always."

Randy smiled and leaned back in his chair, tipping the runners to the rear. "The cows can have problems sometimes; if you see one calving and the pads of the calf are up, then it's backwards and you have to go in there and pull it."

Randy was enjoying the look on Vic's face as his sister joined us in a rocking chair a little ways off, still humming, and it was only now that I recognized the tune as "Dry Bones."

"I bring them into the calving shed, lay them down, and then pull the calves, sometimes by hand, sometimes with the calving chains. Sometimes they're coming forward and have a leg back; you'll see that because they'll have the shoulder pushed out. There are all kinds of things that can go wrong, but mostly they don't and things go pretty smoothly." His eyes went toward the building where we'd seen his uncle. "Enic is in there with one of them if you'd like to watch."

"Umm . . . no thanks." She glanced around. "How many cows do you have?"

Randy looked uncomfortable, glanced at me, and then smiled as he sipped his coffee some more.

I nudged Vic with my elbow. "You don't ever ask that."

"What?"

"The size of a man's herd or the size of his spread—it's against the code of the West."

"Why?"

"Because it's like asking a man how much money he has in his wallet or his bank account; it's just not done."

"Oh." She glanced at Randy. "Sorry."

He lowered his mug. "That's okay." He lip-pointed, just as his nephew had, toward a corral where his horse was tied off.

Inside the pen were a couple of calves milling about, crying out now and again. "See those? They're bums; their mothers don't want 'em and the bulls don't make good fathers."

Vic's eyes lingered on the little ones. "What'll happen to them?"

"They're worth a lot of money, so we'll bottle-feed 'em till they can start eating solid food." He leaned back and looked at his sister. "Or Eva will." He shook his head. "It's Taylor's job, but he can't seem to ignore the siren song of the open road. He wanted to get a job in town, and I thought that might slow him down a little . . ." He rested his dark eyes on me. "Where did you find him?"

"Up on Crook Road, about three miles from here."

"He goes and just wanders the hills sometimes; I don't know what the hell he's doing out there   maybe he's got a woman." Randy looked at the broiling thunderheads and inky blackness that stretched the sky toward the mountains like the boy's black eye and then glanced at Eva. "Hey, could we get some more coffee?" He watched as she disappeared back into the house without a word. "I'm not kidding, he runs away all the damn time; does it about every other day, but it's gotten worse since his grandfather died." He rested the mug on the arm of the chair and ran a forefinger over his upper lip. "They were a lot alike; he used to go fishing and hunting with the old man for days. Hell, my parents practically raised him. Eva never got married—never said who the father was."

"What about you?"

"What about me?"

"Been here your whole life?"

He leaned back in his chair again and smiled a sad smile. "I graduated from Bozeman and took a job as a conservationist but figured out before long that I just wasn't cut out for the academic life. Got married, got divorced—no kids." He looked at the rolling hillsides. "Dad getting older and Eva having her problems, I just decided to come back."

We said nothing.

"So . . ." He settled in for the real conversation. "What can you tell me about my father?"

I leaned forward. "Randy, I was hoping we could include your sister in the conversation."

He nodded and called over his shoulder, "Eva!"

There was a moment in which I suppose she was attempting to make it appear as if she hadn't been listening at the screen door. "Yes." She pushed the door open a bit and looked at the porch floor with the coffeepot in her hands.

"So, I'm assuming you're the one who packed his lunch?" I smiled just to let her know this wasn't an episode of *Perry Mason*, as I held out my mug. "The handwriting on the bag was somewhat female."

She studied me as she approached and poured me another. "What are you saying?"

"The preliminary examination seems to indicate that there might have been some mistakes made with his medications, but we haven't been able to reach his physician to confirm what all he was taking. I thought maybe you might know if there was medication in the sack, since you fixed his lunch."

Randy turned to his sister. "Is the tray still up on his nightstand?" She nodded and disappeared. "And get the stuff from the medicine cabinet in the bathroom."

Her voice carried back to us, just as the teenager's had. "All of them?"

"*Haáahe*, we got nothing to hide." He lowered his voice and turned back to look at us. "He got a bottle of some generic Viagra. I don't know if he ever took the stuff, but the bottle's up there—embarrassed my sister. I guess she doesn't know how she got here, or Taylor, for that matter."

"Randy, I have to ask about the possibility of an autopsy."

His handsome face stiffened. "No."

"It might give us some definitive answers on the—"

"My father was religious, almost as bad as my uncle—he's a Traditional and you know what that is."

"I do, and I know they don't like to disturb the body in any way, but . . ."

"Well then, you shouldn't even ask me." He looked in his empty cup. "I worked in a hospital as an intern in the science lab while I was at Montana State, and I know what they do to a body in an autopsy, and I wouldn't have that done to my worst enemy." He glanced at the corrals, and the building where we'd seen his uncle. "Anyway, Enic would never allow for it—never."

I let the dust settle on that one. "You know I can override you on this."

"Only if you suspect something." He studied me. "Do you?"

"Not yet, but I may."

"Henry Standing Bear is a friend of yours, right?"

"Yep."

"You get him to come talk with us, and we'll consider it."

"Deal." I reached down and put my empty cup on the

porch railing. "Speaking of deals, do you know about the one your father had with the Cheyenne Conservancy?"

"Yeah, I know about it. I think he was just feeling guilty about making it off the Rez and being a success. He carried big medicine for the tribe and, as I said, was getting more and more traditional as he got older. He was getting so stiff, he probably would've ended up standing in front of a cigar store." He glanced around, his eyes lingering on the clouds building up on the mountains as if trying to push them east.

Vic, figuring it was time to change the subject again and easier for her than me, asked, "What's the story on your sister?"

His eyes released me with ease and turned to her. "How do you mean?"

"Has she been here her whole life?"

"Pretty much; she took to religion along with Enic. That and looking after Taylor." He glanced over his shoulder, lowered his voice, and became confidential. "She didn't have a good experience in school, just too shy. Nothing drastic; it's just that she likes it here on the ranch and doesn't like everywhere else." He took a breath and settled, looking at the hills where the wind blew the short grass like waves. "She gets worked up about stuff, so they prescribed her these pills which seem to keep her on an even keel." He imitated toking a joint. "That, and a little rocking the ganja."

"So she just stays here, on the ranch?"

"Pretty much." He smiled. "I make her go with me into town once in a while to take Taylor to work or pick him up, just so she sees that there are other people in the world." He looked over and caught us glancing at each other. "It's not what you're thinking; she's not psychologically aberrant. She's just nervous and shy, really shy."

The conversation was cut short by Eva's return; she carried a plastic tray piled with pill containers and a plastic IGA bag. "Would you like me to put these in a sack for you, or do you want to look at them now?"

I shook my head. "The sack is fine—I wouldn't know what I was looking at, anyway."

She dumped them in the bag and handed them to me. "His stomach pills aren't there, so I think he must've had those with him?"

"He did." I got up and straightened my back. "Can I ask a favor, Eva?"

"Yes?"

"Can I have a look at your liquor cabinet?"

She said nothing but glanced back at her brother, who shook his head at us. "No liquor on the place. I mean, there are a few beers in the refrigerator . . ."

"But no hard alcohol?"

"No, why?"

"Your father had a flask on him when he died." They looked at each other, neither of them really seeming all that surprised. "Was he drinking again?"

Randy sighed. "He and Enic both had a problem . . . Well, we thought they had *had* a problem. My uncle drank himself into a hole—that's why he's here—and then he became a Traditional." He turned to his sister. "Do you know where Dad hid it?"

She put her hand to her mouth. "No. No . . ."

"It was rye whiskey, at least that's what was in the flask,

and if my expert is to be trusted, it was the good stuff." I waited. "Do you think he might've had some stashed around here?"

Randy stared at the planks on the porch floor. "That's how Taylor got the black eye . . . He's the one who snuck it in for the old man, but he wouldn't tell me where."

"It's possible that there's something wrong with what's in that bottle, so we'll need to test it against what was in the flask—besides, if it's bad, you're going to want to get rid of it."

"Wait." Eva stood and disappeared into the house again, after a few moments returning with Taylor the Truant under an arm. "The sheriff has something he'd like to ask you."

The young man stood there not looking at me.

"Hey, you helped me find the ranch—you mind helping me find something else?" That piqued his interest, and he looked up at me, all of a sudden a carbon copy of his grandfather. "I'm looking for a bottle of whiskey."

He stared at me.

"A bottle your grandfather might've had hidden around the house somewhere?"

He continued to stare at me.

His mother nudged his shoulder. "I told the sheriff you could find anything; do you know where a bottle like that might be?"

He swallowed and looked at his feet, all of a sudden seeming to be five. "I promised Grandpa I wouldn't tell."

I leaned in a little. "Well, you see, there might be something wrong with what's in that bottle. We need to take it to the lab so that they can find out what might've happened to your grandfather."

There was a long pause as thunder rumbled from the west. "I don't know where it is."

"Are you sure?"

"Yeah."

Randy started to reach over, but I shook my head at him. "That's okay."

Figuring he was released, Taylor turned and walked away, the slap of the screen door his final, teenage response—it was almost as loud as the thunder.

Randy turned and looked at us. "How 'bout I go in there and kick his skinny ass like a rented mule?"

"I'd rather you didn't."

He shook his head. "I'll look, Sheriff." He glanced up at his sister, who rested a hand on his shoulder. "Or Eva will; one way or the other, we'll come up with it." He studied her. "You ever see Dad with a flask?"

"He had that antique one. You know, it was silver, old-timey with a leather beaded cover?"

I nodded. "That's the one." I looked back at Randy. "Do you mind if we take a look at his study?"

He rose and started toward the door. "No, come on in."

He opened the screen, and we followed Randy into an entryway, where he turned to the right into what had been, I was sure, Danny Lone Elk's inner sanctum. Two large windows looked to the south, with a massive, hand-laid fireplace in the corner. There was a substantive rolltop desk between the windows along with an oak library chair. There were fossilized bones and tribal memorabilia everywhere, from dance fans and ceremonial pipes to war shields and feathered lances, but overshadowing all the relics was a huge horned shell from what must have been the largest snapping turtle ever seen in the territory. The carapace was painted and decorated with feathers and beads unlike anything I'd ever seen, and much too large to have ever been used as anything other than a stationary objet d'art.

Randy caught me studying the artifact, resting on a center table with a Plexiglas box over it. "I know, a monster, isn't it?"

"Where did it come from?"

"Here, at first; then it was acquired by the Canadian Museum of History. The tribe went to war, legally that is, and reacquired a lot of these items. Dad kept a few of them with permission, but now that he's gone I guess we'll hand 'em back over to the Culture Commission."

There were some smaller items surrounding the megalith— rattles and dance sticks, all made with turtle parts, each in its own Plexiglas box. "This stuff must be worth a fortune, Randy."

"I guess, but it's the tribe's now. Dad would've wanted it that way."

Eva carefully lifted up one of the Plexiglas boxes and retrieved a rattle adorned with an intricate painting of a turtle shield, feathers, and strips of horsehair and beads. "This . . . This was one of his favorites. I would come in and find him asleep in his chair with this on his chest." There was a pause as she handled the piece, her eyes full of tears. "I used to find him in here asleep with it every day."

She handed it to Vic, who gave it a cursory look and then handed it to me. Running my fingers along the edges of the box-turtle shell, I noticed a smell emanating from the thing, something antiseptic. "What's that smell?"

Randy stepped into the room from the doorway and took the rattle back and placed it on the stand, re-covering it with the Plexiglas. "They disinfected these things when they were in the museum in Canada." He half smiled. "I guess if they hadn't the mites and stuff would have eaten them all up. Smells funny, huh?"

I looked around the room. "Maybe you should ask to keep this one . . . I can't see how the tribe could be upset by you keeping just one."

He nodded. "I might, for Eva, as a remembrance of Dad." He gestured toward the collection. "He kind of had a turtle fixation. Hell, he used to bring the things back and have Eva here cook him up turtle soup on a regular basis."

Vic made a face. "I thought he held them as sacred?"

"Oh, he did. He'd sit on the front porch and talk to the turtles and apologize for eating them. I'm surprised he didn't have Eva cooking up pink elephant stew, what with his hallucinations."

I glanced around, wondering where I'd be if I were a bottle of whiskey. Lucian kept his liquor in a corner cabinet, but I didn't see anything like that in here; the moss-rock fireplace, however, looked remarkably clean for one that worked. "Is that fireplace operational?"

Eva shook her head. "No."

Randy stepped up and used a fingernail to pick at the moss growing on the stone. "He had a spray bottle that he filled up with old beer and sprayed on the mold to keep it alive—drove Eva here crazy."

"Who built it?"

Randy shrugged. "I don't know, why?"

"It's a Rumford design, unique in this territory." From my peripheral vision I could see Vic shaking her head and placing her face in the palm of her hand, but I continued. "Benjamin Thompson, a.k.a. Count Rumford, designed the fireplace that was state-of-the-art in the late eighteenth century." I leaned in and looked up the flue. "Jefferson had them built in Monticello, and Thoreau said they were one of the modern conveniences most taken for granted."

Vic's muffled voice sounded through her fingers. "So?"

I reached a hand up the flue, feeling my way. "The fireplaces were tall and shallow to reflect more heat into the room and had streamlined throats that carried the smoke away, but one of the truly inspired aspects of the design was a shelf that redirected the incoming cold air and then reflected it back up with the heated air from the fire." Finding what I was looking for, I carefully pulled the almost-full bottle of E. H. Taylor Straight Rye from the flue. "Also makes for a magnificent hiding place, when not in use."

Under the gathering gloom of thunderheads and the overcast sky, we said our good-byes. "Hey, Randy, do you mind if we take a look at the dig where they found Jen on our way out?"

He leaned on a post. "Why?"

"No particular reason; it's just that with all the excitement the other day, we didn't get close enough to see anything, and with all the excitement in town now, I'd like to talk about it from a more informed position."

"Sure." He pointed a finger at me. "No souvenirs, though."

"I promise."

"You better hurry; that storm's coming in and the washes flood if there's enough rain, and those roads get like axle grease once they get wet." He studied the angry skies. "You think you can find it from here?"

We started off the porch. "You can loan us your nephew."

He laughed as his sister followed us to the edge of the porch, clutching the coffee mugs to her chest with a worried look. "I want to apologize for Taylor. He's having a really hard time with his grandpa's death."

Randy draped his arm over her shoulder. "You better get going."

Eva continued, "Even to the point where he thinks . . ."

He interrupted, "They don't need to hear that stuff."

Vic, never one to shy away from asking a question, didn't. "What stuff?"

The woman's head dropped, but we could still hear her voice. "He keeps saying that he sees things."

"Eva, they're going to think we're all crazy."

She looked up past us where the thick smell of ozone permeated the air. "That he keeps seeing his grandfather standing on the hills out here . . . watching him."

6

"I am officially creeped out."

"Why?"

She shook her head and then turned to look at me as if I were the sole member and president of the Absaroka County chapter of stupid. "Umm . . . that kid is having the same visions you are."

Without thinking, I found myself looking in the rearview mirror to make sure that Taylor wasn't running along behind us. "It's a pretty generic vision."

"Maybe the two of you are tuned into the same channel from strange." She lodged her boots onto my dash. "I notice you didn't want to hang around and discuss it with him. You know, compare notes?" I ignored her chatter and watched as she scanned the hills in the available light that made them glow just before the storm. "I want a vision of my own."

"Well, you go ahead and get yourself one."

"Is that how it works?"

I tried not to smile as we sped along with the wind gusts buffeting the truck. "I don't think so."

She turned in the seat and stared at me. "Well, fuck special you. How come you and the kid get to run around communing with the netherworld while the rest of us mere mortals slog along?"

I humped my shoulders in a shrug. "How should I know how it works?"

"Because you have them like clockwork, like the eleven o'clock news."

I actually gave it some thought as I slowed for one of the few turns on the road. "Maybe you should talk to Henry."

"He can give me a vision?"

"I doubt it, but if you're looking to have one, he might help you find it in yourself."

She turned further in the seat. "That doesn't sound hopeful."

"I think some people are more susceptible."

Her tone sharpened. "What, I'm not susceptible?"

"You're pretty rational."

"What's that got to do with it?"

"I think you have to be open to . . . I guess, influences."

"Bullshit."

"No, that's not what I mean."

"No, I mean it's still bullshit that you get to have visions and I don't."

I glanced at her. "You might do well to keep in mind that every time these types of things have happened to me I've been somewhat impaired."

She sighed. "As in ready to die?"

"Something like that."

She went back to looking out the windshield. "Yeah, well, I'm not so sure I want a vision if I have to be bleeding to death to get it."

I watched her as we sped along, her eyelids drooping the way they always did whenever we were on one of our extended county tours. I began wondering how much sleep she was getting given the psychological toll of the last few months.

I was feeling a little unmoored myself and was thinking that even with all the complications, I was looking forward to seeing Cady and Lola. I would have preferred a more quiet time with them, but those seemed to be rarer and rarer these days.

I spotted the gate where we'd gone through the first time, when we'd first seen the dinosaur dig site, and slowed the Bullet, but now three strands of barbed wire blocked our way. I pulled to a stop and climbed out as Dog whined and I shushed him, trying to let my undersheriff grab a few winks. The gate was an old lever type, and I flipped it and dragged the pole and wire wide enough to drive through.

I stood there for a moment wondering if we really had time for this kind of goose chase—the wind was picking up and the storm had eaten the mountains. It was probably less than a half hour away, but seeing as how we were already here, I figured we could take the extra time. I would just make sure I parked far away from any washes, so that we'd be able to make it back to town.

I watched the clouds and remembered something Lucian, the old Doolittle Raider, had told me once, that if we could see what the wind was doing up there, none of us would ever get on a plane again.

Momentarily distracted, I had a feeling I was being watched, and turned on a cowboy heel, floating my gaze over the undulating hills. Maybe that's what happens when you invest so much of yourself in something; whether it is a person or a place, your soul is loath to leave it. I looked for Danny's outline on those hills and thought maybe his ghost or spirit was still here, looking over the place that had been his. Maybe you stayed until you realized it wasn't yours anymore and then you went on your way.

Vic studied me as I got back in the truck. "So, what about the daughter?" It was as though she had been reading my mind; maybe she was getting closer to a vision than she thought.

"Cady?"

"Eva."

Maybe not. "What about her?"

She yawned and covered it with a hand, singing in a fine soprano voice she'd inherited from her mother: *"Dem bones, dem bones, dem dry bones . . .* A little strange, wouldn't you say?"

I pulled through the gate, got out and closed it, and drove toward the ridge where Taylor had taken a few potshots at Omar's armored SUV. "I guess."

"Don't you think we should follow up and see who's prescribing her with Fukitol and why?"

"I would imagine that Free Bird, Danny Lone Elk's doctor up in Hardin, is prescribing for her, too, and in answer to your next question, no, Isaac didn't mention having gotten hold of him, so I'd imagine he hasn't answered his call just yet."

"Are we going to Hardin?"

"Not unless we have to—it's not exactly Paris."

She spoke philosophically: "I haven't ever been."

"Paris?"

She punched my shoulder. "Hardin."

"Well, like I said, don't get your hopes up." I eased the truck to a stop and the three of us climbed out, carefully following the two-track up the hillside to Jen, the dinosaur's next-to-last resting place.

I noticed Vic had left her jacket in the truck. "Are you sure you don't want to bring your coat?" I gestured toward the dark clouds, strung in front of the Bighorns like a royal curtain, to the purple born. "It might get a little rough before long."

She kept coming. "I'm not planning on spending the night."

The afternoon air was cooling rapidly, and I was starting to think that it might not be rain but rather hail that we might be getting, as I stopped by the large wooden box that the paleontologists used to store their tools.

She puffed up behind me and rested an elbow on the crate, which was as big as a refrigerator. "Well, we can use the humidity."

I started, turned, and looked at her.

"What? You say that all the time . . . I'm trying to get with the western code thing, okay?" She pushed off the box and passed me, and I watched the back of her as she worked her way up the trail toward the dig.

When I caught up with her, she was standing next to a depression in the top of the ridge where the ground and surrounding rock was terraced in all directions. You could see that the majority of the *T. rex* was still there, somewhat uncovered but very much intact, minus the head, of course.

The great creature was turned in on herself with the massive pelvis at the center and the elongated tail circling up and over the back. There were a few other bones, a large femur and vertebrae, scattered a little away, and I couldn't help but walk to the overhang where Jen had surprised Jennifer. It was as if the old girl had tucked herself into a modified fetal position. It was difficult to imagine anything that could kill the undisputed seven-ton queen of her time, but life had a way perhaps even then of humbling all of us. From personal experience, I was pretty sure it must've had something to do with her offspring, one of the more than a few thoughts I decided to keep from present company.

I called Vic over to a small trail that led toward a narrow gap and the underside of the cliff. She joined me, and I pointed up to where the two-talon claw appeared to be reaching out from within the rock and time and space. "Look."

"Holy shit." She stretched out a hand, touching the nearest claw, and it was almost as if some interspecies karma was taking place. It wasn't a reach to see that DNA strand that might've somehow connected them, not hard to see Vic's most ancient lineage being a tyrannosaur. Evidently, her line of thought was running along the same trail. "So, if I was a *T. rex*, what were you?"

I played along. "Probably a brontosaurus—they call them apatosaurus these days—means deceptive lizard, by the way."

"What, they got married and changed their names?"

"Remember Cope and Marsh?"

"Oh, no."

"Yep, Marsh was in such a hurry to scoop Cope that he classified a smaller, juvenile version of the same creature as a completely different species; he called the juvenile an apatosaurus and then the much larger, eighty-foot adult a brontosaurus."

"The one that's on the Sinclair Oil signs?"

"Yep." I stooped and picked up a few stones as Dog came over and sniffed the area. "To add insult to injury, in 1970, paleontologists discovered that Marsh had taken a skull from another dig and had put it on the skeleton of the apatosaurus at the Peabody Museum at Yale."

"So, why do we still call it a brontosaurus?"

"Because we are used to calling it that and because this particular specimen is more like a thunder lizard than a deceptive one. I mean, at eighty feet and thirty tons, how deceptive could you be?"

She nodded but seemed restless. "I'm going back up topside. You coming?"

"In a minute."

She disappeared, and Dog started to follow but then lingered with me.

Thinking about the passage of time and what a blink we were in the history of this planet, I reached up to touch one of Jen's claws. Dinosaurs walked the face of the earth for approximately 165 million years, whereas we have been here for only two hundred thousand. To put that in context, if the dinosaurs had been here a week, we would have been here for only the last two minutes. And yet for all their longevity, they were gone, and no one really seemed to know why.

I thought about what Jennifer had said about the big beasts and how they likely ate each other, even family.

As I looked out over the high plains and felt the weight of the oncoming storm at my back, it wasn't difficult to feel small, transient, and ephemeral. I thought about the tenuous threads that held us here, that kept us going. I thought about the women in my life and what magnificent, life-engendering creatures they were. I'd like to think that Jen had been like that—that it was more important what you did with your life than how it ended or what somebody did with your bones long afterward. Still, her head rested in my jail's holding cell. I couldn't help but think that she deserved something better than that.

I guess I hoped that she'd end up at the High Plains Dinosaur Museum or with the Cheyenne Conservancy—somewhere near her home—but it didn't look good.

I watched as a few hailstones the size of BBs struck the rocks outside the overhang, and I could almost feel the sagebrush holding its breath in anticipation of an ice storm. In the distance, lightning struck a point down near the Powder Breaks, and I started thinking that it might be best for us to get out of the two-track before the deluge began.

I looked around, but Dog was gone, probably following Vic, so I flipped up the collar of my old canvas hunting jacket and tugged my hat down tight against the gusting wind and the ice pellet buckshot.

Stumbling a few times, I looked to the west and could see the sky was a wall of purple and black, the only thing defining it the diagonal striping that indicated precipitation.

Thinking Vic and Dog might've shown more sense than I had, I went to the edge of the ridge and looked at the truck. Moving over a little, I peered down through the top of the windshield as the hail bounced off it with an unnatural, metallic ping.

There was no one inside.

The wind was really picking up, and I looked in all directions but could still see nothing. I pulled my gloves from my pockets and slipped them on—it was May in Wyoming, but I'd known spring storms to blow in with the ferocity of February, so I decided I'd better gather both Vic and Dog as quickly as I could find them.

There was a knoll at one end of the ridge, and I figured that was the spot where I'd be able to see the surrounding area. It was possible that my undersheriff had slipped and fallen down one of the steep hillsides, but I couldn't be sure unless I could spot her, and it was doing nothing but getting darker.

I zipped my jacket and made my way upward as quickly as I could, slipping on the wet surface of the rocks as the hail melted into sleet. A small panic was setting in as I scrambled the short distance, and it seemed to take forever. The air from my lungs was billowing like a bison's and clouding from the drop in temperature as I made it to the top.

Nothing.

Some of the hail was hitting the rocks and bouncing like marbles, while some exploded into tiny, icy shrapnel. Visibility was still dropping as I stumbled down a slope of scrabble, kicking some rocks loose and watching them fall some twenty feet to the ground below the ledge where I stood.

It was then that I noticed something beside my boot and stooped to pick it up. It was a piece of cardboard, sopping but still legible, and I read CASH PRIZES, PLAY MONEY in old-fashioned print; at the bottom was the outline of a coin and the words MALLO CUP, 5 POINTS.

As another lightning strike flashed to the east, the thunder shook the ridge where I stood with a resounding shudder like the footstep of a sauropod, and I thought I might've seen something or someone to the east on the opposite side of the narrow canyon. I took a step forward to the very edge of the drop-off as the hail continued to bounce around me like I was a target in a shooting gallery, the roar of the impact drowning out everything else.

There was someone standing at the very top of the other ridge with arms outspread like an eagle attempting to take flight. Evidently, she was trying to summon up a vision after all. I looked around but couldn't see Dog.

I brought my hands up alongside my mouth and shouted, "Vic!"

The shadowy figure didn't move.

"Vic!?"

Whoever it was turned and looked at me. I waved but stopped in midmotion when it became clear that it wasn't she.

He was bigger, much bigger, and his hair was longer and he stood there looking at me. Confused, I thought of the giant Crow Indian who had saved my life in the Bighorn Mountains a few seasons back. "Virgil?" I felt rooted to the spot as the world shifted with a maelstrom of angry weather that couldn't decide if it wanted to blow, rain, sleet, hail, or snow, so settled on all five.

I glanced at the distance between the two ledges, but it had to be at least twenty feet; no way I was jumping that. Racing my eyes around the hillside, I spotted a rutted deer trail leading into the gulley below. It was a good eighth of a mile, part of it downhill, part of it up, but I was determined to face him.

He hadn't moved when I started down, but by now the ground was turning white with sleet, and the soles of my boots acted like skis as I negotiated the narrow path.

I struggled to stay upright but finally gave in and began sliding along on the seat of my pants. My clothes were soaked by the time I got to even ground. The view was obstructed by the fall of the slope, and I couldn't see him anymore, so I grabbed stalks of sagebrush to help pull myself along. The hail striking the ground was as large as golf balls now, the strikes feeling as if I had taken a shortcut onto a driving range.

There was another rock shelf, and as I got near the top, I could hear barking over the incessant sound of the storm; maybe I wasn't chasing ghosts and it was Vic and Dog after all.

I was trying to figure a way around the ledge when something shot out from underneath it and ran directly into me, knocking me backward. I grabbed at it with both hands and it yelped a yelp I recognized, so I eased my grip. "Good boy, easy, easy . . ."

I struggled up on one knee and covered the side of my face with my gloved hand, reaching out to him with the other, and he took my hand in his mouth and began gently pulling me. "What are you doing?"

He whined but wouldn't let go of my hand.

"All right, all right, where are we going?" I followed him toward the overhang, giving one last glance up the hillside in hopes of seeing the figure again, but there was no one there.

Ducking under the rocks, I was glad to get away from the hail. It was dark, but I could see where sections of the rock strata had broken and been pushed toward the opening, leaving an alcove of surprising size. Somebody had used it as a campsite, because there were the burnt remains of a fire.

Dog kept pulling, until I could see that he was taking me to Vic, who lay crouched on her side, shivering and holding her head, blood dripping from her hair. He released me as I knelt beside her, huddled against the back rock wall, pulled her into my chest, and swept an arm around her shoulders. "What the hell happened to you?"

Her teeth were chattering as she spoke. "I fucking fell."

I breathed a laugh and gathered her closer, trying to fight the drop in her core temperature. "You should've worn your jacket."

She clutched me. "No shit."

"Did you break anything?"

"My ankle—I think I turned my ankle." She glanced up at me. "My head hurts, but I think I just bumped it."

I looked at her matted hair. "There's a lot of blood, but it's a head wound and they tend to do that."

She still shivered hard enough to break her teeth. "Where's Dog?"

"He's right here. You're lucky I came over this way and that Dog found me and brought me to you." I looked out from under the outcropping and could see that the hail had subsided but that a torrent of a thunderstorm was now washing the air like a chorus of vertical fire hoses.

"Why did you come over this way?"

Stripping off my jacket, I wrapped it around her before stepping toward the opening where I was able to stand up straight. I thought about the quad sheets on the wall at our substation in Powder Junction, the ones that told me where the major washes were in this part of my county.

I waited a moment before answering. "You wouldn't believe me if I told you."

The mouth of the overhang lit like a flashbulb, and she sat

up a little in reaction, clutching my wet coat around her as the thunder followed. "What's the matter?"

"I think this canyon is a wash."

She struggled up a little more. "Meaning?"

"We're likely to have a couple of millions of gallons of water come rushing through before long." I shook my head. "That water's been coming down on the mountains for hours, along with what's been dumped out here."

She glanced around. "Can't we just stay in this shelter?"

We were surrounded on three sides, and I started making some quick calculations. "No. If it comes, it's going to scour this canyon like a toilet flushing." I cocked an ear, but there was no way I was going to hear the water until it was too late. "We've got to get to higher ground."

I moved to the back of the cave and tried to get her onto her feet, but it was difficult. She bit her lip to the point that I started thinking she was going to take a hunk out of it.

"Damn it."

I wrapped my arm around her back and under her far arm. "How bad?"

"Not bad enough to stay in here and fucking drown." I limped her forward and looked at Dog, who had started growling. Vic looked at me as I stared at him. "That can't be good."

"No." I reached down and pulled his ear in an attempt to get his attention. "Hey, you need to get out of here, too, do you hear me?" He continued to grumble. "Listen to me: when we go out of here, I want you to just climb up the hill and get away. Don't worry about us, but I can't carry the both of you, all right?"

He continued to look out into the cascading water, the low-pitched noise still rumbling from his chest.

Vic brought her face forward. "I know you think he under-stands everything you say, but short of a honey-baked ham, I think your best bet is to get us out of here and he'll follow."

"You're probably right." I took a step forward but was fro-zen by what I saw in a flash of lightning; the impromptu river was only a few feet below the lip of the overhang's floor.

Vic followed my eyes as the thunder echoed off the rock walls. "Oh, shit."

Realizing we had only minutes, I turned right and then left, trying to spot a way out, but the rock was solid at the sides. My eyes went to the overhanging ledge, and I came up with a desperate idea. "I'm putting you over the top."

"What?"

"I'll lift you up, and you can climb without putting weight on that ankle, and then I'll either take Dog with me or lift him up to you."

She looked doubtful. "He must weigh a hundred and fifty pounds."

I nodded. "That's all right; I'll lift and he'll scramble so both of you will get out."

"And what about you?"

"I'll be fine. I can climb my way around the side and scram-ble up—I just can't do it carrying both of you."

As much as she hated it, she knew I was right. She hopped forward on the one good leg and turned to look at me. "You didn't answer my question."

I laced my fingers together, providing a stirrup from which I could lift her easily. "Which question?"

She rested her hands on my shoulders. "Why did you come this way?"

I raised my face to look at her. "It doesn't matter."

"You saw him again, didn't you?" The tarnished gold eyes bore into mine, and I could tell for maybe once in my life that she wasn't joking. "Danny Lone Elk—you saw him again."

I stood there with my laced fingers and stooped shoulders, staring at her and finally nodding. "I did."

She said the next words carefully. "I saw him, too."

I thought I might've misunderstood her. "What?"

"Danny Lone Elk, dressed exactly like he was when we fished him out of the Turtle Pond. He was standing on the ridge and I saw him. That's why I fell—I couldn't believe it and wasn't watching where I was going and slipped off the ledge."

I shook my head. "I think you're hanging out with me too much. C'mon!"

She slipped the distressed limb into my cupped hands but then thought again and used her left. "I'm thinking I'll get better purchase if I try with my good ankle."

I nodded. "Let's go."

She stepped up, and I lifted her skyward into the falling rain as she traced her hands across the top in an attempt to find something to hold on to. A few pieces of rock scaled from above, and I kept my face down, trying to limit the damage.

"I can't get any leverage!"

I pushed her up further, but it seemed as if I was still holding all of her weight. I stood there, trying not to move, but I knew there was a limit to how long I could hold her.

Dog stayed at my side, but his attention was still directed up, almost as if there was something he was focused on; I just hoped it wasn't the floodwaters preparing to wash us away any second.

There was another flash, and as I looked past Vic's legs, an image burned into my retinas—the black silhouette of a large Indian standing on the ledge across the canyon, his dark, wet hair covering his face as he breathed with an incredible effort, his shoulders drawing back and then collapsing with each breath.

I blinked, but whether it was from the blinding effects of the lightning or the inky darkness of the storm, I couldn't see anything. "Vic?"

Her legs moved a little, but I could feel her slipping as the thunder shook the ground. I had to make sure I pulled her in if she started to go backward into the rushing water, which was now lapping at my feet.

Dog's barking grew to a frenzy as I stood there like a sitting and likely drowned duck. I stared into the darkness and laughed, wanting to scream at the ghost of Danny Lone Elk to help us.

There was another extended zigzag of lightning that ran the ridge overhead, and I could see that there was no one standing in the spot where I'd seen something before.

Nothing.

I was about to drop my head and concentrate on the task at hand when, in the very last bit of illumination, I saw him leap from the far ledge and seemingly float across the canyon like a mountain lion, finally disappearing overhead as rocks slid down onto us.

Unbelievable.

Dog was going crazy as the thunder provided a counterpoint to the impossible, when suddenly Vic's weight vanished, and I was standing there with nothing in my arms. Whatever it was, it had taken her.

There was another blink of lightning, and a powerful hand, caked with mud and blood, thrust down from the ledge almost as if from a grave in the sky. It was as large as my own, broad and muscled, and was flexing as if to indicate that I better hand something else up and right soon.

Without pause, I grabbed Dog and lifted him. The hand grabbed his collar while the other buried its powerful fingers into the thick fur of the animal's back, and he too vanished with a yelp.

A few more rocks slid from above, and I looked down to see a rush of water flowing against my legs and figured I'd better try my luck with the rocks to either side. I had just waded to my left when the hand appeared again.

I laughed. It was one thing to lift a hundred-and-thirty-pound woman, and even another to lift a hundred-and-fifty-pound dog, but I was something altogether different. The hand flexed, and I figured what the hell—if the ghost of Danny Lone Elk thought he was strong enough to reach out from the Camp of the Dead and save me from a watery grave, then who was I to argue?

Throwing a hand up, I felt the powerful fingers clasp mine like cables and, unbelievably, felt my feet leave the ground as if I were being hoisted by the sky crane of a Sikorsky helicopter.

I jammed my armpit into the shale, as the other hand grasped my upper arm like a number 6 bear trap and pulled me over the edge. The rain poured all around us, and the lightning flamed again and glowed, illuminating the perfect, flashing grin in the dark, shrouded face of Henry Standing Bear.

7

I set the bag full of Danny Lone Elk's prescription drugs between my boots and leaned forward on the Durant Memorial Hospital waiting room sofa. Pulling the Mallo Cup play money card from my pocket, I studied it. "So, it wasn't you?"

The Cheyenne Nation played with the bandage on his hand where he'd received a few stitches in honor of his rough landing across the canyon cliffs, and stretched the expandable wrap so that the bandage was looser. "Of course not."

"How did you know where we were?"

"I called Ruby, and she said you had gone to the Lone Elk Ranch to ask Randy some questions. I thought I might be of help, so I went there and they told me you had gone to the dig site." The Bear reached down and thumped Dog on his side, which was built like a barrel. "When I got there, your truck was parked but the three of you were gone, and it was hailing, sleeting, and raining, so I hiked up the ridge and that is when I heard this one barking."

I continued to study the card in my hands. "Lucky us."

He smiled. "Lucky all of you, except for your truck."

I glanced out at my dented vehicle, the sheet metal marked like a kid with the chicken pox. "Yep, I guess I'm going to have to get some bodywork done." I also looked at his battered ranch truck, parked beside mine. "Good thing you were driving Rezdawg. No breakdowns?"

He shook his head. "No, the rain puts out the fires under the hood."

I nodded and eased back into the sofa, for once the only one without wounds. "So it wasn't you out on the ridge, which begs the question."

He nodded. "You say the young man, Taylor, has had these same visions?"

"Yep."

"And Vic?"

"Yep."

He turned to look at me. "And you?"

"Yep."

He looked at the mauve carpet, the mauve walls, the mauve furniture, and then back at me, probably just trying to focus on something that wasn't mauve. "Interesting. You see, without his eyes, Danny's spirit is condemned to wander this plane of existence without rest."

"Well, he's been getting around a lot lately."

He grunted. "For a blind dead man?"

"Yep." I sat forward. "So, this is touchy stuff, huh?"

"It can be." He looked up at the ceiling. "Randy is now the leader of the family, but his uncle Enic is the religious one. Since Randy does not care about such things, he has given him that mantle. We will have to do numerous transfer rites to prepare Danny for the Hanging Road and the Camp of the Dead, along with a wake for the white man's heaven."

"Even if the blinding was accidental?"

"Do we know that for sure?"

I nodded. "According to Isaac. But you can have a look at the body yourself, seeing as we're in the hospital."

His voice took on a serious tone. "If the blinding was accidental, it could be even more serious." He cocked his head. "Acts of man are one thing but acts of nature another. Turtles are big medicine, and there will be questions as to how this could have come to be."

"Autopsy?"

He smiled and shook his head. "Not likely with him being a Traditional." He looked at me. "Why? You suspect that somebody also took his life?"

"Maybe." I picked up the bag of drugs and tossed them onto the sofa. "So, were the Lone Elks surprised to see you?"

"Why?"

"Your name came up in the conversation when we were down there."

He flexed the hand that had lifted all three of us to safety. "Ahhh . . ."

I stood and, walking to the plate-glass window, gazed at the steady rain. "Why would someone be impersonating Danny Lone Elk?" The Bear turned to look at me. "Don't tell me the thought hasn't crossed your mind."

He shrugged. "It is possible, I suppose."

I turned and showed him the Mallo Cup card that I'd found near the dig. "Is this supposed to mean something other than you have accumulated five points toward a five-hundred-point two-dollar rebate?"

"When I was on the mountain with Virgil White Buffalo, he was eating Mallo Cups and saying they were his favorites. He even left me one at the top of Cloud Peak."

Henry reached down and brushed his thumb on the fur between Dog's eyes. "I do not suppose you know if this one saw him?"

Before I could answer, David Nickerson came through the swinging doors, spoke briefly with Janine, my dispatcher's granddaughter and the hospital receptionist, and then approached us. "Well, we're not going to have to put her down."

"That's good news."

"But she's getting the boot and crutches."

"Oh, that's not going to be fun."

David smiled and shook his head. "She's not a good patient."

The Cheyenne Nation stood and handed me back the card. "You noticed?"

"When we manipulated the ankle, I'm not sure I've ever heard language like that in those combinations since high school football."

"In that particular discipline, she's kind of an artist in her own right." Thinking it might be wise to check the progress of the plane coming into Sheridan, I pulled out my pocket watch, though I was pretty sure that it was likely to be delayed because of the weather. "Can we see her?"

"Sure."

I stuffed the candy card in my jacket pocket. "Can I bring Dog?"

———

Vic was sitting on a gurney in the open area of the ER with some curtains partially pulled to afford her a little privacy but doing little to protect the ears of her fellow patients.

"Motherfucker."

Her classification was seemingly directed at Henry, who placed a hand on his chest in all innocence. "*Moi?*"

"What the hell were you doing out there impersonating Danny Lone Elk?"

"It was not I."

"Bullshit."

"It wasn't him." I raised a hand in his defense. "When he got there, he arrived from the same direction that we came from." I walked over to the gurney and examined the bandage wrapped around her skull, Dog following, placing his heavy head next to her hand. "When you saw the figure, where was it?"

Not taking her eyes off the Bear, she responded, "On that ridge across the canyon."

"Well, when I first saw him he jumped the cliffs from the west, and I don't think anybody in their right mind would make that jump once let alone two times."

Henry grunted. "In all actuality, the western cliff is slightly higher than the one under which the three of you were taking cover. I do not think you could make that same jump in the other direction—at least I could not." He held up his bandaged hand. "I barely made it once."

She folded her arms. "I take back the motherfucker."

"Thank you." He smiled. "I have a question for you."

"Shoot."

He lip-pointed at Dog. "Did he see Danny, too?"

Vic looked at Dog and then back at the Cheyenne Nation. "He did; he barked at whoever it was when I was standing there—barked more than once."

The Bear spread his hands. "Human."

I glanced at him. "You're sure?"

"Of course not."

"Well, that's helpful."

"Animals react differently. There is an old wives' tale that if an animal responds to a spirit, then you can look between the animal's ears and see that spirit."

Vic ventured an opinion. "Old wives are full of shit."

"A lot of the time I'm afraid they are, yes."

I glanced at the ER doctor, who seemed to be enjoying the conversation. "Dr. Dave, is your accomplice in billing around?" He looked at me blankly. "Isaac?"

"Oh, he's taking a nap in his office."

"Could you go get him? I've got a few questions I need to ask."

He was disappointed to leave.

I turned back to the Bear. "So what's your basis for thinking the figure was living?"

He shrugged. "Two different species seeing the same apparition at the same time is rather unlikely."

"But not impossible."

"No." He started to push his hair back but was impaired by the stitches, so he reached down and placed his hands on the railing of the gurney instead. "But there is a more important question here."

"Who would benefit from Danny Lone Elk still being alive?"

He smiled the paper-cut-thin signature smile. "More important, who would benefit from *you* believing Danny Lone Elk is still alive?"

"Was Enic at the house when you stopped?"

He thought about it. "Why Enic?"

"Because he's physically the closest to Danny; he lives there, and in that he might now be part owner of the ranch, he might have a hand in this."

"That's quite a leap. Enic, like Danny, went through a period where he drank heavily, but to my knowledge he has never done anything illegal."

"Randy mentioned something about him having a drinking problem in his past."

He nodded. "A long time ago—that is what led him to the path he walks now. He was drunk up in Billings and got into a fight with a group of men who beat him senseless. He was able to drag himself to an abandoned car where he slept that night . . ." He paused. ". . . in January, when the temperature dropped to minus twenty-seven degrees." He exhaled strongly, as if trying to get the smell of the story from his nostrils. "And in answer to your question, no, I did not see Enic when I was there. The only ones I spoke to were Randy and Eva."

"Well, in his defense, he was supposedly in the calving shed when we left, which makes it hard to believe that he could've gotten down to the site and positioned himself in the time it took us to get there."

Vic was petting Dog and glancing between the two of us.

"Hey, Henry, you ever heard of a doctor up on the Rez by the name of Joseph Free Bird?"

Covering his face with his good hand, he croaked, "Oh,

no." He peered at us through his fingers. "How is he involved with this?"

"He was Danny Lone Elk's doctor."

"Not Indian—he is a nutcase drug dealer, a plastic medicine man, and a charlatan at that."

"Evidently he's doctor enough to have a license to write prescriptions."

The Cheyenne Nation shook his head. "He lives in Hardin and has what he calls a clinic there. He pretends to care for people who are Traditional and has a mail-order business where he sells bags of buffalo shit and other assorted items as medicinal. There's also a rumor that he traffics in drugs with the Tre Tre Nomads."

I glanced at Vic. "Maybe we can get a second opinion on your ankle."

"Fuck you."

"I've attempted to reach him by phone four times now, Walter, but he doesn't appear to want to talk to me, or maybe it's because you are involved?" Isaac had entered the room and continued around Henry to look at the patient as I handed him the bag of prescription drugs. "This isn't buffalo dung, is it?"

"Danny's medications."

The doc opened the bag as Nickerson reappeared at the door. "Did we get a confirmation on whether dogs can see ghosts when we can't?"

I shot a look at him.

He raised a hand. "Just wondering." He retreated through the door. "I've got some rye whiskey to go test."

Isaac looked through the bag of medications, adjusted his

thick glasses, and made a face. "I'm not sure what half of these are, let alone if they should be prescribed in combination with each other."

Vic poked me with one of her crutches. "We're going to Hardin, aren't we, aren't we?"

I sighed. "Try not to be so excited about it."

When we got back to the office, it was easier to just carry Vic from the truck than let her manage in the rain, and when we approached the door, both Robert Hall and Bob Delude held it wide for the four of us.

Robert shook his head, stepping aside as Bob ushered us in. "Is this the kind of service you get in this outfit, 'cause I'm signing up."

"I thought Mr. Trost gave you guys your walking papers."

Robert shut the door after Henry, who was carrying the crutches and was rewarded with having Dog shake off on him. "The commandant says to hang, so we're hanging." He shrugged toward the courthouse lawn. "The rain appears to have cut down on the protesters."

"Which of you guys pissed Trost off?"

They each pointed at the other.

I continued up the stairs with Vic, Dog in tow, and paused at the top to call down to them, "Well, come on up, we've got coffee."

The troopers trooped up the steps as I deposited Vic on the wooden bench, and, turning to face the power-that-is, nodded to Ruby.

"I heard you almost drowned."

I gestured toward Henry as he gave Vic back her crutches. "Wasn't my idea, but thanks for sending the cavalry."

The HPs helped themselves to some of my dispatcher's coffee, Bob pouring for the two of them.

"Speaking of, where are Eliot Ness and the rest of the Untouchables, anyway?"

Ruby shook her head in disgust. "They're in the back with more stuff."

"More? We don't have any room for more."

"That's what I told them, but they came in with more and put it in the rest of the holding cells."

I shook my head. "Well, that's it then, we might as well close up shop because we can't arrest anybody—we don't have anywhere to put them."

Vic pulled herself up, and Henry helped her with the crutches. "I'm going home and nurse my ankle with a bottle of wine. If anybody wants me, tell them to fuck off."

I spoke after her as she crutched down the hall, "You're not going to the airport with me?"

She called back, gesturing toward the HPs, "I figure you can handle it yourself. Hell, take the Dudley Do-Rights with you."

When we got back to the holding cells, there was nowhere to stand, so we stood in the doorway and watched as McGroder and his men continued to catalogue, list, and take pictures of everything they had confiscated from the High Plains Dinosaur Museum. "You guys are putting me out of business. I don't have any place for the bad guys."

The agent in charge stood, stretching his back, and I noticed that now they were wearing their polo shirts and rain-proof windbreakers with the three-letter insignia on the back. "What about the jail downstairs?"

"That's for serious customers. I try and keep the hoi polloi up here."

McGroder's smile grew as he noticed my companion, struggled his way through some boxes, and stuck out his hand to the Cheyenne Nation. "Mr. Standing Bear, sir, good to see you."

Henry shook his hand. "Agent."

He gestured toward me. "I understand you had to save his life again?"

The Bear nodded. "It is becoming something of a habit."

"Sheriff." The voice rang from somewhere within one of the cells, but I couldn't see him.

"Deputy U.S. Attorney."

"Can I have a word with you?"

I looked around for some sort of path. "Certainly, but you'll have to come out here, since I can't get in there."

After a moment, he appeared around the corner, and I noticed that today he wasn't wearing makeup. "I'd like to speak with you in private."

I glanced around at the boxes. "Doesn't seem possible."

"Now."

I thought I might've misheard him. "Excuse me?"

He emphasized each word. "Right. Now."

I stood there looking at him, aware that nobody else in the room was moving. "Well, go ahead then."

A smug look seeped across his face as he stared at me. "I think you might prefer we did it in private."

"I'll do my own thinking. How can I help you, Mr. Trost?"

He glanced around and then, satisfied that he'd given

enough of a dramatic pause, continued. "I don't think you're taking our case very seriously."

I waited the exact same amount of time before replying. "Our case."

He gestured around the room at the copious boxes and files. "Jen."

I wanted to laugh but figured that wasn't likely to make the situation any better. "Acting Deputy Attorney, I have made my time, staff, and facility available to you. What else exactly is it you need?"

"Your complete attention."

"Oh, you've got it right now."

"I mean for the tenure of the investigation."

"Well, you see, I do have other responsibilities, one of which concerns, as you have noted, a potential homicide, and I think that takes precedence over your sixty-five-million-year-old cold case." He didn't say anything, so I continued. "Why don't you tell me exactly what the problem here is, and then we can both get on with our jobs."

"I was not impressed with your performance this morning."

"At the press conference."

"Yes."

"Performance."

"Yes."

"Mr. Trost, in case you aren't aware, my job is to enforce the laws and protect the lives and property of the people of Absaroka County; anything beyond that is my prerogative. I have conveyed to you and your department the utmost in professional courtesy and will continue to do so as long as it doesn't interfere with the performance of my sworn duties."

His smile faded. "I've got another press conference with a few national outlets this afternoon, and I'd like you to be there."

"I have other responsibilities."

This time he paused even longer before speaking. "I suggest you reorganize your schedule."

"I have an appointment that can't be broken." And with that, I turned and walked out of the room.

On the drive to Sheridan, the Bear, having decided to keep me company, gave me his take on the brief exchange. "I think it is safe to assume that you've been removed from his Christmas card list."

"That's all right, I'm not real fond of him, either."

"I also think you should anticipate a call from the attorney general of the state of Wyoming."

"That's okay, him I like."

He glanced out the window at Lake DeSmet, the rain having let up a bit, with glimmers of the afternoon sun reflecting off the surface of the water in a brassy gold. "Thank you for caring about Danny Lone Elk." He reached back and scratched under Dog's chin. "I know you are under a lot of pressure right now, so if no one else has said it—thank you."

I brushed off the kindness, slightly embarrassed. "Well, it might all be a part of the same case."

"Maybe, and then again, maybe not."

Anxious to change the subject, I asked about the cursory observations he'd made of Danny's body while I'd collected Vic and her paraphernalia. "So, did the turtles do it?"

"The turtles did it."

I thought about it. "I'm not sure why, but that makes me feel better."

"I am not so sure why, either." He turned in the seat to look at me. "And I am not sure why you do."

"Oh."

"Now, on to important matters." He glanced out the windshield at the fresh, newly washed landscape. "Is Vic coming to terms with her little brother marrying and having a child with your daughter?"

I hadn't told anyone about the damage done to my undersheriff or the fact that she had lost a child and now could have none, but it seemed like the Bear was intuiting, something he was pretty good at. "She doesn't have a lot of say in it, and Michael just goes with the flow . . . It's one of his many good qualities."

"The whole family is coming?"

"Just Cady and the baby. Michael was scheduled for some time off, but from what I understand, he's got a new sergeant who's trying to make things hard on him, so he's having to pull second watch for the next week."

"Life in the Philadelphia Police Department."

"Especially if you are the son of the Chief of Detectives North."

He nodded and took a deep breath. "Your granddaughter is five months old. She needs a name."

I made a face the way I always did whenever I was reminded that my granddaughter was named for a '59 Thunderbird convertible. "She's got a name. In case you've forgotten, she's named after your damn car."

"I mean a real name."

Henry Standing Bear, Heads Man of the Dog Soldier Society, Dog Soldier Clan, was offering my granddaughter a Cheyenne name. "Don't you think she's a little young?"

He shrugged. "We're all here, and if you make a run up to Hardin, we could stop in Lame Deer and arrange something with Lonnie and the tribe." He turned his head and looked out the window. "Are you heading up tomorrow?"

I smiled. "That's what I was thinking."

"I will come and make arrangements."

"I'll buy you breakfast at the Blue Cow Café."

"Deal."

Cady's Cheyenne name was Sweet Grass Woman, and I wondered if it would have an effect on the choice for Lola. "Have you been thinking about a name?"

"Yes."

"Care to share it with me?"

"No."

"Okay." We drove on, and, thinking I was making small talk, I asked, "So, what do you think of my granddaughter?"

"She is a great deal like you."

I felt a sharp wave of fleeting self-satisfaction. "You think?"

"Yes, and it will lead to problems with her mother."

I glanced at him. "Huh?"

"Your granddaughter and you are too much alike, and you will be something of a burden to her for the majority of your lives."

I laughed and drove on. "She's only five months old, and you haven't seen her since she was a newborn—you don't think you might be jumping the gun here a little bit?"

"I have seen the two of you together."

"I thought we got along pretty well."

"Yes, and she will come to see you as the sun, the moon, the stars, and all that is." He still didn't look at me. "And this will be very hard for you to live up to; eventually you will fail and she will have to reassess, which will be difficult for her."

"Well, thanks for the vote of confidence on both our parts." I glanced at him again. "So when is this cataclysmic event supposed to happen, when she's nine months old?"

He shot me a look from the corner of one eye.

"You know, between you, Danny Lone Elk, and Virgil White Buffalo, I could use a good word every now and then from the great beyond, okay?"

To everyone's surprise, including the airline's, the flight from Denver arrived on time.

Henry and I were both standing there watching the turbo-prop unload. Not unexpectedly, my daughter and grand-daughter were the last ones off the plane, a gentleman I knew helping Cady carry the paraphernalia down the steps. Lola was screeching, but I was able to say hello to Dennis Kervin, an attorney from Durant.

He handed Henry a diaper bag and other assorted essentials, Cady following. "That granddaughter of yours has the lungs of a Metropolitan Opera star."

"Sorry about that."

I wasn't able to add more as a tall redhead with cool, gray eyes unceremoniously handed me the screaming bundle along with her cell phone. "Here, take her. I need a minute." She turned and marched off toward the bathrooms.

"Why do I have your cell phone?"

"Because there are three messages from the Philadelphia Police Department, and if I answer it and it's my husband, in the mood I'm in, I'm going to give him an earful." She called back over her shoulder, "Answer it if you want to, and while you're at it, tell him I want a divorce and he can have custody of Ethel Merman there."

I deposited the phone in my jacket pocket and considered my granddaughter. The little bundle's cries became so shrill that I was sure she was going to rupture something. I turned to look at the Bear and began to bounce up and down ever so slightly. "She does have a set of lungs on her."

He reached out and settled me with a hand on my shoulder. "She just came in on a turbulence-ridden airplane, Walt, perhaps she would like to be held still."

He had a point. I placed two fingers on the edge of the blanket and pulled it down so that I could see her chocolate-brown eyes, an anomaly in my family. She was sweating from exertion, but I tipped her up a bit more and brought her a little closer.

They tell you about how your life changes in ways you'd never suspect when you have children, but I think it might be even worse with grandchildren. Maybe because it's parenting one step removed, or maybe it's the novelty of it being a part-time job, but whatever it was, it hit me like a tsunami when I looked at her. "You're upsetting your mother."

Instantly, she stopped crying and stared at me.

"I don't mind. You can scream all you like as far as I'm concerned, but you also have to stop when we get to the truck because you'll scare Dog."

She blinked her eyes, and a bubble of drool collected at the corner of her tiny mouth.

"You need to be on your best behavior, especially since you haven't met Dog yet."

She continued to stare at me, her mouth moving just a little as if chewing my words.

I glanced at the Cheyenne Nation. "See, we are simpatico."

He studied the two of us like specimens. "Um hmm."

The phone in my pocket began vibrating and suddenly started playing some sort of hip-hop song. I handed Lola to Henry and began fishing the thing out. "I better get that and let him know that his family is here safe, if pissed."

Looking at the screen, which did, indeed, read PHILADEL-PHIA POLICE DEPARTMENT, even I was able to discern the green ANSWER button. "Hey, is this about those unpaid parking tickets?"

There was a long pause, and then an unfamiliar voice responded. "Hello? This is Chaplain Anthony Keen, and I'd like to speak with Cady Moretti, if I could, please?"

A chaplain.

"I'm afraid she's indisposed at the moment. I'm her father, Absaroka County Sheriff Walt Longmire. Can I help you?"

"I need to speak with Mrs. Moretti, if I could, please?"

"Look, she'll be back in just a minute . . . What's going on?"

"You say you're her father?"

"I am."

The pause was longer this time. "There's been an incident involving her husband, Patrolman Michael Moretti."

"What kind of incident, Chaplain?"

"You're her father, his father-in-law?"

"Yes, damn it."

"He's been shot in the line of duty."

I felt that quarter shift in all points of reference as I formed the next words carefully. "How bad?"

This was the longest pause so far, and I had time to look over and see Cady standing an arm's length away, staring at me as she reached for the phone. "Sheriff Longmire, I'm very sorry."

8

Dog lay on the sofa while the Bear and I sat on the floor on either side of the Pack 'n Play and watched Lola chew on the corner of a blanket Saizarbitoria had been kind enough to provide. "How is the family?"

"I don't know." I glanced toward the bedroom, where I could barely hear Cady. "She's talking to Michael's mother right now."

"Lena?"

I was having a hard time concentrating and forgot that the two had met in Philadelphia what seemed a century ago but was actually just a couple of years. "Yep."

"How did it happen?"

I thought about what Cady had told me after she had spoken with the chaplain. "Routine traffic stop at Fifth and Lombard. He pulled a guy over for a broken headlight, walked up to the window . . ."

"So, it was a random incident."

"Yep, at least . . ." I looked at him. "Why do you ask that?"

Lola made a noise, and the Cheyenne Nation reached out and gave her a stuffed horse rattle that looked as if it belonged in a museum. "Do they have the assailant in custody?"

"I don't know." I leaned against Dog's sofa and, with my hands in my lap, sat there thinking about the late nights Martha had suffered through when I was being patched up by EMTs, in emergency rooms, or worse, not hearing anything. It's part of the contract, and those who serve are not the ones who receive the worst of it; those who stand and wait for that phone call or the knock on the door that tells you that the other half of you won't be coming home, ever—those are the ones who live through a kind of pain that most will never know.

"I made chicken tomatillo soup while the two of you were talking. I will put it in the refrigerator if no one is hungry."

I focused my eyes on him. "You should go home—you've done so much."

"I will wait until she gets off the phone."

I glanced at the door leading to my bedroom. "That could be half the night."

"I have nothing but time."

I couldn't hear her voice any more. "Maybe I should go in there."

"I do not think so."

I stared at my hands, finally reaching up and petting Dog so that they had something to do. "I'm kind of at a loss, Henry."

"I can tell." He waited for a moment. "Do you suppose anyone has told Vic?"

I was jarred by the thought. "I don't know . . ."

"Would you like me to drive into town and tell her?"

I thought about it. "No, she's probably asleep—she's been through so much already today, and I wouldn't be surprised if her phone was turned off. She tends to do that when she's drinking a bottle of wine." I smiled. "I think she gets into trouble when she has a little too much and the phone is available—I've been the recipient of some of those calls."

"Hmm." He grunted, picked up the rattle, and wriggled it, further entrancing my granddaughter. Lola giggled with delight, which made the scenario all the worse.

"I'll go over there first thing in the morning—she usually sleeps late when she's not on duty—after we get everything settled here." I looked back at him. "If things are ever settled here again."

The floor creaked, and I looked up to see Cady, standing with the phone in her hand. I struggled to a standing position and stood there looking at her like an archway with the keystone missing. "Is she okay?"

She leaned against the bathroom door and wrapped her arms around herself. "No, she's not."

We watched as Dog, sensing that someone needed comforting, slipped off the sofa and approached her, burying his head between her legs and standing there threatening to lift her off the ground if she didn't pet him. She finally brought a hand down and scratched his head with her lacquered fingernails, tears falling onto his nose.

Henry saved me with a response. "Is there anything we can do?"

She looked at the wall. "Lena's been trying to get hold of Vic, but she's got her phones turned off. Could someone go over there in the morning and tell her what's going on?"

"I'll take care of it."

Henry spoke softly. "How are you?"

"How do you think I am?"

He nodded and stood, my granddaughter crying out at the loss of him and the horse rattle. The Cheyenne Nation reached down and scooped her up, tucking her on his hip and putting the toy on the kitchen table.

Cady collapsed into herself, taking a step toward him. "Henry, I'm sorry."

He shook his head. "Do not be silly." He stepped toward her and tucked her into his other hip, holding my little family, a family that was even smaller as of today. "We are all here for you, at the beck and call of your slightest wish." He pulled her in even closer and kissed the top of her head. "Because we love you."

Lola wrapped her fingers into her mother's and the Bear's hair, and all I could think was, hang on, little one, hang on to the ones you love because that's all we've got in this world. Never let go.

His voice resounded off the top of Cady's head. "Are you hungry?"

The head shook. "No, thought of food doesn't sit well right now."

"Understandable." Loosening himself, he handed the baby to me and stepped to the counter, opened the refrigerator, and placed the large pot inside. "Remember that this is in here."

We both nodded and watched as he walked to the door. "If you need anything, anything at all, please call me."

Cady responded, knowing the social ethic of the Northern Cheyenne and that he would not return again until invited. "Uncle Bear, come back over for coffee in the morning."

He smiled. "I will."

The door closed, and we were left with ourselves.

I nudged the baby up and smelled her, clean and powdered. She gurgled, and I smiled at her mother. "How 'bout a cup of tea?"

"Tea?"

I raised an eyebrow in an attempt to be funny. "What, I don't seem like a tea guy to you?"

She smiled, humoring me. "No, you don't."

I handed her Lola and began about the business of putting the steam kettle on. "Ruby gave it to me for Christmas; she thinks I drink too much coffee."

"You do drink too much coffee—you have your whole life."

I pulled the teabags from the tin box that had been kept over the refrigerator since her mother had been alive and brought out two mugs, both of them stolen from the Red Pony Bar and Grill. "Your mother once switched to decaf one week without telling me." I set the mugs on the table between us. "I thought I was dying."

The words were out of my mouth before I could whip them back. "I'm so sorry, Cady."

Looking at the surface of the table, she swallowed and hugged Lola a little closer. She finally smiled. "What am I going to do, Dad?"

"Come back to Wyoming."

She seemed shocked by the statement and stood there looking at me. "I meant this week."

"Oh."

Shaking her head, she sat at the table and whispered, "What am I going to do with you? What would I do with me?"

"It's selfish, I know."

"What would I do here, hang out a shingle? Wait for Lola

to grow up and hope she will decide to be a lawyer?" She sadly bounced her on her knee. "Moretti and Longmire?"

I was frozen at that moment, thinking about what Virgil White Buffalo had said on the mountain, his words carrying with the rushing wind that wound to a screech: *She is to be married this summer and when she has the daughter she is now carrying, that daughter, your granddaughter, will carry the wrong man's name . . .* I hadn't understood what it was he was telling me at the time, but maybe the other name my granddaughter would carry would be my own.

"Dad?"

I looked at her. "Sorry, I was just thinking of something . . . something somebody said."

She glanced away with a funny look. "The kettle is steaming."

"Sorry." I got up and went to the stove, took the whistling thing from the burner, and brought it over, filling the mugs. "Moretti and Longmire . . . Kind of has a ring to it."

She shook her head, still bouncing Lola, the baby giggling from the pony ride. "So, what do you think, Monkey—you want to be a lawyer?" The baby immediately wrinkled her face and cried out. "I guess not."

Automatically, I reached across the table and took her, resting her in the crook of my arm, picking up the rattle Henry had used to distract her. "C'mere, you Sweet Pea." She whimpered a little but then settled down and stuffed the horse's nose into her mouth. "Maybe she'll be a sheriff."

Realizing what I'd just said, I looked and found Cady staring at her mug.

———

In the early morning, after calling Henry to make sure his arrival was imminent, I looked in on my daughter and granddaughter, warm and cuddled together on my bed. Dog and I had taken turns on the sofa; I'd had a troubled night, finding myself standing at the window, looking out at the Wyoming hills with my fingertips against the glass, half waiting to see the great horned owl on the teepee.

I kept thinking how much easier this would have all been if my wife were still here, and how I would've gladly traded places with her if only she could be here to console Cady and care for the baby. Martha was like that—she didn't have to say anything but would simply lay her hand on you and suddenly things were all right.

Grabbing my thermos with too much coffee in it, I pushed the door open and stepped outside, pausing to hold it for Dog but finding my ever-present companion nowhere to be found. Quietly, I whistled, but he still didn't come.

I crossed back toward the open bedroom door and could see that the great beast had crept up onto the bed and was now sleeping with the girls.

Abandoned. Say what you will about canine intelligence, he knew who needed to be comforted and protected. I shook my head, went out the door, and headed for town with a message I sorely did not want to deliver.

When I got to the little Craftsman house on Kisling, Vic was sitting on the front stoop, barefoot except for the protective boot, crutches at her side, and a cigarette swirling a thin plume past her face like the steam kettle from the previous night.

"Need a cup of coffee?"

She took a strong drag on the coffin nail. "I need two days off to go to Philadelphia and kill a cocksucker."

"They catch him?"

"No, that's why I need *two* days."

I sat on the porch, spun off the top of my thermos with the words DRINKING FUEL printed on the side, and poured her a cup. "You're smoking."

She flicked ash into the wet grass. "Thanks, I think you're hot, too." She sipped the coffee. "I'm serious—I need some days."

"Take a month."

She nodded with a curt jerk of her head and took another slug of caffeine. We sat there for a while as she alternately inhaled the cigarette and sipped the coffee. Once or twice she turned and started to say something but then stopped and went back to her two-part job.

"Did you turn your phone on early this morning?"

"Yeah. The thing started ringing as soon as I did—scared the shit out of me."

We sat there for a while more. "Your mother?"

"Father."

Knowing the rocky relationship between Vic and the Chief of Detectives North back in Philadelphia, I was glad I hadn't been here for that phone call. "What have they got?"

"The guy walked away clean."

I studied the side of her face. "Walked? I thought it was a traffic stop."

She turned and looked at me. "He pulled this asshole over, and then another asshole stepped up behind him and shot him in the back; then when he went down, the motherfucker shot him in the face." She stopped talking, and her nostrils flared. "I mean while he's fucking lying there on his back . . . In the face."

"No arrests?"

"No, I told you . . . if I have my way there won't be any, just a brief impression on the muddy banks of the Delaware River before the current carries the body away."

"Plates?"

"Stolen."

"Driver's license, ID on either of the men?"

She puffed the cigarette some more. "A sketchy description from a taxicab driver and a woman looking out her third-floor window."

"Your family on it?"

She shook her head. "Internal Affairs and Admin won't allow for it, but if I know my brothers and my father . . ." She turned and looked at me. "Thirty-two years old."

I took a deep breath. "I know."

"That family thing, it never lets up, huh? I mean, here I am two thousand miles from mine. I know I act like it's not really important to me, but . . ." She sighed. "The ties that bind." She studied my face, and there was a spark of triumph. "I finally came up with one you don't know?" She drained the dregs of her coffee. "Bruce Springsteen."

"Actually, it's a hymn from 1872 by John Fawcett, 'Blest Be the Tie That Binds.' "

"Fuck." She held the chrome cup out to me. "How's Cady?"

I refilled her and then put the cap on and set the thermos between us. "As well as can be expected, I guess. She's holding on to Lola for dear life."

"She flying back today?"

"I would imagine so."

"Maybe I can just piggyback with the two of them."

"I'm sure she would appreciate it."

She nodded and stubbed the cigarette out on the concrete. "I'm looking for a way to think good things."

"Me, too."

She struggled up, and I fetched the crutches for her. "I guess I don't get to go to Hardin, huh?"

"We'll always have Hardin."

I opened the door for her, and she lodged the pads under her arms. "Is it nice in the spring?"

"Like Paris."

She nodded and hopped into the house as I stood there holding the storm door. "They don't get something on this, I'm going to need you to come to Philadelphia."

I breathed a laugh. "It's the fifth largest police force in the country and they've got really good people to . . ." She turned to look at me, and we stood there staring at each other. "Of course I will."

She allowed the glass door to close silently between us.

Ruby was the only one in the office when I got there, and I explained the situation as she followed me to the back. "What are you going to do?"

"I need to go to Hardin and look up this Joseph Free Bird, but . . ." I sat in my chair and looked out the window at the sky with hard-edged clouds evaporating into shades of early morning blue. "I don't know—I don't think I can leave this situation with Danny Lone Elk, Trost, the FBI . . ."

She stood in front of my desk. "What does Cady want you to do?"

"She hasn't said."

"Then you have to do the hardest thing and wait."

I nodded and scrubbed my hands across my face. "I'm tired, Ruby."

"Why don't you take a nap before everyone gets here?"

I laughed. "Oh, that'd look good: me in here sleeping on the taxpayer's dollar."

She studied me, the picture of empathy. "Dime—the taxpayer's dime. They don't pay you enough for it to be a dollar." She folded her arms. "Walter, considering the circumstance, I don't think anyone would fault you in anything you do."

I sat there for a long time, but she wouldn't go away. "I wish Martha were here."

She broke a sob and then stifled it quickly. "Oh, Walter."

"It just seems like I made this deal with the universe to serve and protect, and in return, little by little, I get everything I care about taken away from me."

"You need to stop this talk now."

I stood and walked to the window, clenching fists, the sound like studded tires on a roadway. "That's fine if the fates want to monkey around with me—but there my daughter is with a brand-new baby and no husband." I turned toward her. "I'll tell you, if I knew which cosmic office out there to go to, I'd do it and grab some winged or horned son-of-a-bitch by his throat and throw him out his window."

She smiled a sad smile. "My money's on you."

I tried to stretch my shoulders, feeling like one massive, tangled knot.

We could both hear a couple of people entering from outside and then trooping up the steps. Ruby turned toward the door. "I better go do my job."

"Earn your dime's worth?"

She nodded. "Yes." She started to go but stopped, and I could see the tears in her eyes. "Please try and keep your sense of humor, Walter, for all of us, but especially for yourself. You become most frightening when you misplace it."

I turned back to the window, all at once seeing the ghostly image of myself. "Yes, ma'am."

I could hear people talking in the outside office and felt someone watching me at the doorway. I turned to see the Bobs, looking like very large, forged-steel andirons.

"Hey, because we're getting toward the end of our forty-and-found, the commandant keeps givin' us these babysitting jobs, and we're getting kind of bored with it." Robert cleared his throat. "Let's go to Hardin, Montana, Sheriff."

Bob interrupted him. "And let's go there at a hundred and twenty miles an hour."

Boy howdy.

At a hundred and twenty, the sweeping hillsides of the Little Big Horn country seemed like the banked turns on a fictional Montana International Speedway. I glanced over and could see Robert's hands relaxed on the wheel as the motor on the big utility Interceptor roared like a treed cat.

I spoke through the steel grating from the back of the vehicle. "What kind of motor does this thing have?"

"Hell if I know. Bob?"

His partner turned to look at me. "I don't know—you open the hood and all you see is plumbing and electronics. Not as sweet as that '66 LeMans of mine, but she by-gawd moves, doesn't she?"

"Yep." Both men were studiously avoiding the subject of my daughter or of Michael's death. "Did either of you guys call Montana to tell them we were on their turf?"

They looked at each other and then Bob glanced back at me. "We really didn't see any reason for bothering them."

"Right."

Traveling at high speed across the Crow Reservation, I thought about the truncated conversation I'd had with Cady and thought about calling her back but figured there wasn't any reception even if the HPs had a phone I could borrow. My daughter was with Henry, the best person I knew to be with when in a tight spot, and I figured it might be best to give her a little time to make arrangements without me hovering over her.

I thought about Lena, Cady's mother-in-law and Lola's grandmother, and Vic and Michael's mother, and the hardship she must be going through—the loss of a child. I couldn't think of anything worse.

"So, who is this jaybird, anyway?"

I looked at Bob. "His name is Joseph Free Bird, a supposed doctor, but involved with illegal drugs associated with the Tre Tre Nomads, an Indian gang up here and over on Pine Ridge. Henry says he's NN."

"What's NN?"

"Non-Native, but all I'm interested in is his connection to Danny Lone Elk."

Robert passed an eighteen-wheeler like a Saturn rocket. "The rancher who owned the *T. rex?*"

Bob made a face. "That's an odd connection."

"That's why we're going to Hardin."

Robert called over his shoulder, "Surprise, we're there."

Slowing the vehicle to a somewhat reasonable speed, the HP ducked the nose of the thing with a touch of the brakes and made a left, heading into the town of Chi-jew-ja, as the Crow called it.

We cruised down old Highway 87, then took a right on North Center Avenue and then another right as we slowed down and arrived at the industrial section of town, the Three Rivers prison facility looming straight ahead.

Hardin had already hit hard times when a for profit prison management corporation out of Texas convinced the powers that be that a high-security facility would be a good idea for the town's economy and could employ a hundred locals in an area already saddled with 10 percent unemployment.

It sounded too good to be true.

It was.

Sitting on grazing land usually inhabited only by prong-horn antelope, Three Rivers was a ghost facility, 96,000 square feet of state-of-the-art prison capable of holding 464 inmates, the glinting razor-wire spirals guarding only the animals, the thing sitting empty for more than ten years.

Hardin sued the state of Montana for its legislative mixed message of support, given even though it is against Montana law to incarcerate prisoners from out of state. Amazingly, the tiny town won the case, but not so amazingly, the settlement didn't cover the $27 million worth of bonds that had gone defunct.

There was a glimmer of hope that the project would be resurrected when the federal government announced that the Guantanamo Bay facility in Cuba was to be closed, but the three-man Montana congressional delegation was pretty quick to put the kibosh on bringing al-Qaeda to Big Sky Country.

Reading the address from the slip of paper that Isaac Bloomfield had given me, I told Robert to stop at what looked to be an abandoned trucking port, probably built as part of the prison complex, complete with loading bays, ramps, and a few abandoned vehicles in assorted states of disrepair.

He wheeled into the parking lot next to a black, lifted half-ton with heavily tinted windows. "This the place?"

Bob swiveled the computer on the center console and began typing in the plate number; after a moment, the information ran across the screen, along with a picture of a severe-looking individual with long hair and a thin face and neck. "Ladies and germs, may I present Joseph Free Bird." He turned to look at me. "What the hell kind of bullshit name is that?"

Robert laughed. "Must be a Lynyrd Skynyrd fan."

I stared at the two comics through the steel grate. "You guys want to let me out?"

The Bobs looked at each other again. "Robert, I think he's trying to keep all the fun to himself."

"Say it ain't so, Bob."

"Open the door."

They both turned and looked at me, Robert nudging his partner in noncrime. "He's kind of cranky; I'm thinking we shouldn't let him out of the unit—he's likely to do damage to the citizenry."

"I'm liable to do damage to this shiny new Interceptor with

this .45 I've got on my hip if you two jackboots don't let me out of this damn car."

They got out, and Bob opened the rear passenger-side door.

"I don't suppose I could convince you guys to stay out here?"

Bob looked at his buddy across the shiny black sheet metal. "I'm beginning to think he doesn't enjoy our company, Robert."

"I think you're right, Bob."

I glanced at the loading dock and the wire-covered glass in the office door. "Gimme five minutes and then you guys can come in."

Robert shook his head at his partner and then at me. "Why?"

"Because I think I'm likely to exercise a little badass, and I'd just as soon there be as few witnesses as possible."

Bob lifted his space-age chronograph and punched a few buttons on his wrist. "You got five minutes and twenty seconds since I think it'll take you that long to get to the door."

I started walking.

If the place had ever been a thriving trucking port, it had fallen on hard times. There wasn't any sign that indicated there was a business present, but the number matched the one on the paper, so I checked the knob—it was locked. Ignoring the hidebound ideas of breaking and entering, inadmissible evidence, and the forty-odd civil restrictions on what I was doing, I used the ever-handy 13-D search warrant.

The door bounced off the wall, but I caught it on the re-bound, palming it back open and walking into what must've once been a reception or dispatching area. There was no equipment, not even a phone, and there was trash in ruptured bags sitting along the walls and spilling onto the floor.

If Free Bird Enterprises was a going concern, it wasn't evident here.

There was some kind of old-time rock and roll playing from further inside the building, so I went around a battered counter toward another wire-glass-paned door, this time unlocked, and, pushing it open, I stepped into a short hallway with an old punch clock on the wall and two doors marked HIS and HERS.

The music was coming from my left where the hallway opened up into a massive room, built large enough to hold the containers of at least a half-dozen eighteen-wheelers. In the nearest bay there was a nonoperable conveyer belt with stacks and stacks of cardboard packing supplies and four young Native teenagers working away, putting what I assumed was the buffalo chip and lawn clipping samplers in boxes.

I took a few more steps and loudly cleared my throat.

One of the young men, wearing a do-rag and a multitude of tattoos, looked up, saw me, and froze, but then nudged the guy working beside him. The second guy disappeared, and suddenly the music stopped and an older man came over and looked at me. He had the ubiquitous pasty face of a white guy, a glazed look, and the ponytail that Lucian would say made it easier to identify a genuine horse's ass.

"Hey, can I help you?"

I pulled my jacket back to reveal not only my star, but also the Colt on my hip. "I'm looking for Joseph Free Bird."

He glanced around, and I wasn't sure if he thought he could make a run for it or was going to try to finger one of the kids. "Um . . . that's me."

If I was looking for a tough guy to vent my rage on, he

wasn't it. "I kind of figured." I took a step forward. "Walt Longmire, sheriff of Absaroka County, Wyoming."

It was about that time that the second kid pulled something out of his pants and dropped his hand alongside his leg.

Dipping a hand to my own sidearm, I looked at him with intent. "At the risk of sounding a little dramatic, how about you show me what you just pulled out of your pants."

He glanced at the others and then back at me.

"If you don't show me what you've got in your hand right now, I'm going to have to pull mine—and I bet mine's bigger."

He still didn't move.

"Did you hear me?" I waited a second more and then leveled the big Colt at him. "Show me your hands."

He finally spoke, his eyes wide. "It's not a gun." He glanced down at his side. "Um, it looks like a gun, but it's not. Honest, it's a paintball gun, but it looks real."

"Bring it up slow with your finger away from the trigger, got me?"

"Yeah."

He did as I said, and even from this distance, I could see the red plastic trim around the muzzle indicating it wasn't real. As he held it in front of him, I became aware of two very large men standing behind the group with their own weapons drawn.

"Why in the heck are you carrying that thing?"

"Protection."

I reholstered my sidearm as the Bobs came up from behind, slipped the toy away from the kid, and tossed it into one of the boxes full of Styrofoam packing peanuts.

"More likely it'll get you killed."

"Damn kid. I just about sent what little brains you got to . . ." Robert shook his head as he flipped the flap on one of the boxes. "Alicia Hammonds, Wetumpka, Alabama."

"Yeah, he's a patient of mine but most of what I sell him these days is turtle food."

We were sitting halfway inside a cavernous tractor trailer with the sour smell of fresh-cut truck skids in our nostrils; at least that's what I hoped the smell was. He was sitting on a stack of them as I stood, glancing out the back where the Bobs patted down the rest of the gang.

"Turtle food?"

He nodded his head. "Yeah, he buys the stuff by the fifty-pound bag." He gestured toward his accomplices. "One of my guys drives a pickup full down once a month."

"But he was a patient of yours?"

"Yeah, kind of. I had to close the clinic, but I still have my mail-order business and provide to a few of my regular clients."

"Provide what?"

He grinned at his work boots. "Whatever they need."

"So, if I were to contact the Montana Board of Pharmacy, they could provide me with your certification and licensing information?"

He pulled at the collar of his stained T-shirt. "Um, not really . . . I might've let that lapse."

"Uh huh."

He nodded his head again. "Most of what I provide is holistic, all-natural remedies." He leaned back against the interior of the trailer and glanced up at me. "Look, man, Danny was having some problems with life and stuff, and I was just trying to help."

"What kinds of problems, other than those diagnosed by licensed physicians?"

He stared at me. "He was . . . This is going to sound crazy, but he was seeing things."

I stood there. "Seeing what?"

"People and shit, man."

I thought about the conversation Danny and I had had all those years ago. "Dead people."

"Yeah, dead people . . . How did you know that?" He watched me as I broke eye contact with him. "Hey, Sheriff, if you're having problems, I've got some stuff that'll "

I cut off the sales pitch. "What I'm interested in are the medicines you were providing Danny Lone Elk."

"Were?"

"He's dead, and it's a possibility that he was poisoned. What were you providing him with?"

He nodded his head—must've been a habit. "I was giving it to him for his ulcers; it was the Chinese stuff, which is what I sell to a lot of my patients because it's cheaper than the American stuff. I mean, that's where I get most of the drugs I provide." He ran a hand through his thinning hair and tugged on his ponytail. "Look, Sheriff, I don't offer dangerous drugs; I leave that to the real pill pushers."

"Were you giving him anything that might've contained mercury?"

"No. Look, Sheriff, I don't know anything about Danny's medical history, so—"

"That's why we have the whole legal prescription medicine thing, so that the doctors and pharmacists can get together and come to a consensus on what's safe to give a patient." I leaned my back against the interior wall of the trailer. "What about his daughter, Eva?"

"What about her?"

I glanced at my fingernails, perfecting my nonchalance. "Joe, if I get bored with this conversation I'm going to take you over to the Big Horn County jail and hand you over to my good friend, Sheriff Wesley Best Bales." I waited as he fought with himself. "I understand it's fish and Tater Tots on Fridays."

"I um . . . Hey, it's legal in Montana."

I gestured toward some of the bags on the conveyer belt. "Medical marijuana?"

"Yeah."

"I'm no expert, but it looks like lawn clippings."

"It's synthetic marijuana, but you need a carrying agent."

"Lawn clippings?"

He nodded his head again. "Lawn clippings, yeah."

"This is that stuff made in China?"

He studied me. "Hey, yeah. You know about it?"

"Enough to know that it's made from legal substances so that customs can't do anything about it. Every time the government makes it illegal, the chemists just change the chemical formula and make a new drug."

He smiled. "Perfectly legal."

"Perfectly dangerous. Nobody's monitoring this stuff; it's part weed, part cocaine, part crack, part LSD and nobody knows from shipment to shipment what those percentages are."

"Hey, man, it's still legal."

"Eva Lone Elk lives in Wyoming where it is not legal at all."

He picked at a hole in his jeans. "Oh, man, are you really going to bust me on this?"

"Not if you tell me what else you're prescribing for her."

"Chinese Cymbalta—it's just an antidepressant and cheap."

"I'll make you a deal." I pushed off the wall and took a few steps toward the back, pausing a moment for him to stand and join me. "You drop the prescription drugs altogether, and I'll turn a blind eye toward your illegal bullshit business . . ."

"Buffalo shit, man. It's sacred."

I draped an arm over his shoulder and led him to the rear of the trailer, where we stood over the others. "And if I get wind of you continuing to write medications for people or selling this robo-weed, I'm turning you over to the DEA, the Pharm Board, Montana Division of Criminal Investigation, and anybody else I can think of. You got me?"

He nodded. "Yeah, yeah."

We watched as Robert kept an eye on the half-dozen young men and reached down to pick up a few of the darker bags they had been stuffing into the packing boxes. "What in the hell is this stuff?"

Joe Free Bird spoke up in full sales pitch mode. "Medicinal *Bi'Shee* poultices for spiritual and physical well-being."

Bob picked up the nearest bag and read about the all-natural ingredients, making a quick assessment. "Bullshit."

I patted him on the back as we climbed down. "Nope, but you're close."

9

"You know . . ." Bob opened the ziplock bag and sniffed. "I think I've been had."

"Good thing it was a free sample."

There was a break in the series of cloudbursts that were marking the day, and Robert got out and joined his partner. We all began walking toward my office. "You can leave your potpourri in the squad car, and then we can burn it if it gets cold—frontiersmen used to do that with buffalo chips back in the old days."

There was a large black Lincoln parked at the curb behind the other Lola, Henry's Baltic-blue '59 Thunderbird convertible, and I wasn't the only one to notice the state plates as we drew near. Bob closed up his bag and stuffed it in his jacket pocket. "Uh oh."

As we got closer, the tinted back window whirred, and Joe Meyer called out to me merrily, "Where the heck is the sheriff of this damn county, anyway?"

"He was in Montana." I straddled a puddle on the sidewalk and, leaning down, could see two large young men in the front and the elderly statesman seated in the back with a pile of folders in his lap. "What, you brought your homework with you?"

He adjusted his glasses, followed by a helpless gesture, and looked at the piles of paper. "Don't ever let them talk you into being an attorney general, Walt."

"I never wanted to be an attorney, let alone the guy who leads them into battle."

He laughed and looked past me at the two men on the sidewalk. "My goodness, it's the Bobs." He leaned forward. "I've got two of your younger and less experienced cohorts in here; is there any way I could get you to assist them in exploring the culinary splendor of the Busy Bee Café?"

Robert looked at his partner. "What do you say, Bob?"

The other highway patrolman leaned in. "Are they buying?"

The Wyoming AG nodded his head. "Sure, lunch is on the state." I started to straighten when he said quietly, "Can we talk?"

"You bet." As Joe's watchdogs joined their fellow troopers on the sidewalk, I glanced at the thunderheads gathering in the sky again, cracked open the door of the Town Car, and slid into his mobile office. I pulled the door closed behind me and turned to look at him. "Joe, my son-in-law died on duty last night in Philadelphia, so I am in a horrible mood and looking to take it out on somebody. I just thought you should be aware of that fact before we start this conversation."

"Walt." He folded up the papers. "I'm terribly sorry for your loss." Giving me his undivided attention, he put the documents aside. "How's Cady?"

"She had just gotten here with the baby. She's distraught but doing as well as can be expected, I guess."

He nodded and patted the folders and looked out his own

window. "Well, that pretty much takes the wind out of my sails. I came up here to read you the riot act, but now that just doesn't seem appropriate." He watched me, but I said nothing, continuing to stare at the black leather on the seat in front of me—safer that way.

"The kid's a little headstrong . . ."

I grunted. "I assume you are referring to the *acting* deputy United States attorney and not to Cady or Lola?"

Joe took off his glasses and looked at the back of the seat with me. "It's true that he hasn't been confirmed yet, but it would be nice if you two could work together."

"Well." I paused, but then good sense abandoned me and I spoke my mind. "This is a publicity stunt so that man can make a name for himself, and I don't have time for it, especially not now."

"We're talking about fossil remains with a street value of over eight million dollars, and as they say, a million here and a million there . . ."

"Pretty soon you're talking about some serious money." I leaned back in the seat and looked out at Saizarbitoria and Double Tough, who were walking by, peering in the tinted windows. I wondered idly what sort of eyeball DT was sporting today.

"You make good press, Walt. Think of it as giving the guy a leg up."

"How 'bout I give him the boot out instead?"

He frowned. "There are folks in Cheyenne who would appreciate you taking the time to work with him."

"Joe, you keep leaning on me, and I'm going to call Mary and have her lean on you."

At the mention of his wife he held up his hands. "Oh, don't do that." He waited a moment and then added. "In a week, he'll be out of your hair. You know, if we can establish ownership of that giant bag of bones, it'll go to public auction pretty soon."

I stared at him. "There's no way the legal shenanigans will be over pretty soon, Joe."

"They will, if I can get you to help ascertain who has actual ownership—the family, the Conservancy, or the federal government. Then I can do it, and it'll be out of my hair and out of the public eye." His shoulders slumped. "Otherwise, this thing is going to drag on in the courts forever. I hate to light a fire under you at a time like this, but there it is."

"So some venerable organization like the Smithsonian, backed by Exxon/Mobil or Burger King/Pizza Hut, can have Jen?"

"And the owner gets the money." He sighed. "To the winner go the spoils. We are a capitalist society." He leaned back and looked at me. "So, concerning Skip Trost, what can I do to make this happen in an amicable fashion?"

I thought about it and stuck a finger out like a baton. "Remind him he's in my county as a guest."

"Done. Anything else?"

I left the finger out there. "And don't you come back up here to slap my wrists over this again."

He waited a moment and then did a little air clearing. "You know, this is not the way that a sheriff is supposed to speak with his attorney general."

I took a deep breath and blew it out like a valve. "Nope, this is the way I talk to my old friend Joe Meyer, but if you'd like to see how this conversation would go in a professional manner, I can start over from the beginning."

"I think I'll pass." He studied me a bit longer, then pulled the papers from the seat and set them back in his lap. "Besides, I have to be in Evanston this evening for a meeting at the state psychiatric hospital."

"Checking in?"

He opened a folder and began reading. "I think seriously about it sometimes."

I pulled the handle and stepped out onto the sidewalk. "You want me to go down the hill and get the troops?"

"No, I've got enough to keep me busy till they get something to eat. They're good boys—one's in night school over in Laramie getting his law degree."

"What about you?"

"Believe it or not, I have my degree."

"I meant lunch."

"Oh, Mary made me an egg salad sandwich—it's in here someplace." He glanced around, finally spotting a brown paper bag at his feet. "Here it is." He pulled the waxed-paper-wrapped sandwich from the bag, along with a bottle of water. "Would you like a half?"

"No, thanks. Not really hungry today." I leaned in the opening, draping an arm on the door, looking at the last of a breed—a statesman and true champion of the people. "You're a good guy, Joe."

He didn't look up but spoke to the documents in his lap. "So are you, Walt. That's why we do what we do—something I'm sure your son-in-law, after making the sacrifice he has, wherever his spirit is, understands far better than we do." He turned his face toward me, and I could see the sadness there. "Please tell Cady I am so sorry, and if there's anything I can do, anything at all, to please contact me. As a matter of fact, have her call me when she can, if you would."

I nodded.

"Now shut the door so I can concentrate on my work." He raised a fist without looking at me. "Save Jen."

Cady was seated on the wooden bench in the reception area with her belongings around her. I joined her as she talked with Ruby about the flight she would be taking from Sheridan this afternoon. "I explained the situation, and they made a spot for me."

I moved a carry-on and sat in its place. "Short visit."

She turned to look at me as Dog placed his bucket head on her lap. "I'm sorry, Daddy."

"Don't be silly." I put an arm around her and pulled her into inevitable love. "Do you want me to go with you?"

Her voice was muffled against my chest, and her fingers threaded through Dog's hair. "No, there'll be all the preparations to make, and I'll want to spend as much time as I can with Michael's family. Anyway, Vic is going with me." Her hand came up and straightened my shirt. "You don't mind me taking your second in command?"

"Not for this—even wounded she's awfully capable." I looked around. "Where's Lola?"

"In your office, taking a nap with Henry." She pulled back a little and looked up at me. "I guess we'll have to postpone the naming ceremony."

"I'm sure it'll be fine." I glanced up at my dispatcher and

could see she was crying, so I figured I'd better get the ball rolling in a different direction or we'd all be fumbling for tissues. "Hey, what's on the agenda around here?"

Ruby wiped the tears away and slapped her hands in her lap as if the action would dispose of the emotion. She took a deep breath and adjusted her glasses. "Joe Meyer is here, looking for you."

"Already took care of the attorney general; he was sitting in his car and caught me—evidently everybody thinks we're a drive-through." Cady breathed a laugh, but it was hollow. "Speaking of, I'll drive you over to Sheridan."

"That's okay. Henry says he'll do it."

"I saw that he broke out Lola's namesake."

"He said that she should go to the airport in style." Cady swallowed as she glanced out the window. "But I don't think we're going to get a chance to put the top down."

"No, doesn't look good." I thought about how the Bear, knowing what was for the best, sometimes stepped in for me. He would be able to talk to her about the pain of a fresh loss, something I was not as capable of doing. "Ruby, what's the weather going to be like?"

Addicted to the metallic Norwegian voice of our NOAA radio, Ruby always knew the score. "Rain, with the really bad thunderstorms hitting us tonight."

I turned back to Cady. "Glad you are leaving this afternoon, then."

She nodded. "I think Michael's family is going to need me back there."

"Yep." I waited a second before adding, "Promise me you'll take care of yourself?"

"I will."

"No, I mean it."

She paused a moment and gave me a funny look. "I promise, Dad."

With a final squeeze, I stood. "Well, I'm going to get one last cuddle with that granddaughter of mine before the three of you take flight."

She smiled up at me, and I took my leave, Dog staying with her. I quietly approached the doorway of my office and peeked around the jamb to see the Cheyenne Nation reclined in my chair with Lola lying on his chest, slowly rising and falling with each of his breaths, her tiny hands twined into his long hair.

I was about to back out when his voice rumbled, "The best reason I can think of for having children is that it is a marvelous excuse for taking naps."

I stepped into the room, sat on one of my visitor chairs, and glanced around, not used to seeing my office from this perspective. "You mind if I ask you a question?" He stared at me. "Last night, why did you ask if Michael's death was a random incident?"

He waited a moment and then said the two words I was hoping he wouldn't: "Tomás Bidarte."

We sat there listening to the ticking of my wall clock and the breathing of my granddaughter. "So, you don't think he's through after hiring Delgatos to try and kill me."

"No, and if this is still Asociación Punto Muerto, then the contract on you is yet unfulfilled."

I could sense conflicting feelings surging through the tectonic plates of my emotions like lava. I wasn't sure I wanted to hear the rest of what he had to say, but it's a long, red road with no turns when you're dealing with the Cheyenne Nation. "Just for the sake of argument, why Michael?"

"To hurt Cady and therefore you, and Vic."

"Why hurt Vic?"

"She is the one who shot him."

"Two birds, one stone, without ever being in Wyoming." I thought about it, looking at the floor as if expecting it to swallow me up. "A plague on both your houses."

"Yes."

"Continuing with our theme for argument's sake—do you think he's done?"

"No."

"What do I do?"

He carefully stood and crossed around my desk to lower Lola into my arms against my chest where she didn't even stir. He turned his back to us and stepped toward the windows. "You have two choices: you can either stay here and present yourself and your loved ones as targets, waiting for him to show again—"

"Or?"

He turned to look at me with one very dark eye. "Kill him."

I stared at him for a long while and then gently laughed, so as not to disturb the baby. "Don't you think I'm a little long in the tooth to be playing international hit man?"

He didn't blink. "I can take care of this for you."

The full realization of what he was prepared to do settled on our friendship. "I would never ask you to do something like that."

"That is why I would do it."

There was nothing I wanted more than Tomás Bidarte, the man who had done more damage to me and mine than anybody on the face of the earth, dead, but not like this. "No."

He stepped back to the edge of my desk and sat, crossing his arms and looking down at me. "You do not have the luxury of doing nothing."

"I'll wait and see if our suspicions about Michael's death are correct, and if they are . . ." I sighed. "Then I'll do something."

"What will you do?"

"I'll burn that bridge when I come to it." Lola stirred, and I hugged her a little closer. "I am sworn to uphold the law, Henry—I'm not a hired killer."

"No, but you are up against one, and I am offering to stop him."

"You know, you're not as young as you used to be, either." I shook my head. "You're not my ethical default, Henry, you're my friend—one of the loved ones you were talking about. I'll do this, but I'll do it my way or else my whole life has been a joke." I looked down at the tiny, sleeping body on my chest. "If I find out he's behind this, I will bring the concentrated effort of everything I am and have against him, but not until I'm sure."

"Of what? That he is a killer?"

"That he's responsible." Studying the swirls of brown hair that were, at the age of five months, just now creeping over her ears, I kept my eyes on the top of my granddaughter's head.

He reached out one of his powerful hands, the fingertips gently touching the child. "If something happens to this one . . ." He nodded his head toward the front office. ". . . your philosophy will no longer hold sway."

I looked up at him, making sure he understood. "No, it won't."

Watching the Thunderbird pull away in the drizzle, I felt my heart beat against my rib cage like an animal fighting for its freedom. The Cheyenne Nation was going to pick up Vic and, while helping her with her crutches and baggage, talk to her about our suppositions. I had a suspicion that she had already figured out that Bidarte was involved, but better to make sure she was forewarned and forearmed.

A lot of people might underestimate my undersheriff because she was wounded; a lot of people are morons.

Dog whined, and I patted his head. "Just you and me, pal." I became aware of someone standing behind me and turned to find McGroder adjusting his umbrella. "And the FBI."

"I hear you had a death in the family."

I nodded and turned to face him. "My son-in-law, Vic's brother."

"I'm sorry. Anything I can do?"

We both stood there for a while, neither of us sure of what to say next. "Well, do you have any connections in Mexico City?"

"Me personally? No." He took his sunglasses off and shoved them in the case, all the while petting Dog, who wagged like a windshield wiper. "I'm a domestic guy, but I've got friends in high places over at the CIA, NSA, and State." He continued to study me. "You got trouble?"

"Yep."

"Cop trouble?"

I brought my eyes up and looked toward the horizon like some third lead in a B Western. "No."

"Oh, real trouble." He pulled Dog's ear. "Seeing as how you kept me from bleeding to death up on the mountain, I don't think I could deny you much. Why don't you tell me the entire story and I'll see what I can do."

I nodded and began the saga of Tomás Bidarte as the three of us walked back up the steps.

"Walt? Walt!" Mike and I both turned as a highly agitated Dave Baumann hurried to the base of the steps and put a hand on the railing. "Jen's missing."

Dog barked, and McGroder and I looked at each other and then looked back at him. "What?"

"Jen, she's missing."

"You mean the body?"

He looked confused. "What?"

"We've got the head." I turned to look at the FBI man. "Don't we?"

Baumann flapped his hands. "Not the *T. rex*, my assistant, the paleontologist, Jennifer."

I stepped back down and got a read on just how upset he was. "What do you mean *missing*. Since when?"

"Last night at the museum was the last time I saw her. She didn't show today, so I tried calling her cell and her home phones, but nobody answered at either one. Then I texted her, and she always answers." He glanced down Main Street. "I was going to go out to her place, but then I got worried that maybe I should have somebody with me."

"Does she live out at her father's at Lake DeSmet?"

"Yes, the old rock shop."

I turned to McGroder and gestured toward Dog. "You want to go with me? I'm fresh out of sidekicks with opposable thumbs."

"But I'm having such a good time cataloging all this guy's crap back in the holding cells." He paused in mock quandary. "You bet your ass." He pulled a cell phone from his jacket as all four of us jumped in my truck, pulling out as the rain picked up again, and headed north of town. "Jarod? Yeah, it's me." There was a pause. "What? No. Look, I'm headed out of town a few miles and just wanted to check in . . . Yes. Maybe an hour." There was another, longer pause. "Well, tell him it has to do with the case. No, don't put him on." Then the third, and longest pause. "Because the acting deputy douchebag is a pain in my ass." A short pause. "No, don't tell him that." He ended the call and looked at me. "Kids these days."

I glanced over my shoulder at Baumann, looking a little uncomfortable with Dog sitting beside him. "Did you talk to her after she left the museum yesterday?"

"No, but she sent me a text message that she was looking through her computer files trying to find the one with Danny on it where we agreed to the arrangements about the dinosaur."

I nodded and took the ramp onto the highway. "Does she live out there alone?"

"Yes."

"Try her on the phone again, before I burn up the gas to find out she was taking a shower."

He began calling under protest. "She would never just leave." He shot a look at McGroder. "Not with them here." He waited a while and then left a message: "Jen, this is the third time I've called you, but I just wanted to make sure you were all right? Hello? Hello?" Shaking his head, he looked at me in the rearview mirror. "Nothing."

"Was she all right when she left last night?"

He shook his head. "Not particularly, but she's rarely all right so it's hard to tell."

"Was she upset about anything in particular, other than the obvious?"

He glanced at McGroder. "You mean other than these guys taking Jen?"

"Yep." The agent in charge glanced at me with a funny look on his face, so I asked, "What?"

He glanced back at Baumann. "Um, the deputy attorney might've dropped a subpoena on her last night."

"What?"

He ran a hand through his crew cut. "Well, she was the first one to see the damn thing; I mean she found it, right? He's probably going to want her to testify."

Dave threw himself back in his seat as Dog shifted away and looked at him. "Against us?"

The FBI man shrugged. "For, against, whatever."

"It's not like she was going anywhere."

"Look, subpoenas are like hemorrhoids: everybody's gonna get one sooner or later." He gestured toward me. "Even the sheriff, here." He glanced back at Dave. "Don't take it personally."

Baumann folded his arms. "I won't, but it's Jen and she would have."

I took the exit at Lake DeSmet and drove the rest of the way past the marina and the housing developments that now dotted the shore of the 3,600-acre lake nestled in the undrained basin between Piney and Boxelder Creeks, its two major tributaries at the base of the Bighorns. Named for Father Jean DeSmet, the first recorded Catholic priest to visit the region, the lake is the result of a massive coal seam fire. After the seam burned, the bottom of the basin collapsed and slowly filled with water from the area.

We drove past the Lake Stop store where McGroder noticed a large sign adorned with Smetty, the long-necked dinosaur that circled the print and winked at passersby. "What the heck is a Smetty?"

"The local monster that supposedly lives in the lake." I glanced at him as I pulled my truck up to the rock shop. "In the late 1800s the lake had a surprisingly high salt content, and the Indians believed there was a lost tunnel connecting it to the Pacific Ocean. The legend gave rise to a number of stories of a creature similar to the Loch Ness monster, Smetty being the most popular."

The FBI man turned to the scientist. "So, what are the chances that Smetty is real?"

Dave shook his head as I shut the Bullet down. "None."

McGroder looked at him a little quizzically. "How come?"

Dave huffed, "All right, setting aside the fact that this thing, probably an elasmosaurus, died off in the later Cretaceous period millions of years ago . . . even if one of these things survived, how the hell would it have lived in there for sixty-six million years?"

McGroder took on the role of devil's advocate. "I don't know—what's the life span of one of those Elmo-sauruses, anyway?"

Dave palmed his face. "About thirty, if they're lucky—real lucky."

I held Dog's collar as the two of them got out. "You stay in here, buddy. At least until we find out what's going on."

Mike thought about it. "Maybe it's a family of them."

Dave palmed his face again. "These marine reptiles were close to sixty feet long and weighed around fifteen tons." He gestured toward the waves scalped by the Wyoming wind. "There aren't and never have been enough fish in that body of water to keep one of those damn things alive for a week, let alone families of them for millions of years."

The FBI man looked at the water the way men have since they crawled out of it. "Well, you never know."

Baumann looked at him incredulously. "Yeah, you do. That's the thing about science; you can figure things out with what we call facts. I swear that's the reason I don't specialize in marine reptiles. You'd be hard pressed to find a single, mouth-breathing moron that believes that somewhere on the planet there's probably a tyrannosaurus walking around, but the vocal minority of so-called experts that believe that some species of sea serpents has survived to the modern day never ceases to amaze me."

As Dave began winding his way through the mazelike area in front of the rock shop, McGroder watched him depart and then gazed at the massive lake, his imagination transporting him to a place where science refused to carry water. "You never know."

I shook my head and followed Dino-Dave.

Beginning as an Airstream trailer, the Lake DeSmet Rock Shop had been here for years and had grown exponentially from its humble beginnings to a fenced rabbit warren of tables made from concrete blocks and wide barn planks. There were rocks of all types everywhere, and say what you want about the product, nobody seemed to care that the things were sitting about in the weather. I guess if the rocks had survived for millions of years lying around on the ground, they could probably withstand a little sun and rain. There were signs all over the place, proclaiming GEODES $1 APIECE, MINERALS & GEMS!

Baumann was banging on the warped screen door, paint flakes dropping as he knocked. "Jen, it's Dave, are you in there?"

"Kind of hard on the FBI, weren't you?"

"He's an idiot." He rapped smartly on the door again.

"What about that fish that they caught off the coast of Africa back in the thirties? Everybody thought those things died off in the Cretaceous period, right?"

"You know, you bring up some of the strangest stuff." He continued knocking. "It's not the same—this is not a fish." He turned back to the door. "You know, I almost wish they hadn't found that damned Coelacanth—all it's done is embolden all these crypto zoologists, creationists, and snake-oil salesmen who somehow believe that finding living dinosaurs will somehow invalidate the theory of evolution, which it won't."

I studied him. "Wishing they'd not found a specimen? That doesn't sound particularly scientific, Dave."

"You know, Sheriff, I've always thought of you as being an intelligent man."

I sighed. "Don't get me wrong; I agree with all the things you're saying. It's just that the scientific method, like the prin-

ciples of detection, rely on that magnificent process called theory—a thought supported by empirical fact. But that's the
wonderful thing about facts—they keep turning up and, like
theories, they evolve."

He finally smiled. "Maybe I should have you come and do
the talks at the museum."

"No, thanks. I've got a pretty good day job." I reached past
him and banged on the door with the force of having done it
a great deal more than the curator. "Jennifer, it's Sheriff Walt
Longmire—can you come to the door?"

There was no response.

I knocked again and watched as McGroder walked up.
"What's happening?"

"So far, nothing."

He stood there for a moment more and then turned and
walked away, continuing on around the building.

"Jen, it's the sheriff. Open up."

Still nothing.

I pushed past Dave and placed both hands on the knob of
the dilapidated inside door.

"What are you doing?"

"Opening it."

"Can you do that without a warrant?"

"If invited, yes." I called out. "Hello, anybody home?"

A voice shouted from the other side of the building. "Sure,
come on in."

I pressed my shoulder against the facing and popped the
door, swinging the thing wide as Dave stuck his head back in
my line of sight. "You can't do that; that was that FBI agent
that said that."

"Did you see him say it?"

"Well, no . . ."

I stepped into the crowded front room. "Then it's a theory, huh?"

The Lake DeSmet Rock Shop had perhaps seen better days. There was an old cash register from the seventies that looked inoperable crouched on a vintage, oak-framed display counter that held a number of old rocks, minerals, agates, and a few of what appeared to be gold-panning kits.

Dave shrugged. "Jen kind of let the place go after her dad died, but she can't seem to get rid of any of the stuff." I stepped around the counter and picked up a phone by the cord. "I don't think it's connected—she uses her cell phone."

I listened to it for a second and then hung it up on the wall cradle. "Well, it's certainly not connected now." I moved on to the noncommercial portion of the place and used an arm to part a beaded curtain. The windows had mustard-colored sheets draped over them, giving the room a dark but golden cast. The furniture was old, chenille-covered stuff from the thirties, with tattered Indian blankets thrown everywhere in a failing attempt to guard against the dog hair.

There was an opening to the right that revealed a kitchen, so I stepped in that direction but still didn't see anything that looked out of the ordinary. There was a door leading to another storage area and possibly the back, and another across the main room that probably led to the bedroom.

The only newer items in the living room were a large flat-screen television and a desk with some electrical cords lying on the surface. I glanced around but couldn't really see anything out of place or signs of a struggle. "Did she mention anything about going anywhere—staying with somebody?"

Dave stood in the doorway, holding the beaded curtain in his hands, evidently reluctant to enter. "No."

"Did you check the museum?"

"I did earlier." He shook his head. "She's been disappearing a lot lately."

"Call again."

He pulled out his cell and hit speed dial. "If she was there, she'd have her cell phone on her."

"Maybe she's charging it in her van, which, by the way, doesn't appear to be here." There was a Northern Cheyenne Fancy Dance fan under a Plexiglas cover on a side table, and I removed the top to look at the thing. Ancient, the seed beads were encrusted with ash and the feathers tattered, but it was still beautiful.

"Don't touch that!"

I turned to Dave. "Sorry. It's sacred?"

"It's poisoned is what it is." He eyed me as I carefully replaced the top. "That one was recovered from the Peabody Museum at Yale. The things are coated with dangerous amounts of arsenic, lead, mercury, and other heavy metals. Back in the nineteenth and twentieth centuries the museums used about a hundred different pesticides to keep insects and rodents from eating the things."

I studied the artifact. "Where did Jennifer get it?"

"Hell if I know." He gestured with his phone. "Nothing, just the answering machine."

I started toward the door to the left that hung partially

closed and pushed the thing open slowly—there was an old four-poster bed that had been slept in and an ashtray sitting on the nightstand, full of butts. There was a mess, but nothing to indicate foul play.

A large dog bed was on the floor by a dresser, a few chew toys lying about. I glanced back through the doorway. "She has a Tibetan mastiff, right?"

He nodded.

"Not here, either."

"Hey, Sheriff?"

I glanced at the museum curator. "Was that you or is that McGroder?"

"McGroder, and it's not a theory; I can see him."

I stepped out of the bedroom. Mike was standing by the back door, his sunglasses in his hand. "You'd better come see this."

I gave Baumann a look as I passed, but he seemed content to stay where he was.

McGroder stepped back through more tables piled with rocks before stopping in what appeared to be a mudroom that was lined with old, paned windows that had been nailed together. "The door was ajar." The agent tucked his regulation Ray-Bans in his jacket pocket. "Honest." Pointing to the steps outside where it looked like someone had taken a hammer, or a rock for that matter, to a piece of electronics, he leaned against the back doorjamb. "I think that's what's left of a desktop computer."

I kneeled down and picked up the pieces. "Have you got people who can patch it back together and get the information out of it—video files, specifically?"

He shook his head, doubtful. "I'll have Jarod look at it, but I wouldn't hold out much hope."

My attention was drawn to a collection of brown drops on the chipped linoleum, about the amount that might be held in an eyedropper.

McGroder's voice echoed my thoughts. "You thinking what I'm thinking?" He took a step toward me. "I mean I haven't been in the field for a while, but that is what I think it is, right?"

10

"I'm trying to figure out who would benefit from both Danny Lone Elk's death and Jennifer Watt's disappearance."

Lucian sipped from the plastic cup that had been on his tray but ignored the so-called food and glanced at his granddaughter, Lana Baroja, who stood with Henry, both of them leaning against the wall. "I'm tryin' to figure out who benefited from you lazy bastards not bringing me anything to put in this horseshit orange juice." He placed his book on his chest and looked at the cup. "God, that tastes nasty. What is that, Tang? Damned astronauts should've left that on the moon." He held the cup out to me. "Here, taste this."

Clever that way, I declined. "No, thanks." I sat back in the visitor chair and listened to it squeal in protest. "I guess you didn't learn anything from this last experience, huh?"

"What, to not drink poisoned liquor?" He gestured toward the Bear, watching him with a bemused expression. "Indians've known that for centuries, right?" The old sheriff's eyes dropped to his tray, and he made a peace offering. "You want some . . . hell, I don't know what it is, Ladies' Wear, but you can have it if you want."

The Cheyenne Nation shook his head. "No, thank you."

Lana pushed off the wall and crossed to put a hand on Lucian's shoulder. "I'm getting out of here so that you fellows can talk shop."

I got up with my hat in my hands, uncomfortable at having taken her seat, even at her insistence. I guess I was looking tired. "How's the Basque bakery business?"

She smiled at my mention of her going concern. "Like everything else, picking up with the tourists."

"Good."

"We've got an impromptu jazz trio on Friday nights, and I hear you do a mean Ramsey Lewis impression of 'Wade in the Water.'"

I stretched my fingers as if covering a few octaves. "I don't know—my fingers are getting a little stiff these days."

"You should stop by." She moved to go but then paused and looked at me. "Did you know I bought that house that's been for sale forever—the Victorian on the corner of West Hart over by the golf course?"

Aware that she had received a healthy inheritance from her grandmother a few years ago, I knew her sole financial future was not tied to the bakery. "The Buell Mansion?"

She looked embarrassed. "Well, I wouldn't exactly call it a mansion, especially with the work that has to be done." She playfully slapped my shoulder and pointed a warning finger at the Bear, who pointed one back at her like they were a matched set of crossed sabers. "Take care of my grandfather; he's the only family I've got left."

I watched her head out the door and turned to look at the old sheriff. "She's coming up in the world, huh?"

He shrugged. "Wants to remodel the carriage house behind the place and move me in there."

"Sounds like a good deal."

He frowned. "I like my freedom."

I studied the man who'd been born when automobiles had been a novelty. "Um, I don't think she'll put a curfew on you."

"I guess if you can't get rid of the family skeleton, then you might as well give it a place to live."

I waited a moment and then asked, "How are you feeling?"

"Fit as a fiddle and ready for love." He picked up *The Middle Parts of Fortune* by Frederic Manning, and looked at me. "Why'd you come in here?"

"Isaac said he could run a quick analysis on the blood flakes we found at the Lake DeSmet Rock Shop and get us a preliminary, so I thought we'd check and see if you were dead yet."

"Not yet." The gimlet gleam returned to his eyes as he set the WWI memoir on the nightstand. "Make you a deal?"

"What?"

"Get me out of here, and I'll help you with the case."

Just what I needed. "I'll think about it."

He set the plastic cup down on the tray with a flair of finality and crossed his arms. "Then the hell with the lot of you." He glanced around as the Cheyenne Nation moved to the window and sat on the ledge. "Where's my damn leg?"

Henry smiled. "I do not have the slightest of ideas."

The room was silent for a while, and then Lucian leaned toward me in a conspiratorial manner. "C'mon, get me out of here. It's just that observation shit. Hell, you don't stay in here for more than twenty minutes, and I been in here bein' observed for over twenty-four hours."

"No."

He didn't move but his voice dropped a few octaves, and he attempted to sound innocent. "I'm gonna start causing trouble."

I turned and looked at the Bear, both of us knowing the width and breadth of the type of trouble of which Lucian Connally was capable. "Lucian, it's not up to me. What if I took you out of here, and you had another attack on the sidewalk?"

He worked his jaw. "There'd be a great deal of celebration in some quarters."

"Not from your granddaughter." The first lesson of sheriffing—when in doubt, defer. "If Isaac says you can go, then you can go."

"All right then." Satisfied with the track of the conversation, he leaned back onto his stack of pillows. "Lot of blood?"

"A few drops."

"Any other traces?"

"Nope."

He thought about it. "No drip, spray, or splash?"

"Nothing."

He ruminated on the scene he hadn't seen. "That's queer."

"I thought so, too."

"Thinkin' somebody just cut themselves beatin' the livin' daylights out of that computer." I nodded and let him continue to think. "So you got the Highway Patrol out on the girl's vehicle?"

"Yep."

He shook his head. "Well, it ain't gonna do you a hell of a lot of good either way; them triple A with guns couldn't slap their ass with a patented ass-slapping machine." He thought about it a while longer. "You want my learned opinion on this?"

"Sure."

"Runner."

I crossed my scuffed boots and studied him. "I thought about that."

"Got served a subpoena by the FB of I and figured she was going to have to testify against her friends over there at Jurassic Park."

"The High Plains Dinosaur Museum."

"Pile of bones in an old carpet store is what I call it. Whatever. She took that vehicle of hers and has it parked in the middle of nowhere. Hell, she's one of those archeology types, so she's sittin' out there somewhere with a pith helmet, a piña colitis, and toilet paper." He glanced up at Henry. "In my experience, a woman won't go anywhere there isn't toilet paper."

I looked back at the Bear, who shook his head at the malapropism.

The old sheriff continued. "I bet if you check the grocery stores around here, they'll tell you that she loaded up and headed out for the territories."

"What about the blood?"

"Hell, I don't know. Maybe that dog of hers killed a pack rat back there or something."

I shook my head. "There would have been more of a mess."

"Well, maybe somebody butchered a western cottontail."

The door opened, and the chief of medicine entered the room and adjusted his glasses, but before he could say anything, Lucian spoke. "Isaac, I gotta get out of here." He gestured toward me. "The current sheriff and full-time layabout and his redskin sidekick need my help."

The old doctor glanced at us. "Is that true?"

Both Henry and I answered simultaneously and with a great deal of emphasis. "No."

He shook his head at Lucian and adjusted his glasses. "It's blood, all right."

"How old?"

"Less than twenty-four hours."

I turned to look at Henry, who in turn looked at Isaac. "Human?"

"Within the ABO group with two distinct antigens and antibodies, B-type. With my limited facilities it could also be another primate, but here in Wyoming monkeys are rare so the chances of that are slim."

Lucian pushed his rolling tray away. "Well, thanks a lot, Doc. You just shot my theory in the ass." He looked at me, snapped his fingers, and pointed one at me like a gun. "She got a pet monkey?"

"No."

He dropped the weapon and turned back to Isaac. "What the hell else can you tell us?"

Isaac pulled his ever-present clipboard up and pretended to read from it. "Female, blonde, approximately twenty-six to twenty-eight years of age . . ."

"Damn, you're kidding."

He lowered the clipboard. "Yes, I am."

Lucian turned to me. "You know, the smart-ass quotient in this county has sure gone up since you took over."

I stood, and Lucian cleared his throat, which forced me to direct my attention to the doc, as much as I was trying to avoid it. "Isaac, he wants to know if you'll release him."

"Please."

I stared at him, hoping I had misheard. "What?"

"Please get him out of here this afternoon—I've got two RNs in this wing who are threatening to put him out of their misery." He gestured toward the door. "If he stays any longer, I really can't vouch for his safety."

"So, what are you going to do?"

Sharing the information that my son-in-law had been killed might not have been prudent, but it didn't seem right not to tell him, as Lucian was Cady's unofficial great uncle and ersatz grandfather. "Wait for word from Philadelphia to see if there's anything odd about what happened."

He sat back in his seat as I made the turn on Fort and drove on toward the first grocery store on the way toward the mountains. "I don't have to tell you what I'd do if somebody shot my son-in-law."

"No, you don't—you'd go to Philadelphia and shoot somebody whether it was the right person or not."

"Makes you feel better when you shoot people . . . You ought to try it sometime."

I pulled up and waited at one of our three stoplights. "I've shot people before, old man, and the last thing it ever made me feel was better."

He turned and looked at the Cheyenne Nation. "What do you say?"

"Leave him out of this."

He nodded as he turned back in the seat. "That's just what I thought."

"When I first started out, you taught me to make sure I was right and then go ahead with all of my abilities. Well, this is the make-sure-I'm-right part. I'm not going to go kill a man because I'm angry about losing Michael."

"The son of a bitch has already got an irrevocable contract out on you, and you don't think that's reason enough to go exterminate his ass?"

"If I go after him, it'll be for a specific reason and not a general feeling."

"Well, till that time, you and yours are going to be marching around like tin bears in a shooting gallery." He glanced back at the Bear. "No offense."

Henry rumbled, "None taken."

I pulled my truck into the grocery store lot and saw the SAVE JEN! banner on the side of the building.

The old sheriff leaned forward, looking through the top of the windshield in the other direction and pointing toward the towering fork and spoon with the words SETTINGS FOR YOUR TABLE outside the IGA where we sometimes shanghaied jurors for court duty. "I remember around the Fourth of July back in '60 when Robert Taylor backed his Cadillac into that sign."

"No, you don't."

He turned to look at me, the indignation sharp in his eyes. "The hell I don't; it was a big ol' boat of a thing, white convertible with a red and white interior."

I pulled my truck up in front of the sign and parked. "You might remember the car, but you don't remember the incident because you weren't there."

He unclicked his safety belt, pulled the handle on the door, stepped out with his new four-prong cane, and then opened the suicide door for Henry, who slipped out but left Dog inside. "And how the hell do you know that?"

Having climbed out myself, I came around the front and joined them on the sidewalk. "Because *I* was there, and it was later than that. I remember because he was filming a movie called *Cattle King*."

He shook his head, looking up at the bulbs that ran the circumference of the kitschy sign. "Nope, you didn't start working for me till in the seventies, after Vietnam."

"That's right, but before that I witnessed Robert Taylor backing not only into this sign but also into Ida Purdy's husband's '57 Apache pickup."

We started toward the front of the grocery store, and I slowed to allow Lucian to keep up.

He looked at me. "You know, I'm pretty sure that's the first time I became aware of you." As we stood there, the automatic door slid open and he walked in like he owned the town, which he pretty much had for nigh on sixty years. "Where are the pickled pig's feet in this damned place?"

A long-haired teenage bagger at the checkout raised a fist. "Save Jen!"

I raised a fist in return and watched as Evelyn Clymer, an elderly woman who I remembered used to work at the hardware store but must have changed jobs, smiled at the old sheriff. "Hello, Lucian. We heard you had a stroke?"

He limped toward them. "I did, but it must've been a backstroke because here I am."

The coy smile remained on her lips. "Well, I know that to be the truth."

The teenager looked Native, and when he turned I finally

realized who he was, even though his hair was pulled back and he wore an apron. He spoke to the Bear first. *"Nahkohe, what's up, innit?"*

"Just prowling, Taylor, and you?"

The young Lone Elk leaned against the counter and gestured around him. "Living the dream."

He glanced at me. "Didn't know I had a job at the market?"

I shrugged. "No, I just figured you ran away for a living."

"I mostly walk into town."

"That's close to twelve miles."

He smiled. "I run it most times."

Evelyn rested an elbow on the check-writing stand, propped up her pointed chin with a freckled hand, and glanced over Lucian's shoulder at us. "Something tells me this is a business call."

The old sheriff turned to me. "What's her name?"

"Jennifer Watt, blonde, about five-seven, midtwenties, might've been in here in the last day or so?"

Evelyn shook her head. "Nope, doesn't ring a bell, but I don't know everybody—especially this time of year." She reached behind her and picked up a phone. "Dan, the sheriff and his bodyguards are down here." She hung up, and we watched as a middle-aged man in glasses approached from the offices to our left. "They're looking for a young woman by the name of Watt."

The manager, Dan Crawford, pulled up and raised a fist. "Save Jen!"

I returned the salute; this stuff was wearing me out. "First name Jennifer, works out at the High Plains Dinosaur Museum."

He continued nodding. "She was in here when we opened this morning at six. I thought it was kind of strange in that most people aren't usually in that big of a hurry to buy groceries." He motioned toward the youth. "Taylor was here and spoke with her a long time, as I recall."

We all turned toward him, and he looked pretty unsettled. "Toilet paper—she bought a lot of toilet paper."

I avoided Lucian's eye.

"It's a large county."

Dino-Dave leaned forward and looked at the map unfolded on the hood of my truck, the fuzzy edges of where it was folded betraying its age and use. "I'd imagine you want to concentrate on the areas where we've had digs, the places she'd be most acquainted with?"

The breeze was picking up, and the tail end of the storm that had hit us the day before was subsiding only to kick up its heels a little at the end. I glanced back at the vague shimmer of platinum light that was being swallowed by the mountains, and began wondering if it really was over. "Exactly what I was thinking."

"There's the dig on the northern part of the county that's associated with the University of Montana." He pointed to a different area on the map. "This one is south, down near Powder Junction on property owned by the University of Wyoming in that red Hole-in-the-Wall country." He stood up straight. "If I was looking to get away from everyone . . ." He glanced at McGroder, his arm hanging over my side-view mirror. ". . . you know, till things cooled down, that's where I'd go."

Lucian added his two cents' worth. "Hell, it's where Butch and Sundance holed up."

I noticed Dave didn't mention the site where Jen had been discovered. "Why not the Lone Elk place?"

"That's a working ranch—there are people on it." He pointed back at the map and the site farther south, tapping it with a nail. "That's where I'd be."

"Yep, but is that where you would be if you were Jennifer?"

He looked up. "Well, you have a point; she does have a connection to Jen." He glanced at me. "The tyrannosaur, I mean."

"Right."

"She found it, after all."

I thought about the overhang where we'd taken cover until the flash flood had flushed us out. "Has she ever gone down there and stayed?"

He nodded, thoughtful. "Well, we practically lived down there when we were working the dig, but with the animosity that Randy and his family have shown lately, I find it hard to believe that she would be back down there."

A niggling feeling was working at the back of the reptile stem in my brain, the part of me that was closest in lineage to Jen, the tyrannosaur. "Give me those exact coordinates, and I'll have Saizarbitoria use a GPS to find this spot and we'll go ahead down to the Lone Elk place."

I noticed the acting deputy attorney standing to the side of my truck and looking none too patient. "Sheriff, if I might? I need a word."

"Make it a short one—I've got a missing woman on my hands and a little over four thousand square miles in which to look for her."

He stepped closer and looked up at me with a severe expression. "You missed the press conference."

"Excuse me?"

"The national outlet press conference I arranged."

"I'm not aware of having said that I would be there, Mr. Trost." I thought about the conversation I'd had with Joe Meyer and attempted to suppress my temper. "I'm sure you'll understand when I say that the importance of a missing woman supersedes any obligations I might have to you."

"Some random woman."

I stared at him. "Excuse me?"

"This is some random woman who's missing?"

I stood there for a moment more and then began folding my map. "Not that it matters in the random scope of things, but the woman happens to be Jennifer Watt, the paleontologist who discovered Jen, the fossil remains that are the centerpiece of your investigation."

He was held in check by this information for a moment and then turned to McGroder. "Why was I not told this?"

The special agent frowned. "Um, because we just found out about it."

He turned back to me. "The press conference was embarrassing."

I stuffed the map in the interior pocket of my jacket, nodded, and started for the door of my truck. "I know that; I've been to your press conferences before."

Lucian fumbled with his pipe and tobacco bag but then remembered he was forbidden to smoke in my truck. "Who was that asshole?"

"Somebody I'm supposed to be nice to."

He nodded. "Well, you're doin' a hell of a job."

Henry leaned up between the seats. "Why are you thinking the Lone Elk Ranch?"

I navigated the truck off of the main road and headed out of town south by southeast. "Because, when you hauled us out of that overhang in that back-door canyon, I noticed there were the remains of a campfire, and it looked like someone had done some work to make the place habitable." I wheeled off the road and slowed my acceleration. "In all the excitement of potentially drowning, I kind of forgot about it."

The Bear's eyes went to the windshield and the clouds, tinged mercury of all things, swelling above the hills of the high plains. "You are thinking that she is staying out there periodically?"

"Somebody is."

"Or you think that whoever it is that is impersonating Danny might be living out here?"

"That's a theory. All I know is that somebody's staying out here and we're looking for somebody who we're assuming wants to stay out of sight, so whether it's her or somebody else, maybe we can get some answers."

We discussed the finer points of the investigation until I slowed and pulled up to the gate that led to the dig and stopped.

Lucian looked between the two of us. "Well, why are we sitting here?"

I gestured ahead. "Somebody has to open the gate."

The old sheriff looked at the Bear, who made no attempt to get out, and then back at me. "You two sons-a-bitches are gonna make the one-legged man open the thing?"

Neither of us said anything.

"I'll be damned." He pulled the handle and climbed out, taking his cane with him and slamming the door. "I would like to point out that I almost died and was in the hospital no more than a day ago."

"I am assuming there is a reason you wanted to get rid of him?"

"McGroder made some calls, and he says that Tomás Bidarte is in Nuevo Laredo, Mexico."

He nodded his head and then became motionless, like a hunter in a blind. "Should I be looking for my passport?"

We watched as Lucian made a show of opening the gate and dragging it aside, ever so slowly. "Nope, I'm sticking to my guns. I just wanted you to know." I pulled the truck forward and stopped, watching the old sheriff through the rearview mirror. "We could leave him, but he'd probably shoot at us."

As Lucian hobbled closer, Henry got out of the truck and held the door for him, a chivalrous act that I didn't quite understand until he let Dog out with him and then closed the door.

Lucian rolled down the window, looked at him, and then at Dog. "Where the hell are you and Rin Tin Tin going?"

The Bear ignored him and looked around on the broken turf, grass, and sagebrush. "The ground is still wet, and there are tracks where someone has driven in here recently."

I rose up and looked, and indeed, there were tire tracks going through the gate and veering to the right. He kneeled down and looked in the direction of the tread marks. My eyes played over the area where we'd parked and been shot at before. "That's not in the direction of the site."

He stood and started walking toward the hills the other way with Dog in tow. "No, and more important . . ." He raised a hand and pointed toward a plume of dirty smoke that was spiraling up from the other side of the ridge. ". . . that is more smoke than a campfire would make."

"That ain't smoke signals." Lucian inclined his head toward the darkening sky as the Cheyenne Nation and Dog took off at a good pace, and then turned to look at me. "That's a vehicle fire."

I pulled the truck down into gear and gassed it in an attempt to keep up with Henry and Dog, who were able to take a more direct route over the rock ledges.

Lucian gripped the dash and braced his good leg against the transmission hump in an attempt to stay upright. "Damn, this is rough country."

"Why would you drive out here?"

He shrugged. "To escape a speeding subpoena."

As we pulled around the edge of the ridge and started toward the source of the smoke, I could see tracks where the van must've been intentionally driven off one of the cliffs into the canyon. "Oh, no."

Staying to the right I was able to park pretty close and watched as Henry and Dog stopped at the edge to look down and then disappear over the brink.

Throwing the door open, I followed and could see the old Chevrolet, billowing in flames, lodged in the rocks below with the driver's-side door hanging open. I scrambled after Henry and Dog and then fell on my butt and slid down a scrabble heap.

The heat from the fire was tremendous, but the majority of

the flames were toward the front of the vehicle, making it unlikely that the tank had blown.

Veteran of numerous vehicle fires, I was aware that the majority of them aren't like the ones in the movies; in actuality, the tank melts and then the proper mix of fuel and air combusts since it's the vapors that burn and not the liquid. When they go, an exploding gas tank is more like a flash, not making it, at close range, any less dramatic or dangerous.

I yelled at the Bear as he tried to get closer to the open door. "Henry, don't!" Dog, hearing me, retreated immediately, but my friend was less well behaved. Raising an arm, he attempted to get nearer, but from my perspective, there was no way anyone could be in the gutted hulk and still be alive.

Sliding the rest of the way down, feeling the waves of heat, I collected Dog by his collar and moved down to where the Bear was. "You see anybody?"

He shook his head. "Difficult to say." He moved toward the front and tried to see through the shattered windshield, but like me, could see nothing. "She had a dog?"

"Yep."

He scanned the surrounding area. "Most of the time animals are thrown free or find a way to get away, but they will generally stay in the immediate vicinity."

I glanced down at Dog. "If there was another dog around here he would've been aware of it."

"Yes." Henry watched the fire.

"What are you doing?"

His eyes flicked toward mine. "Smelling."

I immediately caught his meaning. The smell of burning human flesh is particularly pungent, and you can usually make out the one stench from all others. I couldn't smell it, but generally his senses were finer tuned than mine. "Anything?"

"No, but that does not mean she is not in there."

I moved next to him and gripped his shoulder in an attempt to get his attention. "When that tank melts, we're going to be in a bad place." I glanced back up the cliff and could see Lucian standing there with his cane, silhouetted by the last rays of the day making their final eight-minute trips from the sun. I raised a hand to the side of my mouth and yelled to be heard above the roar of the fire, "Call it in and get the fire department out here!"

He kicked a small rock from the edge where it bounced down and slid to a stop just before reaching us, and yelled back, "It'll burn out before they show up."

"Call them!" I turned back to Henry. "Just in case she's in there, I want to save as much evidence as I can."

He nodded, and we stepped back and began the climb up to the rim, finally reaching the edge and standing there, watching the vehicle enveloped in the undulating flames. As I'd figured it would, the tank let go and there was a great *whoosh* as its contents flushed underneath and mushroomed in an orange ball that blew from beneath the van, momentarily lifting it and then allowing it to resettle in the rocks and debris.

I sighed, regretting the loss of the evidence that was cooking in the inferno below, and stepped back still holding Dog's collar. He seemed to show no untoward urge to go down to the fire, so I released him.

Lucian was smoking his pipe, seated in my truck with the

door propped open. I suppose he figured the rules didn't apply when the door was ajar or that there was enough smoke in the immediate vicinity that it really didn't matter. "They're on their way."

"Good."

"Should be here by Thursday."

Henry had wandered to the right and was kneeling, looking at the tracks that led to the edge. Figuring it was the only way I was going to find out what was what, I followed, Dog tagging along.

"Something?"

"She did not hit her brakes."

He looked up at me and then back at the tracks. "Fortunately, you drove parallel to these tread marks without disturbing them." He planed his face to one side, reading the impressions in the grass and sagebrush in the fading light. "There is a spot a little bit further back where the van stopped; it sat there for an extended period and then restarted before driving into the canyon."

I looked at the distance between the canyon lip and us. "So, she did it on purpose?"

He stood and walked past me, stopping again about two-thirds of the way toward the precipice, and then stooped again. "She swerved here."

Lucian joined us from the other direction and watched Henry. "She have second thoughts?"

He ignored the old sheriff and stood, taking a few more steps forward and then, looking at the ground to the left, walked in that direction and then once again kneeled. Dog, taking it as an invitation, approached the Bear, who reached out and scratched the space between the beast's ears. "I do not know if Jennifer or her dog are in there." He glanced over the canyon edge where the flames had grown so high they licked the cooling air, almost as if the crust of the earth had opened up and swallowed the Chevrolet as a tidbit. The fire's orange swirls tasted the air, and it looked like the flame was inside Henry's eyes, lighting his face. "But the driver jumped out here."

11

I don't eat donuts.

The massive tow truck, designed to haul eighteen-wheelers, easily plucked the vehicle from the canyon and, dragging it from the edge, pulled it back a safe distance. We sipped coffee that the firefighters had brought, and Henry had a glazed with sprinkles as I excused myself from the group and carried my cup over to the van to look at the burned-out interior. It had achieved temperatures high enough to melt the metal.

Human skin burns at 248 degrees, but bones don't burn so easily. Crematoriums use ovens approaching 2,000, but bone, containing approximately 60 percent inorganic, noncombustible matter, is capable of surviving even those temperatures. It is so tough that in modern-day crematoriums, after burning the body, the remains are ground in a process that reduces what's left to granules similar to the dried bits in fertilizer.

According to Chaucer, murder will out—and in modern forensics it usually outs with bones.

One of the firefighters brought us fresh coffee and then raised a fist. "Save Jen!"

I raised a weary one back and then waited for him to retreat before asking Henry, "She wasn't in there?"

The Bear, having retrieved the blanket from my truck to use as a cape, was looking particularly period, aside from the Styrofoam cup and the donut. "No."

"Neither was the dog."

"No." He waited a moment and then took a bite, chewed, swallowed, and pronounced, "They landed about forty minutes ago."

I turned and looked at him. "What?"

"Your family, they have arrived in Philadelphia, along with their bodyguard, who, to the best of my knowledge, has not killed anyone yet." He looked thoughtful. "Evidently the undersheriff incurred a brief altercation with a captain of industry over the allotment of overhead storage space, but cooler heads prevailed and the stewardess awarded them first-class seats."

I pulled out my pocket watch and looked at the delicate gold numerals that my grandfather had studied in his time. "Only ten minutes old and already a good day." Pleased with the news, I repocketed my watch and stared at the van's blackened shell, not really seeing it.

"What?"

I turned and looked at my friend. "Hmm?"

"What are you looking at?"

"In case it escaped your attention, the burned hulk in front of us."

"No, that is where your eyes are directed, but what are you looking at?"

I smiled. I had been looking at the moon rising over the Powder River country and the clouds that piled up around it in the blackness with tinged edges dulled like an old coin. I smiled at his catching me. "I was thinking about what I was thinking. You know, asking myself about what I need to do? Where do I want to be right now?"

"Wonder."

I sipped my coffee. "Excuse me?"

"Wonder. There is wonder in you, along with a little impatience. You are standing outside of yourself, looking at yourself, conscious of a rhythm within yourself, several rhythms, and the sound of drums from far away."

I turned and stared at him. "How the hell do you know that?"

He took the last bite of his donut. "You think you are the only one who hears them?"

I took a deep breath and sighed. "Think we're headed for something big?"

He laughed a smile. "That, or something big is headed for us."

"Think we can take it?"

"We have taken it all up until now." He shrugged. "But you need to be careful."

"Of what?"

"Preparing for a battle yet to be fought while in the midst of another."

"Play 'em one at a time, huh?" I smiled and shook my head, staring at the destroyed vehicle and finally seeing it. "Why would she want us to think that she was dead?"

The Bear gestured toward my truck, where the old sheriff was dead asleep. "Perhaps it is as Lucian says—she is attempting to avoid being drawn into the trial—or maybe it is something else."

"Yep, but that's not helping Dino-Dave, as near as I can tell." I took a deep breath and then released it as an elongated and tortured sigh. "What something else?"

"I'd rather not say unless it is confirmed." He licked his fingers and grinned. "So, I am thinking we should be heading over to the Lone Elk place to snoop around."

"Without a warrant?"

"Everything has to be so proper with you." He shook his head and sipped his coffee. "*Beatus homo qui invenit sapientiam.*"

I made a face. "Blessed is the man who invents wisdom?"

"Blessed is the man who *finds* wisdom." He shook his head, dismissing me. "You always act as if you are the only one who *cui* from a classical education."

It wasn't dark at the Lone Elk place; in fact, every light that could be on, was. The lights were glowing not only from both floors of the house but also from the barn and outbuildings. "I don't think we're going to be able to sneak in."

He leaned forward. "No."

Lucian rose up from the back and thrust his head between the seats, moving Dog to the side. "What the hell's going on?"

"Go back to sleep."

His head disappeared. "You'll wake me if we get to shoot somebody?"

"I promise."

"I don't want to miss an opportunity."

"You bet." I pulled the truck into the drive and got half turned before the pack of border collie mixes surrounded the Bullet. I turned to Dog, figuring it was time to release the hound. "Don't eat any of them, all right?"

He responded with a single wag, which was not completely convincing.

I opened my door and watched as the assembled canine mafia swarmed forward and barked. I opened the back door and watched as Dog bounded from the truck and looked at them. The half-dozen dogs froze at the sight of him. The one farthest away ducked its head and started off, but the others held fast just a bit longer as the beast turned his large-muzzled head and started toward them as if in a Jack London novel. This was too much for the pack, and they all widened the area around him. One barked, but Dog turned toward it and it joined the one on the far end in making a move for the porch. All the others, feeling their numerical advantage diminish, started backing away, quietly retreating.

Dog looked up at me.

"One police dog, one riot."

Henry joined me from the front, and after I put Dog back in the truck, we started toward the house. I could hear a lot of shouting inside, and I was beginning to think that we'd stumbled into a domestic situation.

Before we got onto the porch, the front screen door flew open, and Randy limped out, pulling up to keep from running into us. "You found him?"

The Bear and I glanced at each other and then back at him. "Who?"

"Taylor!"

I glanced at Henry again, as he answered, "We saw him at the IGA this morning. He did not come home?"

Randy was massaging his knee, and his butt held the screen door open. "Yeah, but he's gone again." He gestured a thumb over his shoulder. "Eva went in to check on him, and he had disappeared."

I interrupted. "I thought he ran off every twenty minutes. Why is this such a big deal?"

"Never at night; he never runs off at night."

"What, he's afraid of the dark?"

"Yes."

I looked at him. "You're serious?"

"Yes." Randy yelled inside. "Eva, the cops are here."

After a moment, she arrived at her brother's side. "Did you find him?"

"Um, no."

Randy talked out of the side of his mouth to his sister. "He says they saw him at the IGA, but we saw him after that . . ."

"When?"

Her voice was urgent. "He gets home at seven; I guess it was around then."

"Where does he usually go? I mean, before it gets dark."

She threw her hands in the air. "Everywhere, anywhere!"

I gestured toward my truck. "I'll go call it in and get the Highway Patrol and the Bobs to start watching for him. In the meantime there are really only two directions he can go on the main road out here, north and south, and we just came from the south, so I'll try north—sound good?"

"I'll go with you." Randy ducked back in the house, probably to grab his jacket and hat.

"We don't really have room."

He looked at the truck. "I'll ride in the bed. I stove up my leg earlier fighting with a cow, and it feels better standing up anyway." He smiled. "Unless that's against the law."

"I am the law."

We loaded up, leaving Eva on the porch, her hands knotted

in her dress, humming the old spiritual again. I wheeled the three-quarter-ton back up the road as Lucian's voice echoed from the back, "I don't mean to alarm, but there's an Indian standing in the back of your truck."

"We're aware of that. Go back to sleep."

Henry glanced at Randy's legs in the rear window of the cab and then directed the beam of my Maglite on the hills across the road, as I turned the spotlight on and focused it on my side. "A missing woman and a missing young man . . ."

"What are the chances?"

I glanced at the Bear. "That the two of them are together?"

"Yes."

I nodded and trained the spotlight over the hills. "What was the other thought you had?"

"She went missing before he did."

"And he did not seem overly surprised that she was gone."

"Didn't show much emotion either way."

The voice rose from the back again. "Inscrutable, those damned Indians."

I talked over my shoulder. "Old man, if you're going to join in the conversation, sit up."

"Hush. Me and your dog are tryin' to catch a few winks."

The Cheyenne Nation nodded. "We will have to ask Randy."

It was about that time that the aforementioned individual began pounding on the roof of my truck. "Stop, stop!"

I braked, the truck slid on the gravel, Dog yelped, and Lucian slammed into the back of our seat and hit the floor mats. "Damn it to hell!"

I watched as Randy carefully eased himself from the bed and took off at a hitched pace into the hills to our right. I redirected my spotlight in that direction and could see an Appaloosa gelding, saddled, bridled, and munching grass on the other side of the fence—the same horse we'd seen in the corral the other day. He jumped and lifted his head, his reins trailing on the ground, his eyes reflecting gold in the light, and pivoted to the left as Randy approached. The rancher, realizing he'd spooked him, stopped and spoke softly in Cheyenne, whereupon the animal ambled over to him like an old friend.

By the time we got to the fence, he'd led the horse over. "Yours?"

"Yeah, Bambino." He glanced around. "Not Taylor's regular horse, but this one was in the corral and saddled, so he was convenient." He brushed his hand across the velvety nose. "He's got the yips, though; every once in a while he thinks there's a grizzly bear under a Snickers bar wrapper."

"You think Bambino did the two-step, and Taylor got grounded out here?"

"It's more than possible."

"If you were headed out, where would you go?"

He pointed in an easterly direction toward a crutch in the hills. "There's a gully that leads back south and circles around the ranch proper toward the ponds and that dry wash and ridge where we found the *T. rex*."

"Where we found the van."

"What van?"

"Jennifer Watt's, crashed in the canyon, burned."

His face froze. "Holy shit, was she in it?"

Henry interrupted. "No."

He sighed in exasperation. "What the hell was she doing out here, anyway?"

"We were hoping that you might have an answer to that question."

He glanced at Henry. "And why is that?"

My turn. "There just seems to be a lot going on out here at the ranch, and no one seems to know what, who, or why." I waited a moment and then asked, "Where's Enic?"

He stared at me. "What?"

"Your uncle, where is he? With all the hubbub going on, I would've supposed that he was awake."

Randy shrugged. "He never sleeps; at least only an hour or two at a time." He reached out and petted the horse. "Jeez-O-Pete."

"Randy, what's going on?"

Jamming a thumb and forefinger in his eyes, he scrubbed at them. "I don't know, and that's what's got me worried. I mean . . . you don't think I know how this looks with people running around and disappearing?"

The Bear rumbled again, "How does it look?"

"Guilty." He shifted his attention to Bambino and rubbed his withers.

"I mean, ever since Dad's death everything's been kind of weird, and every time I think I've got a handle on things, something else strange happens."

I nodded. "Welcome to my world."

"Maybe it all started with that damn dinosaur . . ." He cast his eyes on me. "Look, there's something I should tell you. Dad was drinking again, and Taylor was hiding the stuff for him. Like I said, he wouldn't tell me where and that's when I hit him. He's pretty much convinced that he's responsible for Dad's death because he kept letting him have the liquor—that may be why it is that he ran off." He held the reins out to me. "Here you go."

I stared at him. "What?"

"There aren't any roads in that direction, so somebody's going to have to do it old-school, and I'm hurt."

I glanced at the Bear, who shook his head. "As much as it pains me to say, you are the better horseman."

I shook my head. "It's an Appaloosa. Isn't that the horse the Cheyenne traditionally rode into battle?"

"It was, because by the time you ride an Appaloosa some distance, you are ready to kill anything."

I sighed, took the leather strips between my fingers, and studied the white in Bambino's eye. "The yips, huh?"

We all decided that Henry would drive Randy back to get his truck and continue north; then he and Lucian would head south and meet me back at the site where Jen the Elder had been found. As a precaution, I took a handheld radio from my truck, just in case I found myself alone standing in a field in the dark with a sore rump.

There was a ruffling in the grass as the wind picked up, and Bambino sidestepped to the right and shook his head, rolling his eyes back to me. I countered: "You know, my grandfather had a horse with a nervous disposition, and whenever he acted up he'd reach out and slap the living daylights out of the back of his head."

We rode along, and I looked down, longing for Dog's companionship, but having realized that the presence of a strange animal might give Bambino more of a motivation to misbehave,

I had left him in the truck—besides, Lucian was using him as a pillow. "Good thing we live in more enlightened times, huh?"

Bambino made no comment.

At the ridge I looked west toward the Bighorns and even in the darkness could make out the tracings of the mountains that suddenly halted at about twelve thousand feet. There was a ceiling over the high plains as far as the nighttime eye could see, a thick confection of black that hid the moon and promised a deluge.

I just hoped that our work was done by the time that someone turned on the faucet and started thinking it had been pretty smart of me to roll up the yellow slicker that now rode on the cantle behind me.

Pulling up, I turned us toward the wind and watched as a strike of lightning hit the flats between Powder Junction and here, the bolt holding like a heavenly finger poking the earth for emphasis. "Wait for it, Bambino . . ."

The thunder rolled up the wide valley between the mountains and the endless ocean of the plains, a soft rumble that built and then subsided like a tidal voice.

The Appaloosa backed up a half step and sashayed to the left as I wrapped the reins in a fist, determined to avoid the horseman's greatest fear, to be left afoot. "Easy."

He tensed, and I caught wind of one of his tricks: getting the rider's weight traveling backward, he would likely launch and leave you tumbling off his rear as he raced for the barn alone.

"You can try that one, little Bambino, but I've seen it before and you'll be dragging two hundred and fifty pounds of very unhappy sheriff." I reached down and petted his neck. "Just so we're clear on this—I will never let go."

Never let go. Those three words echoed in my mind as I turned south, riding the ridge and letting the Appaloosa watch the lightning strikes and get used to the accompanying thunder instead of it overtaking him from the rear.

We joined up with a cattle path and spooked a group of mule deer that had bedded down for the night. Bambino shifted but stayed steady as we continued on, the first sprinkles of the storm reaching us like a dusting from the clouds as they shook themselves off. It felt good, and I thought back at how much time I'd spent in a saddle in my youth, herding cattle with my father and grandfather, the real rancher of the family.

My father had refined the ranch, but my grandfather had built it, aggressively buying property from adjacent families until he had accumulated many thousands of acres. I was on intimate terms with those acres and knew every single stand, swale, gully, and canyon where a cow and calf could hole up and brush pop in the very worst of weather.

Men get on edge doing some kinds of work, while others develop an ability to continue on where others can't. My father was outside working—I was eating breakfast, sitting at the kitchen table in the dim light of my grandfather's home—when the old man told me he didn't particularly care for me and that in his estimation I probably wasn't going to amount to much.

Calving season, and I was fourteen years old.

Staring at him through the pewter condiments holder on the round table as I sipped a glass of buttermilk, I'd mumbled an honest response: "That's all right; as far as I'm concerned you haven't turned out so great either."

He hated everyone but had a special, single-cask-strength

hatred held in reserve for his immediate family. He had kept his son, a natural-born engineer, from continuing with his schooling, instead chaining him to those thousands of acres and a life of agricultural servitude. To give my father his just due, he had not allowed that to poison his own life, his wife's, or mine.

The bulwark against the poison usually held, but every once in a while the old bull and I locked horns. I'd been working seventy-two hours straight without sleep and had been stepped on, kicked, horned, butted, stomped, pinched, swatted, and crushed—and I'd had about enough of his venom.

He showed me his teeth. "I suppose you think you're a man now?"

He was eighty-two years old with a receding hairline and little tufts of hair on the sides of his head that gave the impression that he was an owl—not a wise old owl, but rather the kind that hears small, defenseless things from a great distance. He wore steel-rimmed, round glasses, which did nothing but emphasize the imagery. His eyes were gray, a gift I'd received from him, perhaps the only one.

In the pale light of that morning I'd studied him.

"Stand up."

I sipped my buttermilk.

He stood, and I ignored him.

Still in remarkable shape, he was broad at the beam and winnowed down to nothing but stringy muscle and gall. He came around the table to look down at me.

I tried to feel sorry for him just then, tried to understand where all the anger, recrimination, and bitterness that had eaten up his life had come from. There was talk of a woman other than my long-deceased grandmother, rumors of a dalliance that had somehow been swept away with the years. There were also whispers of a lost act of violence so unspeakable that its utterance still went unvoiced.

With the first swipe, the blue-willow-patterned cup had flown from my hand, knocking over the condiment holder and the sugar bowl and shattering like the fragile relationship between us, spraying its contents across the table and the papered wall.

I stood, the rough-cut joists of the floor creaking beneath me, my nose brushing his as I gathered myself, looking down at him from a four-inch height advantage.

He'd forgotten how big I was, how big I had become, didn't know then how big I would be, but the surprise didn't last and he struck me across the face with his open hand.

It stung, but I didn't show it, only turning my eyes, his eyes, back on him, my expression as neutral as the nickel-plated color we shared.

A thick forefinger, leathery and stiff as a truncheon, bobbed against my chest like a woodpecker having found a soft spot on an otherwise impenetrable tree. "When I say stand . . ."

They say he'd killed a man, numerous men, but I had grown up in a period when the ghosts of a previous era still roamed the plains and had seen enough that those spirits didn't affect me any longer. Say what you will about age and experience, youth and indifference can engender an annoying strength of its own.

"Don't ever do that again." I brushed past him and deliberately walked slowly back to the calving shed where my father still labored.

Later in the morning when we had returned to the house, my grandfather was gone, likely on one of his aberrant rides where he would disappear for hours and then reappear, barking orders as if he'd never left. When we entered the kitchen, the remains of the mug and its contents had dried on the wall and the floor, but where the sugar had dusted the red-and-white-checkered tablecloth, that thick forefinger had traced the words "Never Let Go." Before I could get a good look at it, my father swept the words away and coaxed them back into the open container at the edge of the table like a scouring wind.

Never Let Go.

Those words had haunted me for decades, especially after my grandfather died, and it was only when my father had been approaching his final rest that he told me the significance of the words and the story, a story that had changed the trajectory of my family for generations.

Never Let Go.

Bambino's ears perked at my words; probably wondering why I had made the same statement twice, and I could see the white sickle in his eye. The lightning struck again, closer this time, and he sidetracked and sashayed some more, reversing into his launch position, but I turned his head toward the strike to show him that I wasn't hiding anything. If he shot forward he would have to do it without the benefit of seeing what was ahead of him, and in my experience horses are loath to do that.

"Easy."

The resounding thunder shook the ground, and Bambino circled to the right, slipping off the narrow trail, digging in with his rear hooves and driving up the slope. I gave him his head just a bit and then changed the lead on him in an attempt to get him going in the right direction but also to distract him from any further mischief.

The rain was steady now, and I thought of the slicker behind me on the saddle. It was tempting, but I wasn't sure what kind of response Bambino might have to me suddenly producing a large yellow raincoat and swirling it above his head in the pervasive wind like a banshee. Actually, I knew exactly what Bambino's response would be, and I thought it best to avoid being knocked out of the park.

There was another flash but further away, and the horse seemed to settle again as I leaned a little forward and noticed hoofprints in the dampened earth, coming from the direction where we were headed, the glistening water in the shoe prints looking like semicircles of mercury.

Mercury. I thought about what Dave Baumann had said about the dangerous vapors from Native relics that had been in the hands of museums.

The path stretched to the right in a curve like a woman's hip, and I figured we'd covered a few miles. Before long we would circle around and reach the archeological site, the narrow portion of the canyon, and finally the turtle reservoir where we had found Danny Lone Elk.

Something was nudging at the periphery of my consciousness like a burr under a saddle blanket, a thought that kept intruding until an image appeared—the burnt remains of blackened sandstone and broken pieces of cottonwood and scrub pine.

Thumbing through the dog-eared Rolodex of my mind, I saw a card flip up, and I could again plainly see the overhang in the choked canyon near the site where Henry had pulled Vic and me to safety.

It was raining, you're hurt, where do you go?

I turned the Appaloosa into the wind and increasingly heavy rain, and, slapping his rear, sent him down the trail beside a dry creek bed with a bit more purpose and a good amount of speed, the ground not wet enough yet to impede us.

On cue, static raised the hair of both horse and horseman as a bolt struck the ridge above us, and Bambino redoubled his efforts in getting us on down the trail. The thunder echoed off the rolling hills and the cap of dark, dangerous clouds chased the lightning as if we were in a glass specimen dome.

I crouched in even closer and pulled my hat down tight, aware that the race was indeed on. It was raining in earnest, and I knew by experience that the little canyon was going to be filled with fast-running water.

Henry was probably in the vicinity of the dig, but he hadn't been in the cave and likely wouldn't remember exactly where it was. I thought I would pull the handheld and call in from the next ridge where the reception would probably be better.

Bambino's muscles bunched under me and, watching the westward sky and the chain lightning that streaked over the Bighorn Mountains like white, electric veins, we headed for the ridge that ran to my right. Reaching for the handheld, I could imagine the profile we cut against the black diamond skies.

Never Let Go.

I once found my grandfather on one of his horseback jaunts on a tall bluff north of Buffalo Creek. He had been gone longer than usual, and my father had grown worried. The old man was then almost ninety-seven years old but still insisted on traveling the place alone on horseback—the way he said it was meant to be done.

I'd come up on him from behind, had followed his tracks to a spot he must've come to over and over, the trail well worn from his passing back and forth. There was a stand of pines along a rock outcropping that faced due north toward the Northern Cheyenne Reservation, and he'd pulled his old horse, Starbuck, a big bay stallion, up there and they stood like a Civil War statue.

It was as if they were waiting on something, or someone.

The eyes of both man and horse were focused on the horizon.

I stayed there for ten minutes, watching them, until the sorrel I was riding that day snorted and they both turned to look. They watched us for a moment and then turned back in ultimate dismissal, their eyes returning to that much anticipated something in the distance—something that was coming, or something that never had.

Maybe it was the light or the angle from which I was viewing him, maybe it was the sun or the ever-present Wyoming wind, but I had seen tears in the old man's eyes that day.

It was strangely silent as I unhooked the radio from my belt, the clip springing back with the tiniest of metal sounds, like the detonator on a very large bomb. It was at that moment, with my hand behind me and my weight backward and slightly to one side, that I felt the hair on my body pulse with electricity just as a bolt of lightning struck the rocks about seventy feet to my right like an earth-shattering pickax.

12

I was lying on the wet ground with the sound of hoofbeats rapidly diminishing into the darkness.

I sat up and shook my head, hearing a high-pitched whine that eclipsed the thunder and everything else, truth to be told. Scrubbing my hands across my face, I discovered the reins still wrapped in my right hand, so I draped them over my shoulder and looked around for my hat and the radio, discovering both underneath me. Pulling the small device out, I discovered the source of the noise and examined the broken housing and the few wires and partial circuit board that hung out the side. I clicked the thing on, but no lights illuminated and no sound emitted from it except the screech.

"Great."

I gathered myself. It was slow going, standing, but I did it, feeling a spasm in the small of my back and deep within my horseman's pride as I pulled my hat back on—all hat and no honor.

Rain pulled like curtains across the landscape, and I figured I'd better get moving. Setting off at a hitch—I favored my right hip, which was probably bruised where I'd landed on the radio—and started toward the dinosaur ridge.

I tried to keep it in front of me, although when I had to cross some lower hills, my objective disappeared. I watched with concern as the dry creek bed at the bottom of the ravine to my left began filling, reminding me again that I had limited time.

Trudging on, I started missing the slicker almost more than the horse, but then, speak of the devil, I spotted something on the trail ahead. I bent and picked up the yellow package, cracked and rumpled but still whole.

I unrolled it and slipped my arms in. Fastening it closed, I was a little more protected from the elements and decided that I would follow the creek bed rather than traverse the hill and dale in my attempts at reaching the ridge. The route would be more circuitous and opportunities to fall into the knee deep water more plentiful, but where the stream was coming from was where I wanted to inevitably go, and with the lightning continuing to strike the ridges, I felt a little safer at a lower altitude.

The ground began sucking at my boots, but I kept my footing and only once slid toward the water, partially submerging a size 13. When I righted myself, I could see something big ahead on the trail.

"Bambino?"

It didn't move at first, but then, in the momentary light of another strike, I saw the Appaloosa tense through the thunder and then amble over to me as if all sins were forgiven. I found a crumbling sorghum treat from the pocket of the slicker and held it out to him.

He stretched his neck forward, and I slid a hand up and took hold of his mane. Feeding him the cake to keep him occupied, I examined the bridle and could see that the rings that had held the reins had opened. I pulled them free from my neck, glad that I'd saved them.

The rings proved useless so I threaded the leather strips through the halter portion of the bridle and brought my face close to his, my hat brim dipping forward and releasing a small waterfall that caused him to start. "Let's try and not have any more epic drama, okay?"

I mounted the horse and started off again, perhaps at not so quick a pace but both of us happy enough to have company in the downpour, my hip still sore but better in the saddle than the muck. I led Bambino around another hill and could see the slope of the dinosaur ridge again and the backside where the small canyon tightened and the water was dropping like a miniature Niagara Falls about a story high, pounding into a pool below, the water thundering through the canyon mimicking the heavens.

There was only one problem—I was on the wrong side.

I dismounted, looked at the thigh-deep water that rushed by, and then spoke to the horse. "Hey, partner, how 'bout we take a little swim?" Another strike of lightning hit the ridge above like a reminder.

With a horse, the key in these situations is to not show any hesitation but rather to boldly step forward as if you know what you're doing, which works marvelously if you really do know what you're doing.

"C'mon, boy, we don't have all the time in the world." He took a tentative step forward, and I let out some rein and watched him plant a hoof into the depths.

I guess he was used to the ponds and reservoirs on the

Lone Elk Ranch, because he forded the creek with me like Esther Williams. We were about three-quarters of the way across when I noticed something upstream. At first I thought it was one of Danny's turtles, but the shape was wrong. Whatever it was, it was approaching fast, and I just hoped it wasn't a loose cottonwood branch. Bambino saw it, too, and moved to the left, but this time I had hold of the reins that were sturdily wound through his bridle. I had a choice—either hang on or grab whatever it was that was about to knock me downstream.

It was just about then that I saw the branch had an arm. I dropped the reins and lunged, twisting my fingers into a denim shirt. I planted my feet but slipped and fell in the powerful current, watching as the horse began to climb the bank, shake itself off, and trot away. I tightened my one hand on the garment and pulled the two of us from the creek bed with less than one horsepower.

I lay there on the bank for a second or two, took a few quick breaths, and then rolled over. It was Enic, lying on his back, his face open to the deluging skies. Turning his head, I spilled the water out of his mouth, pushed on his chest, and felt a tremor of movement in his body. When his hands came up weakly, he yanked his head away to the side, coughing and spitting.

I held him there as he continued to convulse and finally emitted a long moan. "Enic?" His eyes wobbled toward mine, and I smiled down at him as another lightning bolt ran the ridge. "Looks like you took a swim."

His eyes were wide and reminded me of Bambino's. "Mmm . . . *Mahk jchi.*"

I shook my head at him. "English, Enic. My Cheyenne isn't that good."

He blinked the rain away from his face, and I leaned forward in an attempt to shield him with the brim of my hat, his hanging from its stampede string.

"The boy . . ." He sputtered the words out. "The canyon where they found the dinosaur. Got them out but then slipped."

"Do you know where they are?"

He coughed and then nodded his head as his hand came up and fingered my raincoat, his teeth bright in the pitch darkness as if illuminated from behind. "Can I borrow that slicker?"

"So, why did they run off?" Maybe it was the lightning strike or the fall, but everything was sounding like I was in a barrel.

The older man, insisting that he knew where they may have gone, slogged along in the steady rain, keeping up a pretty good pace for a guy who'd almost drowned. "Maybe he was protecting the girl from you."

I hustled to keep up and wished I'd brought two slickers. "I'm the one who's trying to find them, lost out here at the ends of the earth."

He grunted. "Or the one trying to keep them from being happy ever after."

With this pronouncement, he turned, trudged the rest of the way up the hill, and paused at the top. "We should get going."

He disappeared over the side, and I had little choice but to follow. Making my way in the greasy grass on the far side of the hill, I called after him again.

He said nothing.

Over hill and dale we trudged along, slipping and sliding until I decided to swing him around and ask, "Enic, where the hell are we going?"

Our noses were very close, and I could see the expressionless look on his face, much like the one that I had seen on Taylor's.

"Take your hand off of me."

"Not till I get some answers." I could feel pressure at my midsection and looked down to see the point of a deer-hoof skinning knife pressed against my shirt. Bringing my face up slowly in the same rhythm as the now distant thunder, I merged the waterspout from the brim of my hat with his and spoke carefully. "You go ahead and do what you need to do, and when you're finished I'm going to shove that skinning knife down your throat, turn it sideways, and yank it back out."

There was another lightning strike, which although distant was bright enough to illuminate an opening in the hillside guarded by a few huge, ancient timbers that marked what looked to be an old mine.

Enic smiled slowly. "You know, I believe you would."

13

We stood at the opening in the hillside, Enic running a hand over the horse that blinked with a sleepy expression on his long face as the old Indian tied him off, out of the rain. "When he runs away there are only three places he goes to and this is one."

"I know how he feels." I glanced up at the heavy, rough-cut timbers and felt like Dante, preparing to enter hell. "Looks old."

"Before my time, but Danny and me, we found it."

"I think I might've seen it when I was a boy." I ran a hand on the wood, moving my hip in an attempt to get it mobile again and failing miserably. "Coal?"

"Maybe."

I thought about the Dead Swede Mine. "Gold?"

He shrugged. "We never found any, and it's not in the right place for that, but I never found no gold nowhere so what do I know?"

Hoping the sun would begin showing a glimmer in the east through a crack in the iron sky, I stared into the inky gloom of the shaft, at least looking forward to getting out of the rain. "So, where are they?"

He shook his head. "It's very deep, and when Danny and I found it we used dynamite to clear the debris so that we could have a way into the larger, natural tunnel inside, maybe carved out from the reservoirs. That's probably where they are."

Just inside the opening there were two broom handles sticking out of a medium-sized plastic garbage can with a lid that had a hole in it along with a lighter. Enic pulled out a sawed-off floor mop that had seen better days and palmed the lighter.

The smell was unmistakable. "Kerosene?"

"Yeah." He held the flame to the mop head and it slowly lit. "One of the torches is missing, so they're in there."

Enic held his up, and I was starting to feel like I was in *The Adventures of Tom Sawyer*. I lifted the lid and pulled the remaining mop from the can, aiming it toward his.

He pulled it away. "You don't trust me?"

I thought about it. "Not really."

"What would the next person do?"

"What, you're planning on a meeting?" I held the thing closer, and he finally lit it, albeit with a frown on his face.

Remarkably, there was no writing on the walls, and the cave was pretty broad. I could see where it narrowed ahead, so I attempted to stay close to Enic; even with my own torch, I wasn't sure if I wanted him too far out of sight.

He turned sideways, keeping the light in front of him, and continued on, looking back only once. "Well, c'mon."

From the angle of the rock, you could see it was the same formation shelf as the ridge that contained Jen, and I couldn't help but wonder what had hollowed the cave out other than human beings. I watched as he squeezed his way through, and as I attempted to negotiate the same space, I could see his torch turn a slight corner and continue on. "Hey, Enic! Slow down, would you?"

The passage was about as wide as a hallway, and I stepped off at a lopsided jog, turning the corner at the end of the thoroughfare just in time to see his torch in the distance. I went around an abutment and found myself in a spacious passage with a smooth floor made out of compacted dirt.

I looked to the right and could see that the path was at least as large as the one I'd just been in, whereas the one to my left was narrow. Picking the one of least resistance, I headed right, figuring that if I didn't see Enic in a straightaway or hit a turn pretty quick, he must've gone to the left.

I continued on, even though I was aware that my shoulders were scraping both walls. I was pleased to see another opening ahead and figured that he must be in there, but he wasn't. The chamber was the size of a one-stall garage with a couple of other tunnels leading in opposite directions but nothing that looked, on closer inspection, promising.

With just a little panic setting in, I retraced my steps back into the original tunnel and struck out back to the area where I'd been. Looking up at the rock ceiling and having faith that it was sturdy, and still hoping that Enic was on the level and that it was only his familiarity with the cave that had caused him to accidentally escape me, I started allowing my thoughts to grow dark. What if he'd turned the corner and then doused his torch, leaving me, well, in the dark?

There was another opening to my right, this one even bigger than the first, but it separated into two tunnels also angling off in opposite directions. I chose the larger one and

switched the torch to my left hand so that I could hold my
.45—better safe than sorry.

Setting off, I suddenly felt my boots splashing in water and
held the torch so that I could see the shiny surface and the
image of myself looking back up at me.

Great.

With retreat being my only other recourse, I started wad-
ing forward, figuring that if the water got thigh deep, I was
turning back, no matter what.

There was a series of bulb sockets overhead in this passage,
strung together with old, cloth-insulated wiring, which led me
to believe that the place had been electrified back in the dirty
thirties or possibly the forties. "Too bad there aren't any bulbs
or a switch."

I continued to study the ceiling and as I did could see that
my torch was making black marks on the roof of the cave.
Stunned that I hadn't thought of it before, I stood there looking at marks on the rock when I noticed that some were
darker. This one time in the cave I was thankful for my size; I
reached up and rubbed a finger on the ceiling and withdrew
with a completely fresh, black fingertip.

Sighing a breath of relief and trusting my black smudge
technique to at least show me where the most recent occu-
pants of the cave had passed, I waded ahead, ignoring the
other passageways.

To my right was what I was pretty sure was a handmade
ladder. As I got closer, I could see that the thing was con-
structed of lodgepole pine, and I was just as glad not to have
been responsible for carrying those into the narrow passageways.

I ran a finger over the rung closest to my face and noticed it was wet; Enic, or somebody, had climbed this way.

The treads were roped on, and the rails of the thing shot up through a break in the rocks above. I slipped my sidearm back into its holster and decided to climb. Placing my boot, dripping with water, on the first rung, I shifted my weight and listened to the loud crack as it spilt in two.

I stood there in the semidark muttering, which had no effect on the broken step whatsoever. Lifting my leg a little higher, I rested my boot on the next rung, this time gently applying my weight until the majority was on the ladder.

Sighing, I lifted myself up, holding the torch in my right hand a little away from the ropes so that I wouldn't set them on fire.

The rung held, and I listened to the wood squeal as I placed my other boot on the next and slowly climbed up with my hip still aching. There was a trapdoor with hinges and a handle at the top of the ladder. From the distance I'd climbed, I calculated that I must be pretty close to the surface.

I thought about pulling my sidearm again, but I was sure that if I made some sort of dramatic entrance, the ladder was likely to buckle and dump me, the torch, and my .45 back in the cave.

Carefully taking the handle, I raised the trapdoor an inch or two so that I could see the interior of what looked to be an old lineman's shack, a small, rough-cut, wooden structure. The portion I could see had an empty bunk against a wall, a closed door, and Enic Lone Elk sitting in a chair in my slicker, a single-barrel shotgun pointed at the opening. "Hi, Sheriff."

"Mind if I climb the rest of the way out?"

"You better—I'm not sure if that ladder will hold you for too much longer."

Lifting the hatch the rest of the way with my right hand, I climbed out and sat on the floor with the torch still in my left, and commented on the small potbellied stove crackling with a few burning logs. "You had time to make a fire?"

He kept the shotgun on me. "Took you a while."

"There were moments when I wasn't sure I was going to make it at all."

He nodded. "Lot of caves down there—we cleared a bunch, but there are a bunch more." He gestured with the single barrel. "Stuff that torch in the fire there."

I did as he said and watched as the flames leapt a little at the introduction of the extra fuel. "You and Danny?"

"We were redoing the floor in this place and found the trap. Pulled it up and discovered the cave down below. Figure they must've used it to get away or store stuff."

"Who?"

"Don't know—found empty bottles of hooch from the twenties, so it might've been used by bootleggers, and who knows before that—maybe Butch Cassidy and the Sundance Kid, for all I know." He gestured with the shotgun again. "Wanna close that thing? Causes a draft."

I closed the door in the floor and reached out to warm my hands near the fire, noticing a pot of coffee on the stove and a few tin cups. "You know, if I hadn't found my way up here, you'd have had a lot of explaining to do."

"You would've just disappeared; people disappear in this country."

"Like Jennifer Watt?" He said nothing, and I poured myself

a cup of coffee and set the pot back on the stove under his careful eye. "And Taylor." I studied him. "What's going on, Enic?"

He unsnapped a few of the clasps on my slicker and pulled a drenched hat from his head, ignoring bad luck and throwing it on the bunk. "You're a smart fella—you tell me."

I sipped the coffee, and it tasted wonderful. "I was just about convincing myself that you didn't have anything to do with the death of your brother."

"I didn't."

I gestured with the cup toward the shotgun. "Then why is one of us having this conversation at gunpoint?"

"Just slowing you down so that the young ones can get away." He didn't move, but his eyes drifted from me toward the fire. "Danny was hard on Randy, and now Randy's hard on that boy. So, I'm putting a stop to it."

"Danny was hard on Randy?"

The older man nodded. "Danny was drinking and worked Randy like a mule but it made him tough, made him capable. Randy's been tough on Taylor, but all it's done is wear the boy down. I knew both Eva and Randy wouldn't want that boy running off with a white girl, so I took a hand."

I nodded. "Where are they headed?"

"None of your business."

"Actually, it is my business. Someone murdered your brother."

"They didn't have anything to do with that."

"Then who did?"

He didn't answer—just sat there with the shotgun pointed at me. I noticed the hammer wasn't pulled back. "Enic, I'm having a hard time believing that you would shoot me."

"Don't want to, but I need you to stay put for a while."

"Then what? There's an APB out on the two of them and every highway patrolman in the territory is going to be looking for whatever vehicle they're in."

"Drink your coffee."

I did and then set the empty cup down on the kindling box. "Enic, I've had a little drama in my family just lately, too. My son-in-law was killed a day ago, shot in a routine traffic stop in Philadelphia where he was a police officer. So, now my daughter is going to have to go through what I've been going through for a bunch of years since my wife died." I rubbed my face with my one hand and then dropped it in my lap with the other one and looked at him. "That's something I wouldn't wish on my worst enemy, let alone the two people more important to me than everything." I sighed and shook my head at the thought of it. "But now there she is with a brand-new daughter and no husband to help her. She needs me, and if you think I'm going to sit here and sip coffee and pass the time of day with you, you've got another think coming."

As I started to stand, he raised the bore of the barrel toward my face. "Hold up right there."

"And it's going to take a hell of a lot more than that shotgun to stop me." I stood. "Besides, my hip hurts and my legs are getting stiff from sitting on this floor." I arched my back and straightened my hat. "I'm stiff all over, but I think I'm mostly tired, tired of everything, to tell the truth." I walked past him as he stood and rested a hand on the doorknob. "You can go ahead and shoot me if you want, but as tired as I am, I can't guarantee that I'll feel it."

It was about then that everything went black and I realized

I'd been wrong about a couple of things—that Enic was not afraid to use that shotgun and that that shotgun had stopped me after all.

Number one: the sudden deceleration or acceleration of the head is pretty important in a concussion, generally occurring when the blow is from the side or from behind with, say, oh, the butt of a single-barreled shotgun.

I tried to rise up on one forearm, but it wouldn't support me, so I just lay there.

Number two: evidence suggests that a good concussive blow that results in a knockout generally has a twisting motion which results in the brain reacting within the skull something like a Mixmaster.

I finally opened my eyes and stared at the floor, expecting pools of blood but not seeing any through the crashing waves of tsunami pain that were attempting to overturn my brain in its pan. Incapable of much else, I rolled over and looked at the ceiling and listened to my breath rattle, the warm air from my lungs creating a cloudy vapor in the now cold interior.

As I thought back, I could only come up with a handful of times this had happened to me, which is good because I felt like my brains were leaking out of my ears.

Sitting up, I noticed that Enic must've covered me with my slicker. I picked up my hat and carefully placed it on my head, avoiding the lump, and rubbed my face. It was still raining, and the fire in the stove was out, the torch end having burned off and fallen to the floor, which gave me an indication of how long I must've been lying there: too long.

Struggling to my feet by sliding my back against the door, I stood, sort of, and looked through the grimy windows; it was still dark out, early morning being my guess—before sunup, at least.

Feeling the bile rising in my throat, I swallowed and stretched my jaw and felt for my .45, relieved to find it still in my holster. Taking a few unsteady steps, I went over to the stove and felt the coffeepot—cold, but still half full. I picked up the tin cup, refilled it, and took a swig to clear the taste from my mouth.

Taking a few steps, I draped the slicker over a shoulder, and threaded an arm through a sleeve, stopping to rest before threading the other. I waited a moment and then buckled the thing closed, flipping up the collar and pulling my hat down in the front.

Grasping the knob, I turned it and stumbled around the door as the wind and rain blew it against me, and I trudged into the dark, not really sure where I was and certainly not sure about where I was going.

The rain wasn't as hard as I remembered it being before, but the wind had picked up. Since it generally came from the northwest, I tacked into it and down a hill onto what appeared to be an old cow path.

Figuring that Enic must've taken Bambino, I decided not to look for him and kept walking, assuming I'd eventually find a road and start my way back toward civilization on foot.

The cow path turned to the left and stayed on the lowland and out of the wind, for which I was thankful. My head was killing me, and all of a sudden, while wiping the rain from my face, I found myself lying on the path, struggling in the mud to stand.

I fell down a few more times but then managed to keep my footing. It felt like I was walking for a hundred miles, but I just ignored time and distance and kept going, hoping I wasn't just walking in circles and not knowing it.

Trudging through the barrow ditch, I climbed up the hillside, and when I got there I kneeled in an attempt to catch my breath and fight back the vertigo.

I breathed heavily, again watching the vapor trail from my nostrils, and stood, at first a little unsteadily but then feeling somewhat better. I noticed that the rhythm of my steps was matching my breathing, possibly the only thing that was keeping me going. I pushed my hat up and gripped my forehead in an attempt to chase off the pain, but it stayed right there with me until I unexpectedly ran into something.

My thighs struck the blunt edge of a solid impediment, and when I tried to grab whatever it was, I slipped and fell backward. I lay in the road thinking I'd better get up before either I drowned like a turkey or something ran over me.

There was a lot of noise, and I swore I could hear voices as somebody, two somebodies actually, picked me up, trailed my arms over their shoulders, and dragged me to the backseat of a car. The Bobs.

I mumbled.

"What'd he say?"

"Something about not letting go."

14

I was seeing double. I shook my head, another mistake in that now my brain felt like it was bouncing around like a sneaker in a washing machine.

"Good thing you've got a hard head." Bob Delude made a face as the Bobs stood at the foot of my hospital bed like bookends.

Sitting the rest of the way up, I could see Henry and Doc Bloomfield at the side of my bed. "You know, I'm really getting tired of waking up in this place." I could feel the bandages wrapped around my skull as I rested back on a collection of pillows. "Has anyone found Jennifer and Taylor?" Henry shrugged, and I looked at the two patrolmen, who followed suit. "What about Enic?"

"Also missing." The Cheyenne Nation sat in the nearest chair. "We were hoping you could tell us where everyone was, but we did find the horse."

"Do me a favor?"

"Yes?"

"Shoot him."

"Too late. We already returned him safe and sound to the corral at the Lone Elk Ranch." He studied me. "Did the horse have something to do with all this?"

"Well, kind of. The biggest problem was Enic." I yawned and could hear cracking noises—probably not a good sign. "My head hurts."

Robert Hall spoke up. "We've got an APB out on the two— should we add Enic?"

"Yep." I glanced around. "Where are my clothes?"

"Locked up." The doc's voice was firm as he pulled at his nose with a thumb and forefinger. "DCI sent back the official report on Danny Lone Elk."

"Now why do I not like the sound of that?"

"All indications are that Danny died of mercury poisoning."

I glanced at the other men in the room, but they seemed as concerned as I was. "Mercury poisoning?"

The doc nodded. "Yes. If you'll remember, I remarked on the flesh shedding at the fingertips?"

"Other symptoms?"

Isaac recited: "Tremors, emotional changes, insomnia, impairment of peripheral vision, headaches, lack of cognitive function—all the things that Danny had been suffering from that lately might've been misconstrued as alcoholism."

"The rattle." They all looked at me. "The turtle rattle that Danny kept getting out and placing on his chest when he took his naps—it had a strong smell to it, and I remember Dave Baumann saying that the things were dangerous because of the residual chemicals that remained from the museums cleaning them. He mentioned mercury, specifically." I happened to catch Henry's eyes as they played out through the dark past the windows. "What?"

He turned to look at me. "Fish." He stood, placing his fingertips on the surface of the glass. "High levels of methylmercury can be retained in fish and shellfish."

I stared at him. "Are you saying that Danny ate enough fish that he—"

"Well, in Danny's case not exactly fish." He turned to look at me. "Turtles."

"Oh, hell." I thought about it. "Didn't Randy say that Eva fixed their dad turtle soup all the time?"

"She did, but still, where is the mercury coming from?"

I watched as Isaac thumbed up his glasses and massaged the bridge of his nose, a habit when in deep thought. "Forty percent of mercury poisoning in the U.S. comes from power plants, but once again, there's nothing like that in the area."

I thought about the conversation I'd had with the Hardin hippy. "Turtle food." They all looked at me. "The herbalist/pharmacologist up in Hardin told me that he sold turtle food to Danny by the truck-load." I turned to the Cheyenne Nation. "What do turtles eat?"

He smiled the thin-lipped smile, the one that cut paper . . . or red tape. "Fish."

"Most of that crap that Free Bird is selling is illegal Chinese stuff, and I'm sure it's probably laced with mercury because it's too bad to sell to humans."

Bob shrugged. "So you think his death actually was an accident?"

"I am not sure, but if somebody knew about the mercury in the feed and subsequently the turtles in combination with the sacred rattle . . . Eva?"

I looked at the Bear. "You think?" I turned to Isaac. "Doc, I need my clothes—now."

As he hurried out, I spoke to the assembled posse. "So, as near as I can tell, Taylor and Jennifer have a thing and Uncle Enic is helping them along." I looked at the Bobs. "Can you guys get down to the Lone Elk place and arrest everybody who is down there?"

They spoke in unison. "Charge?"

"What, since when do you guys need a reason to arrest somebody?" I threw out the first thing that came to mind. "Probable cause."

Bob turned to Robert. "I love probable cause."

Robert nodded and looked back at me as they went out the door. "Me, too. So, not that it's any of our business, but where are you two going?"

"Looking for the starstruck lovers and their guardian. I think I owe Enic a pop in the jaw . . ." As the HPs exited, I turned back to the Cheyenne Nation. "Where are Trost and the FBI?"

Henry folded his hands in his lap. "They were boxing up more of Jen, but it is late and they gave up when they could not get Jay to run the forklift in the rain."

"It's a manhunt—isn't that what the FBI does best?" I pressed my fingers against my right eye, which seemed to want to pop out. "Wait, did you just say it was late?"

Henry looked at his wristwatch. "Close to eleven; Mr. Hall and Mr. Delude found you just before dawn and you have been unconscious all day."

"Oh, no."

Henry frowned. "Yes, you cannot move in your holding cell. From what I understand, Trost has been in negotiation with the DOJ to have Jen stored in the official depository in Bozeman."

"What the hell is he thinking?"

The Bear shrugged. "I guess he has his sights set higher than the Big Empty."

"I'm calling Joe Meyer." I glanced around for a phone but could see only the internal one for the ICU. "As soon as I get my damn pants."

There were some emergency clothes in my office, which was good because the director of the Cheyenne Conservancy and the chief of the Northern Cheyenne tribe, along with their bodyguard, were waiting for me.

I re dressed and limped back into the dispatcher/reception-ist area. Henry was sitting on the bench with Brandon White Buffalo and Lonnie Little Bird, Lolo Long sitting on Ruby's desk, her long legs dangling. "Sheriff."

"Chief. What's up?"

She gestured toward the old man, who smiled. "I'm thinking there's something you should know. Um hmm, yes it is so."

"What's that, Lonnie?"

"There was a meeting a few months ago with the tribal council, and those meetings, they get long, so I sometimes fall asleep. Mm, hmm." He shook his head. "Which is how I got elected chief I suppose; I was asleep and couldn't defend my-self . . ."

"What about the meeting, Lonnie?"

"What?" He looked at me, his mouth moving in an attempt to continue the conversation, but not quite sure what it was.

"The meeting?"

"Oh, yes . . . There was a meeting. Mm, hmm, it is so."

I stood there looking at him for a spell but then finally turned and glanced at Chief Long, who obliged me by reminding him, "The girl, Lonnie."

His head rose back with his mouth open, the thought reforming. "The girl, yes, there was a girl. She came to the first meeting and stood by the door, but then they got her a chair to sit on in the next one, and then by the time we got to the last meeting she was sitting with us at the table during the negotiations."

"Who is 'us'?"

"Danny, the negotiations with Danny about the Cheyenne Conservancy and the dinosaur."

"Yep, but who was the girl?"

"The girl with the camera. Mm, hmm. Yes, it is so."

Lolo added in explanation, "The paleontologist, Jennifer Watt."

"She filmed all three of the meetings?"

Brandon sat forward, his giant hands linked under his chin. "It's true. I remember that there was a blonde woman at the meetings, filming. Evidently she and Danny were very good friends, and he had her film everything."

"Yes." Lolo shrugged. "I didn't think anything about it, but then she went missing along with Taylor and I thought it might be pertinent."

I looked at Henry. "We need to find those two and get those files. Any word from McGroder on the computer?"

"Not that I know."

I glanced back at Chief Long, figuring she probably knew the answer to such things. "How much can you save on one of those cameras?"

"Small, digital?"

"Yep."

"They record onto a memory card, so it's according to how big that is. If one file gets filled it will just flip over to the next."

"Remembering that she films everything, enough so that the files from that meeting could still be in her camera?"

"I would think so."

I turned to Henry. "All right, we've got the two starstruck lovers and their trusty companion; as my go-to guy on all things tracking, where would they be?"

"On the ranch—it is the only place where they would be safe."

"Well, that's only fifteen thousand acres—how would you suggest doing that?"

"Omar and his luxurious Neiman Marcus helicopter."

My stomach flipped. "Tonight?"

"I thought you had gotten enough sleep."

"Flying." I listened to the rain pelting the roof of the old Carnegie library. "In this weather?"

The Bear smiled. "He has flown in worse."

On September 3, 1996, Ron Bower and John Williams broke the round-the-world helicopter record in seventeen days, six hours, and fourteen minutes. They were able to accomplish this feat due to the Bell 430, which had a four-blade, bearingless, hingeless composite main rotor and close to eight hundred horsepower produced by two Rolls-Royce/Allison turboshaft engines. I was listening to the same sort of engines whine as we ducked under the swinging props and climbed into Omar's helicopter, the rain now blowing sideways.

I envied the poncho the Bear had appropriated from the duty closet as I clamored toward a seat. "This fits the parameters of my worst-case scenario."

We thumped into the soft, butter-colored leather of the obscene conveyance as the Cheyenne Nation closed the door behind us.

"Wait. It will most likely get worse."

Omar called over his shoulder, "We in?"

I yelled back. "For better or worse!"

In revenge, he throttled up, and I felt my guts settle into the cradle of my pelvic bones, suddenly rushing up and skyward. "Oh, hell."

The Bear turned and looked between the seats at our pilot. "You know where you are going?"

He nodded, most of his face covered from my view by the massive headset. "Start at the dig site?"

Henry shouted. "We will do a circle out, and if we find nothing then we can begin a grid pattern."

Omar nodded, and we raced over Durant's main street, headed south-southeast. The last time the three of us had been in this self-same helicopter had been in an attempt to save a young man who was being stalked by an unknown sniper in the Cloud Peak Wilderness Area. The weather had been moderate when we'd started, but then a front had come in with snow, sleet, and sixty-mile-an-hour winds that had sent Omar and the Neiman Marcus helicopter down the mountain and Henry and me on a life-threatening hike on snow-covered trails. "Don't get shot this time."

"I intend to do my best."

"And don't sing."

"I did not sing before."

I glanced out the window at the rolling hills we traversed, only a hundred feet or so above the wet, waving grass. "Can't we fly higher, so we don't have to go up and down so much?"

"I think he is attempting to avoid the wind, which is worse higher up."

"Oh."

He glanced out the window on the other side of the helicopter. "It also means the helicopter will fall a shorter distance should something happen."

"Shut up." I fastened my seat belt. "How fast are we going?"

He leaned forward again, reading the instruments over Omar's shoulder. "One hundred and forty knots."

I thought about the rough knowledge I'd received behind the control seats of a B-25 Mitchell by the name of *Steamboat* years ago. "One hundred and sixty one miles an hour?"

He shrugged and went back to looking out the window. "I think he likes to go fast, and since it is his helicopter . . ."

I looked out and was barely able to make out the contours of the land now. "How are we going to see? It's as dark as the insides of a cow out there."

"Omar has assured me that he has enough auxiliary lighting that we should be able to spot them if they are out here. We can search for them until dawn and then refuel and start out again."

He studied me. "How is your stomach?"

"Flipping like a trout."

"Does it help to talk?"

"Some."

"MMO?"

It was a game we had played for as long as I'd been in law enforcement, maybe even a leftover from Vietnam: Motive-Means-Opportunity. "Is it my imagination, or was it on this same helicopter that we last did this?"

He shrugged. "Breaks up the monotony."

"And keeps my mind off my stomach." I settled myself. "Suspects?"

"Jen, Taylor, Enic, Eva, Randy, and your friend, Dino-Dave."

"No one else on the ranch as far as we know."

The Cheyenne Nation nodded toward Omar. "Him."

"He was there, but he doesn't have a motive; anyway, we'll throw him in when we get to opportunity."

A voice suddenly sounded in both our headsets. "You two know I can hear you, right?"

Henry smiled. "Might be an opportunity to ask."

So I did. "Hey, Omar, did you kill Danny?"

"No."

I gestured with my one hand. "He's innocent."

Omar's voice rang again. "I understand your having to ask."

"Thanks." I glanced at Henry as we both removed our headphones and hung them back on the interior hooks. "Jen."

"Low on motive—what would she have to gain?"

"Taylor?"

"We're moving on?"

I shook my head. "No, she had Taylor to gain."

"You think Danny would have prevented the two of them from getting together?"

"Possibly." I tilted my head. "But she was obviously trusted enough by Danny to be invited to all the Cheyenne Conservancy meetings. Two?"

He nodded. "Opportunity?"

"Zero, she didn't live there and wouldn't want to be caught near the pond, as nobody knew about the relationship with Taylor, or so they say." I shook my head. "Randy seemed genuinely surprised."

"All right, we will give Jen a total of two."

"Eva?" I thought about the psychopharmic cloud surrounding the woman. "Who the heck knows?"

"She would keep her son from Jen, and Enic would side with her on traditionalism."

"And the two would override Randy?"

"Yes."

"Give her a three." I looked out the window but still could see nothing but the rain pelting the glass. "Means?"

"She cooked for him."

"Yes." I sighed. "Three."

"Opportunity?"

"Three."

He nodded. "We have a new leader at nine."

I moved on. "Taylor."

"He would get the ranch eventually, but there are two surviving generations ahead of him."

"He'd get the girl."

He shook his head. "Do you think the objections to their May/September relationship were strong enough to kill his grandfather for?"

"Seems like a stretch."

"Give him a one? I am not giving him a zero."

"Means?"

"He had access to the alcohol and the turtle feed."

"He doesn't drive."

"True."

"Two." He glanced back out the window. "Opportunity?"

"He was around the house all the time, when he wasn't running away, and he didn't seem to have too much of a problem shooting at us after we found Danny."

"Two, which gives us five."

"Dino-Dave."

"Killing Danny would only complicate things for him."

I agreed. "One."

"Means?"

"He doesn't live on the ranch; I'd give him another one."

"Opportunity?"

"Same, so we've got an all-time low of three." Suddenly I could feel the aircraft pull up, and we hovered there in the air, probably a hundred feet or so above the ground. Omar motioned toward his earphones and then gestured toward ours.

Henry and I plucked them from the hooks and put them on, adjusting the microphones in front of our mouths as Omar's voice sounded in our ears. "You've got a call from the FBI."

"Yep, I left a message for McGroder on his cell phone. Mike?"

His voice was groggy. Static. "I just got the message to call you."

"Any luck on that computer?"

Static. "No, it's annihilated; any information on the hard drive is corrupted. Sorry . . ."

"Well, that's a disappointment, but I've still got one ace in the hole. Hey, Mike, do you guys have any kind of whizbang satellite gizmo that can pinpoint the location of some suspects out here on the—"

Static. "Where the hell are you?"

"I'm in a helicopter; we're looking for the runaways and Enic, and I was hoping to call in a favor and see if the bureau had any way of helping us track them down."

Static. "Tonight?"

"Well, yep."

Static. "No."

"What do you mean no?"

Static. "I mean no as in you're only going to get satellite reference on a twenty-four-hour basis, and then somebody's going to have to go through the data. Besides, is it still raining?"

"Yep."

Static. "Then you're not going to get anything anyway." He readjusted the phone. "I can locate a guy in Manhattan using his mobile in a third of a second, but out here in God's country? You've got to be kidding." He laughed. "If they were using a cell phone we could get an approximate location from the sending towers, and by approximate, I mean a couple hundred square miles, but since there is no cell service almost anywhere here in Wyoming, they won't be using one—which means we get zippo, nada, zilch."

"Thanks for your help."

Static. "Any time." There was a silence, but then he spoke again. "Look, I'll contact NSA, but I'm promising less than nothing, okay?"

"Better than nothing, I guess."

Static. "Over and out."

I listened to the radio go dead and glanced up at the millionaire pilot. "Omar, how far to the site?"

The nose of the chopper dipped, and we jetted forward. "About two minutes."

As we skimmed along into the rain and the windswept sky, I rapidly moved down the list. "Randy I'm giving a two on motive simply because he would have to kill his uncle as well to get anything out of it." I thought about it. "But there was something Enic said about Danny being hard on Randy."

Henry raised a finger in response. "Also, Enic is a Traditional and possibly more open to the idea of closing out something newfangled like the Cheyenne Conservancy."

"I just don't see those two agreeing on much of anything."

"Around eight million dollars can soothe over a number of differences."

I shook my head. "I'm still giving him a two."

"Means?"

"Gotta give him a three on that."

Opportunity?"

"Three."

"Second place at eight."

"Enic."

"He knew about the relationship, and he's been trying to help them." I reached over and fingered the delicate glass of the bud vases, a strange thing to have onboard a twin-engine, light-medium helicopter, but it had come from Neiman Marcus. "He said something about Eva not being happy about the situation." I sighed. "He gets the ranch, he gets the eight-million-dollar Jen . . . He gets everything."

The Cheyenne Nation nodded. "Three."

"He just doesn't seem like the type; I get the feeling he wouldn't kill his brother."

"He struck you in the back of the head with the stock of a shotgun."

"He could've shot me." I acquiesced. "Three."

"Means?"

"Three."

"Opportunity?"

"Three."

An eyebrow on the Bear crept up like a black caterpillar. "Need I remind you that the game is not Motive-Means-Opportunity, and Feelings."

Boy howdy.

15

"Is it me, or have we stopped?"

The Bear nodded. "I think we are in the process of stopping."

The Bell 430 eased to a hover over the dig site as the northwest wind buffeted the fuselage and Omar eased us downward, suddenly pivoting to the left, his voice a little too excited for my taste. "Sorry, that ridge was a little closer than I thought. We're checking the immediate area from the air and then, if we don't find anything, we begin the circle?"

"I'm open to ideas if you've got a better one."

"Nope—just checking before I turn on the lights."

Henry glanced at me as we swept the immediate vicinity, our eyes getting used to the sudden glaring light. "Enic is armed?"

I nodded. "With a single-barrel shotgun that looked as if it might've come off a Wells Fargo wagon."

"Do you have an extra firearm, just in case?"

I shook my head. "No."

"That's okay, I do." Omar's voice assaulted us, along with the butt-end of a tactical shotgun, complete with a black nylon sling.

"Benelli M4 with all the bells and whistles—nothing lives in two equal parts, unless you get attacked by earthworms."

The Cheyenne Nation took the thing from the front passenger seat and held it gently in his hands, more than a little impressed with the sleek, matte-black 12-gauge. His fingers wrapped around the fore stock near the flashlight below the barrel, and he flipped on the high-intensity light.

"Shades of Vietnam?"

His eyes came up to mine, and he smiled as his free hand pulled the hood of the poncho up over the cloak of dark hair. "Just a little."

"Hey, Omar, nothing moving around here—let's proceed south by southwest and see if we can find a lineman in a hay shack, or something like that."

I figured it was pretty much an impossibility that we might stumble onto the shack even with the lights, but I kept my eyes out the windows, as much as I didn't want to, adjusted the mic, and spoke to Omar. "Follow the drainages; when we found the opening to the mine it was on a hillside with the shack on the ridge above it." I'd just finished speaking when there was a loud thump, the aircraft shuddered, and the searchlights were entwined in a mass of wet, waving grass. "Did we just hit the ground?"

Omar's voice sounded completely calm. "Just grazed a hilltop."

My voice, on the other hand, was not so completely calm. "Let's not do that again, okay?"

Henry glanced over at me, shook his head, and continued looking out the window.

"I know this area pretty well. I've hunted down here and we—"

There was another thump. "Damn it, Omar! Put another twenty feet between us and the ground, would you?" This thump had been different, though. The helicopter shuddered like before, but now there seemed to be an imbalance in the vibrations of the thing. "What the hell was that?"

"Shit." I watched as Omar struggled with the controls, finally easing the craft back in an attempt to hover, but the chopper was having none of it and pitched to the side.

I slammed my shoulder against the door, clamped a hand onto the seat, and, glancing at Henry, noticed he had lost a little of his nonchalance. "What's happening?"

"We hit something, or something has hit us."

I pressed myself even further into the seat, if possible. "Are we going down?" He didn't answer, but there was another shuddering thump and it seemed as if the helicopter was tipping forward even though we were still moving. "Are we on the ground?"

Omar answered. "We are, but we are sliding—better grab on to something."

I reached for the seat in front of me, but we hit the side of the hill before I could hold on. I flew forward, taking Henry with me, and we tumbled into the cockpit with Omar, crushing him into the instrument panel as we flipped over the dash and lodged against the glass.

The good news was that we'd stopped moving.

I yanked my arm free as the Bear carefully placed the shotgun on the seat, then pulled himself into the copilot position and looked at Omar, who was piecing together a strip of flesh at the bridge of his nose that was leaking copious amounts of blood.

Henry disengaged himself from the copilot controls. "Are you all right?"

Omar nodded and started shutting the helicopter down. He gestured toward me. "Yeah, I guess. I was fine until Bigfoot planted a boot in my face as you two went over." He reached down and hit a few more buttons and then spoke into the mic. "Absaroka County Control, we are down. Requesting assistance." He keyed the mic again. "Absaroka County Control?" He listened for a moment and then pulled his trademark black hat from his head and ceremoniously dropped the headset to the floorboards. "Either we're out of range, there is no reception, or the radio is FUBAR."

Lying on the leather-covered dash, I dropped my head back and looked at the rain striking the Plexiglas. "What did we hit—or what hit us?"

Omar gave the flap of flesh one more quick pinch and wiped the blood away with a GORE-TEX sleeve. He put his hat back on, then grabbed a high-intensity flashlight from a console and pulled the lever on the door. "Let's go find out."

The Cheyenne Nation piled out his side with the Benelli, and as comfortable as I was just lying there, my sense of duty called and I dragged myself off the comfy shelf, fell into Omar's seat, and slid out after them. They were looking at the chopper, but, like them, I couldn't see anything beyond the bending of the runners and a little cosmetic damage to the front of the fuselage.

"It looks fine." I glanced at the multimillionaire but noticed he was pointing up.

"Not really."

Henry and I followed his eyes and the beam of the flashlight and could see large chunks broken from the rotors. "I'm no aviation engineer, but that looks bad."

"It is."

"I don't think the county can cover this."

"I've got insurance." Omar walked behind me around the stabilizers as the Bear and I, saying nothing, looked at each other in the rain. After a few seconds, our pilot came back and held out a shredded piece of what looked like rubber-coated cable.

"Power line?"

He nodded. "An old one, copper." He glanced around. "Probably a rural electrification feed from back in the thirties."

"Who the hell would be running electric lines all the way out here back then?"

"Let's go ask them."

"I was thinking you should stay here with the helicopter."

"Like hell."

I turned to look at Henry as he pulled up the hood of his poncho again. I watched as he studied the rotors and then looked over our heads toward the hillside behind us where there was a square outline of a lit, framed window that could be seen on the ridge above us, in what I could only assume was the lineman shack.

"Good job." I punched Omar's shoulder with my fist. "You found it."

He reached back into a storage section of the Bell and pulled out another shotgun exactly like the one he'd given the Cheyenne Nation. "Indeed."

We walked toward the light. "So, how many of those things do you have onboard?"

Omar tucked the second Benelli under his arm and wiped the rain and more blood from his face. "In my experience, you can never have enough AsomBroso tequila or shotguns."

The Bear held back as the pilot stopped for a moment, holding his nose. "The Reserva Del Porto?"

Omar shrugged. "Of course."

Henry called back to him, "The bottle looks like a penis."

He looked up and sniffed. "At eleven hundred dollars a bottle it's fucked me up enough times."

As I pulled up beside him, Henry placed a hand on my chest. "Just as a precaution, I think you should know that I believe someone may have been shooting at the helicopter."

"You see something in the rotors?"

"Maybe."

"Why didn't you say anything?"

"Because I am still not sure; it is possible that it was ball bearings, but since the engines are bearingless, I am thinking it could have been a shotgun."

"Sure about what?" Omar had caught up with us.

"Henry thinks we might've been shot at."

He shook his head. "Bullshit—it was the power line."

The Bear didn't say anything.

"Could it have been both?"

Omar shook his head. "I've been shot at before, and the results are similar but different."

I knew Rhoades's background and was pretty sure he hadn't been in the military. "Where?"

"Kyrgyzstan, hunting Argali sheep. We were in the Batken

Oblast near the Kyrgyz-Tajik border where the land mines are like paving stones. The only way you can get the sheep is with a helicopter, but with all the political and ethnic violence, you're constantly flying into one tribe's or another's airspace—so they shoot at you, and sometimes they get lucky and score a hit." Omar started climbing, and we followed. "Really sucks getting shot down in a minefield."

"I bet."

"Saved my life one time with a bag of bite-size Snickers bars." He paused, tipping his head down and letting the rain run off the brim as I had done numerous times in the last seventy-two hours. "We were able to land this piece of shit Hind and avoid the land mines and what happens? This patrol of Issyk-Kul partisans came marching up to us like the minefield doesn't exist." He shook his head. "I swear, there wasn't a one of them with hair between their legs. They were gonna shoot us, but I happened to have that bag of candy and I swear that's what saved our lives." He laughed and moved ahead. "There was a guy at the Transit Center in Manas near the airport close to Bishkek who gave me the tip. Spooky fucker, but he said you could offer these teenage soldiers your Rolex and they'd look at you like you were an idiot, but pull out candy or soda and you had friends for life."

I stepped back on the shelf a little, remembering the light in the shack's window. "If we cut the power line, how come they still have electricity?"

Henry nodded and started after Omar. "From the quality of the illumination, I would say propane."

I trudged in the mud after them. "From that distance in these conditions you could tell that?"

"Yes."

Omar laughed and called over his shoulder. "Bullshit."

Suddenly, there was an unmistakable blast of a 20-gauge, and shot ricocheted off of everything. I covered my face with an arm as Omar fell onto the ground next to me. "Well, bullshit."

I asked the question you ask in like situations, which always sounds like bad dialogue in a B war movie: "Are you hit?"

He grimaced and clutched at his leg. "No, I was just tired and thought I'd lie down and take a nap."

I sat him on the deer trail and examined the wounds, two small holes that appeared to have struck to the left of center on the femur and lodged in the thigh. "You're lucky—eight inches higher and you'd be singing soprano."

He gritted his teeth and spit out the words, "Well, it hurts like a bitch."

I pulled a bandana from the inside pocket of my jacket underneath my slicker and carefully wrapped it around his leg, tight enough to stem some of the bleeding. I helped him up. "Can you walk?"

"I think so . . ." I released him, and he immediately fell. "I guess not."

Sitting him upright, I looked at the hill, but from this vantage point I couldn't see where the shack was or where the shooter might be. Henry had moved to the right and was studying the rim of the ridge above us. "See anything?"

"Maybe."

"Do you want to go ahead and clear the way, and I'll bring Omar up with me?"

Without answering, he slipped up the side of the hillside like a black ribbon.

I turned back to our wounded comrade. "I'll help you up the hill and out of the rain."

"What if they keep shooting at us?"

"They'll probably hit me first. Anyway, I've got faith in the Bear's abilities in counterinsurgency." Rhoades strung the shotgun over his shoulder, and we trudged up the trail. "But stop saying bullshit; it's bad karma."

"Bullshit."

I had lost track of Henry and just hoped that the shooter had lost track of us. That hope was short-lived, and pellets ricocheted off a rock outcropping to our left but I was less worried when three consecutive rounds from the Benelli M4 riot gun returned the fire.

"Jesus . . . It sounds like Beirut up there." Omar's voice was right in my ear, just as it had been in the chopper.

I kept working us up the path and almost hoped to be shot so that I could take a rest. When we made the small break in the rocks and the flat area at the precipice of the ridge where the shack sat, there was no one around, and light was cascading from the open doorway.

"I don't see a large Indian with a shotgun, do you?"

"No, and I'm hoping that that's a good thing." I was reassured by what sounded like voices and a barking dog coming from inside the shack. We limped to the door and carefully peeked inside. Henry had pinned Enic onto the cot and was attempting to hold him steady as Jennifer's mastiff stood barking in the corner. I entered and looked at the Coleman lantern sitting and hissing on the small table to our left—of course, Henry had been correct.

Omar had limped in beside me. "Did you shoot the Indian?"

Henry threw the words over his shoulder, "I am an Indian. I am allowed to shoot Indians."

I noticed the broken shotgun that Enic had hit me in the head with earlier, lying on the floor, and shrugged Omar onto the only available chair. "That seems exclusively racist to me."

"You can shoot as many white people as you would like."

Enic had looked better. "How is he?"

The Bear had pulled up the older man's shirt, and I could see where the pellets had hit just above the kidney, along his side where they appeared to have missed any solid organs.

I moved closer as the Bear pulled a large packet with a first-aid emblem from the folds of his poncho. "There are two more in the underside of the arm; he was turning when I fired."

The dog continued to bark until I'd finally had enough and yelled at him, "Shut up!" He did and promptly sat and wagged at me. "Good dog." I watched as Omar filched a Band-Aid and applied it to his nose. "Where did you get the first-aid kit?"

"From the helicopter—it was in the compartment next to the flower vases." He glanced at me as he began sorting out ointment, gauze pads, and strips of bandage. "Generally, somebody gets shot when we are involved in these types of adventures, so I thought it best to be prepared."

I knelt down and spoke to the older man as Henry ministered to his wounds. "How are you doing, Enic?"

He replied through gritted teeth, "Hurts."

"I bet it does." I grunted, "You shouldn't shoot at people; it pisses them off, and then they shoot back—it's a lesson we learned in Vietnam."

"I didn't mean to hit any of you."

"That's the problem with shotguns in the dark—they're kind of an indiscriminate weapon." I pulled up the tinderbox and fed some twigs and crumpled, yellowed newspapers into the stove in an attempt to get a fire going. "Did you shoot at the helicopter, Enic?"

He winced some more and then settled as Henry studied the damage. "A little."

"Hmm." Omar handed me a fancy lighter, and I started the fire, slowly adding a few larger pieces, including the broken stock of Enic's 20-gauge. "Last time I was here you hit me in the head with this thing, then you shoot our helicopter down and fill Omar here full of lead." I broke off the rest of the stock and threw it in the stove. "There, that should slow down all the shooting."

The older man jerked a little as the Cheyenne Nation poked at his side. "I did it."

"Did what?"

After a moment, he spoke again. "Killed my brother."

"And why would you do that?"

"I . . . I got tired of him."

"After seventy years, you got tired of him?"

"Yes."

I sighed. "Enic, you may be the worst liar I've ever met, and that's saying something 'cause I've met some doozies." I studied him, but he wouldn't make eye contact with me anymore. "Who are you protecting? I mean, this can't be just about helping the two young people, can it?"

The Bear stood and looked down at him. "You need proper medical attention, something you are not likely to get unless you start answering Walt's questions."

Enic turned his face away from us and remained silent.

The Cheyenne Nation held his hand out to me. "Do you have your pocket knife?"

"Actually, he's got a nifty skinning knife, don't you, Enic?"

The Cheyenne Nation extended a hand, and the older man struggled to slip the weapon from his back pocket. The Bear held the blade into the fire as Enic's curiosity got the better of him and he turned back to look at us. "What are you doing?"

"Sterilizing this knife before I cut the lead out of you." Henry watched the older man's eyes widen just a bit and then pulled his own elk-handled bowie from the small of his back. "Or I can use this one." Enic studied the eight-inch blade. "It is sharper, but I do not think it is made for delicate work."

I joined in, helping to make the case more intimidating. "We have to get the pellets out because of lead poisoning."

Enic gestured toward Omar. "What about him?"

I shrugged. "He's got only two pellets in him and you've got five, so you get to go first." I smiled. "That way Henry can practice."

He scooted a little away as the Bear drew the blade from the fire. "I think I would rather wait for a proper doctor."

I shook my head and rose, implying that I was going to hold him while Henry did impromptu surgery. "We don't know how long we're going to be out here looking for your family, so I guess we're going to have to get all western on this, as Doc Bloomfield would say."

Henry approached with the skinning knife held at the ready. "Time to get the lead out."

The older man was sweating and had somehow plastered

himself into the corner with his back against the wall, his heavy boots turned toward us. "It was Taylor."

"What?"

He swallowed. "Taylor thought that he had killed his grandfather by giving him the alcohol—I don't know where he got the idea."

I slumped and looked at Henry. "Where are Taylor and Jennifer?"

He had an answer for that but not a particularly satisfactory one. "I don't know."

I gestured for Henry to tend to Omar as I sat on the edge of the cot and palmed my face with my hand. "Enic, as I've said, I've got a lot of personal drama going on in my life right now, and I haven't gotten a lot of sleep, but the thing I'm really tired of is your family, and if I don't start getting absolute compliance from you, I'm going to lock all of you up for the rest of your squirrelly lives." I took a long pause and snuck a look at him through my fingers. "Now, I'll ask again, where are the rest of your family?"

"We can call the house."

I stared at him. "What?"

He fumbled in his pocket. "I have Taylor's cell phone."

I took it and looked at the blue and white Cheyenne flag cover. "What good is that going to do us?"

"This is the only spot on the ranch that gets reception."

I turned in time to see that both Henry and Omar had their phones out and were looking at me with affirmation on their faces. "It is true, I have three bars."

I sighed. "One of you call 911 and then get Ruby and the other try and get the Bobs and find out where they are."

Quick on the dial, Omar hit 911 and looked up at me. "Who are you calling?"

I handed the thing back to Enic. "Eva, please."

Henry was dialing as Enic hit a single button and handed it back to me. "What would you like me to tell the Bobs?"

Holding up a finger, I took the phone and held it to my ear. It rang three times and then went to a message, whereupon I disconnected and handed it back to Enic. "No one's answering. Where's the nearest road leading to this trailhead?"

He raised a hand and pointed over my shoulder. "The one to the Turtle Pond, four miles that way."

Back to the beginning. I reached for Omar's phone. "Bobs?"

"As per your request."

I held the thing to my ear. "Robert, are you guys at the Lone Elk place?"

"Yeah."

"Have you seen Eva and Randy?"

"Yeah."

"Where?"

There was some talk in the background. "In the backseat of our unit—Randy got a little mouthy, so Bob cuffed him."

"Do you guys think you can find the Turtle Pond?"

"The Turtle Pond?" There was more noise in the background, and I could hear whichever Bob it was on the line speak to the detainees in the backseat. "Well, we can go there, or we will not pass Go and not collect two hundred dollars and go straight to jail. Which would you prefer?" There was some more conversation. "We'll meet you at the Turtle Pond. You need anything else?"

"EMTs and such, but I think I've got Ruby on the other line."

"Roger that."

"Or Bob that, whichever comes first." I handed the phone back to Omar, exchanging it for Henry's. "Ruby, we've got two men with shotgun wounds and need medical personnel out at the Turtle Pond where we found Danny Lone Elk—can you get somebody out there?"

McGroder's voice broke in. "What happened to the helicopter?"

"It's, um, indisposed."

Ruby came back on. "Is it you and Henry who are shot?"

"Amazingly enough—" I glanced at the two wounded men. "—no."

I listened as she spoke with McGroder and then returned. "The AIC says he's pinpointed where you are from the four cell phone signals and can plot where the Turtle Pond is exactly, so there will be no problem in finding it."

I shook my head at the far-ranging abilities of modern technology. "That'd be great. We'll get there as quick as we can." I ended the call and looked at Enic, something niggling at the edges of my thought processes. "Okay. They must be around here somewhere if you've got her dog."

"No, I'm keeping him, but they're gone."

"Do you have a number for Jen?"

"No."

"When did you get Taylor's phone?"

He paused for a long moment, too long. "He gave it to me so he could call when they were safe."

The niggling kept working as I tried to get an answer out of the old coot. "Enic, at this point I'm not after either Taylor or Jen concerning any criminal offense. I just want to make sure they're safe and maybe get them home." He said nothing, and I was stuck, standing there with the niggling thought and nowhere to go. It was something on the phone, something McGroder had said. Or was it Ruby? Or maybe something Ruby had said about McGroder.

Four cell phones.

I turned and looked at Omar, then at Henry's phone in my hand, then at Enic, and then down at the trapdoor on which I now stood.

16

"If he tries anything, can I shoot him?"

I pulled the trapdoor but avoided looking down into the darkness I'd escaped only a day ago, listening to the rain continue to pound the shack's corrugated tin roof. "No."

Omar straightened his leg and made a face. "Can I shoot him if he doesn't try anything?"

I dropped down on one knee and stared into the abyss. "No, Henry says we can shoot as many white people as we want, but no Indians."

He slumped back in his chair. "Oh, all right."

The Cheyenne Nation crouched at the other side of the opening, his Benelli cradled loosely in his hands as I asked Enic one last time, "They're not armed, right?" The older man didn't answer. "I don't suppose you'd like to give them another call and warn them that we're coming down just to bring them back to safety?"

The older man pointed at Omar but still didn't say anything.

"Look, nobody is going to hurt anybody, okay?" I stood and took the 12-gauge from the multimillionaire.

"Hey!" He reached after it.

"I need it—it's got a flashlight."

"You're going to leave me here without anything to defend myself?"

I glanced at Enic. "He's over seventy years old and has been shot a multitude of times."

Henry looked up at me. "What are we looking at down here?"

"I think it was an old coal mine, but Enic said that back in the day the Hole-in-the-Wall boys used it to evade the law." I thought about what it had been like in the tunnels. "There are a few narrow spots, but I made it through—there's water, which has probably gotten worse since it's been raining for days now."

"How deep?"

"Up to your shins, but like I said, probably deeper by now."

"Any big drop-offs?"

"Not that I saw, but I was stumbling down there with a flaming mop in my hands, so it's possible I missed something."

Henry turned toward Enic and spoke in Cheyenne in words I did not know, but in a tone I did. *"Áahtomónėstse . . . Hena'háanehe, ma'háhkéso. Né'áahtovvėstse néstaéváhósévóomåtse."*

The older man looked at him for a long while and then replied in a low voice with more words I didn't know. The Bear interrupted him once, but then Enic repeated what he'd said and after a moment, Henry nodded and began climbing down into the hole.

"Be careful of the ladder, it . . ." As these words came out of my mouth there was a loud cracking sound and the splashing thump of my friend hitting the water. ". . . has some weak rungs."

His voice echoed up. *"Hahóo, ma'xhevéesevo'htse ooa'hé'e . . ."*

I didn't know what that meant either, but Enic was smiling as I lowered myself over the edge and eased my weight onto the ladder, careful to negotiate the broken steps. "Make a hole and make it wide." By the time I got to the bottom, I was knee-deep in the water. I turned and faced the dripping Cheyenne Nation. "You all right?"

"Nothing is hurt beyond my pride." He began casting the beam of his shotgun flashlight down the cavern behind me. "Where does that go?"

"I don't know, I got to here and went up. I was following the smoke marks on the ceiling from the other direction."

"And what is there?"

I thought about the layout of the caves and tried to remember. "It circles around to the right where there's a larger area, but then it squeezes in and turns to the right again and comes out of the hillside below the shack."

He shone the beam of the light on the surface of the water. "There is a current moving past you toward the area of the cave in which you have not been. If the water is flowing in that direction it must be lower and most likely of a larger capacity than the area you described."

"So you think the cave gets bigger in that direction?"

"I hope." He moved past me, shining the muzzle of the shotgun and consequently the flashlight ahead of him. "Neither one of us are exactly tunnel rats."

I followed, shining the light behind me only once and then flashing my own beam to the sides just in case we might've missed something, but he pulled up short, and I almost ran into him. "What?"

He stood there, silent, but then finally spoke, "Do you hear something?" He leaned forward, pointing the shotgun down the cavern, the light bouncing off the walls ahead.

"Nope."

He took another step forward but then retreated a half stride. "It is deeper here." The Bear continued to shine the beam into the darkness but eventually the light was swallowed up. "Did you hear that?"

"What?"

He said nothing but pointed the beam along one side of the tunnel where another jagged ledge protruded from the side like the one I'd encountered before. The ledge continued on into the darkness.

There was a sound in the distance.

"Did you . . ."

"Yep, I heard that." I swallowed. "Someone shouting." I moved past him onto the ledge, the sharp edges breaking off with my weight and falling into the water. I pressed my back against the rock and sidestepped my way down the narrow area, alternatively shining the beam attached to my shotgun onto the ledge and then into the darkness ahead.

Henry moved in behind me, and as we made our way slowly forward, I could clearly hear someone yelling. Cupping a hand near my mouth, I yelled back. "Taylor, is that you?" Thankfully, the ledge got broader, and I could concentrate the light forward where it appeared to hit a wall of solid rock on the far side of an open pool. "Hang on, we're coming!"

The voice came from my left. "We're over here!"

Creeping forward a little, I could see around an abutment where the two young lovers were clutching each other on a much larger ledge that slanted back into the rock, illuminated by another Coleman lantern. "What the heck are you doing over there?"

He stood and nodded toward the water twenty feet between us, sipping something from a Styrofoam cup and holding the fourth cell phone. "We waded over a little way back when the water was shallower."

I nodded. "Well, we'll get in and bring you two back over to this side."

He pocketed the phone. "You can't."

"Why?"

In answer, he tossed the white foam cup into the water between us, and we watched as it circled briefly and then submerged with a shudder and disappeared. "It's a sinkhole—it's where all the water goes, and I don't think it's a good place."

The Bear stepped up to the edge and then kneeled, dipping his arm in as far as it would reach. There was a sudden tug, and I grabbed his shoulder with my good hand to keep him from pitching in. He looked up at me. "The current is strong just beneath the surface, which leads me to believe that the hole is not small."

"Large enough to be sucked down into?"

He breathed a laugh. "Possibly, possibly not."

I looked at the distance between them and us. "Well, hell." Once again, I found myself willing to negotiate a timeshare on a portion of my soul, this time for a twenty-eight-foot, forty-eight-thread, right-twist lariat. Looking for anything that would be helpful, I played the beam of the light around, suddenly reflecting on the wires of the old electric lights that draped across the ceiling, the empty sockets looking like exclamation points.

I turned to Henry. "If I boost you up, can you grab that electric cable and yank it down?" I held the light on my face with the barrel of the Benelli shotgun alongside it and looked at him. "If you've got a better idea, I'd love to hear it."

Setting the shotgun to the side and making a stirrup with my laced fingers, I watched as he steadied himself by grabbing a rock nub and reached out and up to take hold of the end of the seventy-year-old conduit. He yanked, and the clips driven into the rock pulled away, the length of wire holding together.

The Bear held the cable in his hands and started looping it. "I find it hard to believe that this wire is still whole."

"Solid, braided copper cable—unless there was a break in the rubber housing it couldn't corrode and degenerate."

"Like what the helicopter blades hit?"

I nodded.

"We go over there, or they come over here?"

I looked at him. "I said it probably hadn't degenerated too much—I didn't say that it was indestructible." I glanced at the young couple. "They weigh a hell of a lot less than the two of us."

I stooped by the water and looked over at them. "Taylor, you two are going to have to come to us."

"And how are we going to do that?"

"I'll throw you this wire. Tie it off on one of the rock out-croppings on your side and make sure it's solid. Hold on to the cable and don't let go, no matter what happens."

"Okay."

"Have Jennifer go first." He nodded, I tossed, and we watched as he fastened the cable and assisted her in getting ahold of it as I pulled it tight and looped it over a cornice to my right. "You're going to have to work your way across the wire, and we'll grab you when you get close enough, but most of the time you're going to be on your own. You might dip into the water, but whatever you do, don't let go of the cable—got it?"

She nodded and then looked at me. "What about my camera?"

"What?"

"My video camera—I don't want to drop it in the water."

"You've got it with you?" I thought about throwing her in the water but then had a thought. "Just out of curiosity, does that thing still have evidence on it?"

"Yes."

"Toss it to me."

"You'll drop it in the water."

"Why would I do that?"

"So that the federal government can have Jen."

"I wouldn't do that."

"You're all working together against us."

I cocked my head. "Who is us?"

"The Lone Elk family."

"And when did you become a member of said family?"

She held out a hand with, what I assumed, was a wedding ring on it. "Taylor and I were married yesterday."

I sighed and thought about how even more complicated things had just gotten. "Throw me the damn camera."

She looked at the rushing water for a moment. "I can't— I'm not that good at throwing things."

"Have Taylor throw it."

She looked dubious but then handed it over to him in a moment of trust. I watched as Henry moved to the edge and prepared to catch it, catching items being in his background.

Taylor tossed it, and the Bear swiped it in midair. He gave it to me, and I carefully put it in the breast pocket of my jacket with the thought that being the highest spot, it would be the safest.

I motioned for Jennifer to get with it. "C'mon, the water's doing nothing but getting deeper and swifter."

She was in pretty good shape and relatively athletic, so she didn't have too much trouble shimmying along the cable with only her back and rear end getting dipped. "This water is cold!"

"Just keep moving." The Cheyenne Nation reached out a hand and grabbed her by the scruff of the neck, the collar of her jacket safely in his iron grip. Like a crane, the Bear easily lifted her onto the ledge beside me.

We all turned to look at Taylor, who stood there without moving, and I could tell something was wrong. "C'mon, it's your turn." He didn't move but just kept looking at the swirling water that led to nowhere, and I was getting a bad feeling. "Let's go, Taylor." He nodded briefly, as if he were making his mind up about something, something that was embedding a terrible resolution in him. "Taylor?"

His face rose, and I was sure he'd made up his mind. "I killed my grandfather."

Jen stepped forward. "No!"

I held her with one arm as Henry, looking at the young man, stood in front of us. "What are you talking about, Taylor?"

He swallowed. "I gave him his whiskey just that once." He looked at us for a moment, but then his eyes went back to the water. "I thought it would help, you know, make him feel better . . ."

He didn't say anything else but just kept looking into the

swirling darkness and then turned his eyes to Jennifer. "I really love you, you know?"

She pulled against my arm, but I held her fast. "Taylor?"

I watched as he leaned forward a little, almost as if ready to jump. "The whiskey was laced with mercury. Your grandfather died of mercury poisoning. It had nothing to do with the liquor itself, honest."

"You're just trying to keep me from doing what I need to do."

I gestured toward the Bear. "Henry was there when Isaac Bloomfield told us, right?"

The Cheyenne Nation stood at the edge, and I knew what he was contemplating, but it was too far. "Yes."

"The whiskey wasn't the cause of his death, Taylor—we wouldn't lie to you."

"Tell my mother I'm sorry." With that, he stepped into the void and dropped into the fast-running water.

Henry leapt in after him like a war lance and disappeared after the young man faster than a great white shark could've ever hoped to.

I pulled the loop from the cornice and let it drop into the water after them and then relooped the thing in hopes that the Bear would be able to grab the young man and the cable. Jennifer was screaming, and I was about to make the dive myself.

I pushed her back and moved forward, thinking that my next breath was probably my last when suddenly Taylor was thrust from the surface in a military press and handed to me.

I grabbed the wayward youth and extended my hand to the giant that rose up from the depths, the water at his waist. He stood there with his wet hair draping his head like a cloak. "It is only deep on that end, and as near as I can tell the drain hole is about the size of a small trash-can lid."

We pulled my truck up to the Turtle Pond just as dawn began to break and a few shards of pewter began chipping away the ironclad underside of the clouds. The Wyoming Highway Patrol cruiser sat with its warning lights tracing the hillsides and reflecting their colors onto the surface of the pond as Bob Delude came over and dripped in my rolled-down window. "Looks like it might rain."

I thanked him for thinking of us and parking my truck on the road as close to the shack as possible. "I appreciate that both of you uphold the eight core values of Integrity, Courage, Discipline, Loyalty, Diligence, Humility, Optimism, and Conviction that are integral to the success of the agency and a hallmark of the Wyoming Highway Patrol."

"Just tell Lucian to stop referring to us as triple A with guns." He laughed. "McGroder figured that if the going got rough, that's where you'd be coming out." He glanced in the back at the huddled Lone Elks, and finally at Omar, who was sitting between Henry and me. "Looks like it got rough, all right."

I threw a thumb toward the back. "Enic shot the helicopter and Omar, Henry shot Enic, and then we had to go spelunking for Taylor and Jennifer."

He shook his head. "His mother is fit to be tied."

"I bet." I glanced at the Highway Patrol car. "They say anything else?"

"They've just been bitching about being held, but I told

them it was for their own safety." He glanced over his shoulder. "Is it all right if I let them out so that they can come see that the boy wonder is safe and sound? 'Cause if that prick Randy kicks the back of my seat one more time, I'm going to find a hole to stuff him into."

I thought about it as the rain settled into a light sprinkle. "Sure."

As I got out, I flipped the safety strap on my holster, checked my .45, and then reholstered it. Bob approached the cruiser, opened the back door, and let Eva and Randy out. Thunder sounded over the high plains, and the smell of the wet grass and sage was intoxicating. I climbed out, opening the rear door and inviting the Lone Elk clan to get out of the vehicle. "C'mon, let's have a little family reunion."

Eva rushed over and grabbed Taylor's face and held it close to hers. "Where have you been?"

He said nothing, but as she pulled his face down to her shoulder, she saw Jennifer. "What are you doing here?"

I interrupted. "Um, there have been some developments, Eva. It would appear that these two have gotten married."

Yanking him out at arm's reach, she glared at him. "You're seventeen. You can't get married without my consent!"

The teenager nodded toward the older man still seated on the edge of the backseat of my truck. "Uncle Enic signed the papers."

I interrupted. "You three can work this out later, because right now we've got a more pressing question as to why Taylor attempted suicide."

Eva turned to me. "He what?"

"Taylor here attempted to drown himself about ninety minutes ago."

She turned to look at him. "What?"

I stepped between her and the boy, keeping my right hip toward Randy. "He said that somebody advised him to run because he gave his grandfather the whiskey and that's what killed him. He also says that neither he nor Jennifer destroyed her computer back at the rock shop."

I felt the tug as Randy, even handcuffed, deftly pulled the Colt from my holster and backed away from all of us. The Bobs immediately went for their sidearms, but I raised a hand and they stopped.

It was one of those moments where everything kind of comes to a halt; the breeze had stopped and it was almost as if the mist had frozen in midair. "What are you doing, Randy?"

He glanced at me, but his eyes shifted back to the Bobs. "I'm not taking the blame for this."

Taylor took a step toward him, dumbstruck. "You told me—"

"Shut up, I didn't tell you anything."

I squared off, placing myself between him and the rest of his family. "Then why are you holding my gun, Randy?"

He backed away toward the Turtle Pond. "I'm not getting railroaded."

I shook my head and stepped toward him. "You're not—I really already knew it was you, because you're the one who always placed that ceremonial turtle rattle in your father's hands when he was sleeping, and you're the only one in the family who would've known about the dangerous amounts of arsenic, lead, DDT, and mercury that those artifacts have after having been treated by the museums." I took another step toward him. "It was only after Dave told me about the contamination that I started putting two and two together, but the only ones I could think of who would possibly know about that problem were Dave and Jennifer here. But then I remembered that you had worked in the labs up in Bozeman."

"Stay back."

I took another step forward, forcing him to the edge of the pond. "And the two of them would never have had the access to your father like you."

He glanced at the Bobs, both still with their hands on their sidearms. "Don't either of you move."

I, on the other hand, took another step, narrowing the twelve feet between us. "Those years after college you said you had a job up in Montana? I've got a sneaking suspicion it was doing archival work. When you told me you didn't want me touching the rattle, it wasn't so much because it was a treasured family relic, was it?"

He raised the barrel of my Colt, pointing it directly at my face. "You don't have any proof."

"Not a lot, which is why I didn't arrest you before now, but once Taylor here tells us it was you who talked him into giving your father the poisoned whiskey, we'll be well on our way—besides, innocent men don't grab an officer's gun and point it at him."

He pulled the hammer back on my Colt. "I'm going to do more than that."

I took another step toward him. "You got greedy, didn't you? The rattle and the mercury-laced turtle food had been doing their work for a year's time, ever since you found out about your father's meetings with the Conservancy, but once the dinosaur was discovered you thought you'd speed things up, huh? The Conservancy was going to get the ranch, the museum was going to take Jen, and you'd be left with nothing. But what if you could stop that from happening? The clock was ticking. Danny could sign the papers any day, you thought, so you decided to help things along by putting mercury in the flask. Lucian drank some, but his stomach wasn't acidic enough to cause the mercury or the arsenic to absorb enough to kill him."

"I don't want to shoot you, Walt, but I will."

I took another step, bringing me within arm's reach. "It makes me sad to think of that old man out wandering the countryside with symptoms of alcoholism even when he wasn't drinking, talking to himself, and being baffled by the fact that every time he woke up in his chair he was holding that magical turtle rattle."

"Don't come any closer."

"I'm betting that your father was only tempted this once." I sighed. "The first time I met him he told me that he worried about disappointing his ancestors." I took the final step, pressing my chest against the barrel of my .45 and looking him in the eye. "I think that's something you should've considered."

He pulled the trigger, and we both stood there looking at each other, the loud click of the hammer falling on an empty chamber sounding like the turning of a key that could never be reversed.

"You should have trusted your father to not disinherit you, Randy. He wasn't going to cede the ranch to the Cheyenne

Conservancy and leave all of you penniless. He knew that none of you really wanted to be here, so he was planning to sell the ranch to the Conservancy and give you the proceeds. That is, until Jen was discovered, and he decided to give the ranch to the Conservancy and divide the proceeds from Jen among all four of you. I guess he figured more than two million apiece was pretty good." Calmly placing my hand over the slide action, I twisted the weapon away from him, took the magazine from my pocket where it had been all along, replaced it in my sidearm, and slipped the 1911 snug in my holster.

I started back toward the others, but the lesser part of my nature took hold and I stopped. I took a deep breath and expulsed it with my words. "I don't normally do these types of things, but I'm really tired and I've had a bad couple of days."

Putting everything I had into it, I spun around with a haymaker that caught him on his chin's sweet spot, sending him backward where he flattened out with his heels four feet from the bank, hitting the surface of the Turtle Pond like a depth charge.

As I walked past the others toward my truck, I made my final pronouncement on the matter: "You can fish him out or you can let the turtles have him—I really don't care."

EPILOGUE

We were all sitting at the Red Pony Bar and Grill, because it was the only place that had a television where we could all fit. The auction was being held in New York and most of the components of what was the largest and most complete tyrannosaurus ever discovered, named Jen for the young woman who had found her, now rested on red velvet-cushioned metal cradles.

Say what you wanted about the auction house, the largest broker of fine goods on the planet, they knew how to put on a show.

At least I'd gotten my holding cells back.

I had a front-row seat at the bar because I'd gotten there early along with Ruby and Lucian, my two cohorts. And thank goodness we'd gotten there when we did because I was pretty sure that the entire population of Durant and the Northern Cheyenne Reservation were now in the bar, many of them wearing the green and white SAVE JEN T-shirts the vendors had been selling on Main Street.

It didn't look good.

There were at least four major museums worldwide that were seeking the acquisition, some with silent partners from the private sector, some private collections, and even a Dubai sheik who wanted her for the entryway of his mansion. The High Plains Dinosaur Museum had a contingency in New York, but their hopes weren't too high—the little museum just didn't have the pockets needed for this kind of endeavor.

I'd caught a glimpse of Dave Baumann and some of his backers from the Wyoming oil and gas community in the crowd in Manhattan, but they looked somewhat out of their depth.

The Cheyenne Nation rested a cold can of Rainier in front of me, and then I watched as he stretched high for the top shelf where he kept the good stuff, including the bottle of Pappy Van Winkle's Family Reserve twenty-three-year-old. I turned to my old boss. "Are you sure you want to try that stuff again? The last round of rye didn't agree with you."

He watched as the Bear turned and poured him three fingers, straight up. "Gotta stay in practice."

The Cheyenne Nation returned the bottle to the top shelf and then poured a club soda for Ruby, who as far as I knew had never been in the Red Pony before. She lowered her voice and leaned in to me. "What is Dino-Dave's limit?"

I took a sip of my beer and rested it back on the bar, also keeping my voice low, so that the figure wouldn't become public knowledge. "He says he and his partners can go six point two, but nothing more than that."

Lucian spoke out loud before sipping his liquor. "Six million dollars for that bunch of bones?"

So much for keeping it quiet.

Ruby sighed. "So, that won't be enough?"

I shook my head. "Probably not."

The auctioneer approached the podium and addressed the room, welcoming all the bidders and explaining the rules, especially those for the bank of phones with operators in the gallery to the right. It would appear that the auction for Jen would be worldwide.

The Bear continued to serve the legions as a few people patted me on the back. "I spoke with Dave and some of the others, and they seemed sure it would go over eight."

"Maybe nine." I turned on my stool and found Agent in Charge McGroder smiling at me. He was truly undercover, if a little incongruous, in a polo shirt and a light windbreaker. He had left after the ruckus had faded, but I guess was back for the show. He raised a fist. "Save Jen."

I returned the salute, but with little enthusiasm. "What the heck are you doing here?"

"Oh, I thought I'd come back up, take a few days, and get a little fishing in."

I smiled at him. "And watch a dinosaur get sold?" We shook hands. "Where are your other agents?"

"They don't fish."

"They hardly eat, as I recall."

He nodded and motioned to the Bear for a beer. "Heard anything from your buddy, Skip Trost?"

"No—when the media dried up he disappeared."

"In more ways than one."

I turned on my stool and looked at him. "Meaning?"

He leaned in between Ruby and me, taking the proffered can from the proprietor. "Joe Meyer requested that he be removed."

I was stunned. "You're kidding."

"As you well know, Joe holds some sway back in Washington, and I guess he didn't give Trost the best of report cards—what the AG giveth, the AG taketh away." McGroder sipped his beer. "It's a powerful position, even on a state scale."

"Well, I'll be damned." Over my shoulder, I could see the auction was about to begin, but Henry stood by the cash register with the phone receiver in his hand, motioning to me. Foolishly, I pointed to myself and he nodded, too much noise to speak. I stood and stepped around McGroder. "Save my seat for me, would you?"

He slipped in and sat as I made my way down the bar and turned the corner near the back door, Henry meeting me with the phone, which he handed to me without comment. I held the receiver to my ear and gave the Bear's usual salutation. "Red Pony Bar and Grill and continual soiree."

"You moonlighting?"

I laughed. "Well, howdy, Mr. Attorney General, we were just talking about you."

"You and your constituency watching this auction?"

I glanced up at the TV. "Looks like it's about to get underway."

"Well, I don't want to keep you, but I've got a question."

"Shoot."

"Do you think your daughter would like to come work for me as an assistant attorney in the Criminal Division?"

Of all the things the highest law enforcement official in the state could've asked, that was the last I'd expected. I cleared my throat, just to give myself a little time. Thinking about what I wanted to say next, I mumbled a response. "I'm not sure."

"I don't want to offer it to her if you think she wouldn't consider the position."

I thought about the Greatest Legal Mind of Our Time. "Well, she's got a will of her own."

"I realize she's going through a lot right now, and I don't want to add to those pressures."

"How long would she have to decide?"

"Long as she wants."

"Well." I sighed. "I think you should ask her."

"I was kind of hoping *you* would."

I laughed. "Oh, no. I don't want her to think I had anything to do with this."

He was silent for a moment. "If you don't mind my asking, as one old bull to another, is it something you would be in favor of?"

I felt my eyes tear and my breath catch in my throat as I stood there leaning against the bar for support. I was thinking that he'd had this in mind since our conversation in his car in front of my office that day. Faced with a Machiavellian master, I did the easiest thing and just fell back on the truth. "More than anything in the world, Joe."

"I thought about sticking her in Water and Natural Resources or Tort Litigation, but I thought she might turn me down." There was a pause. "Anyway, I like the idea of the two of you locking horns every once in a blue moon. You got a number I can call?"

I recited Cady's cell phone number and listened as the attorney general scribbled it down. "I should warn you, she's kind of a pain in the ass."

"Like her old man?" He laughed. "Get back to your auction,

and I hope you win your dinosaur. Save Jen." The phone went dead, and I turned to find my oldest and dearest friend next to my elbow.

"What did the AG want?"

"Cady."

He thought about it and smiled, giving me the impression that he'd already figured that was what Joe Meyer had had in mind—the Bear, always five moves ahead. "Hmm . . . It would be nice to have the two of them nearer."

I hung the phone up and leaned against the jutting jaw of the cash register. "I guess Cheyenne is nearer. Don't know, Henry, she's so used to the big city, and Cheyenne is just Des Moines with a rodeo."

He patted my shoulder as he moved past with another beer and a glass of wine, picked up the remote from the counter, and turned up the volume on the TV. "Trust me, she'll be fine."

The dulcet tones of the auctioneer, with his prim and proper British—possibly not so prim and proper Australian—accent filled the crowded confines of the Red Pony, and the crowd grew quieter. "And here she is, the star of the evening, the undisputed queen of the Cretaceous period and the most recognizable dinosaur in popular culture. Jen, as she is affectionately known, was found in Absaroka County, Wyoming, by a young woman named Jennifer Watt and her dog, Brody, and from these humble beginnings has been determined to be the largest and most intact specimen of her kind ever to be discovered."

Lucian looked across the bar at me. "Did that limey just call us humble?"

"I believe he did."

"Cocksucker."

Ruby reached past McGroder and swatted him. "Watch your language."

The auctioneer continued. "The apex predator of her time, Jen is over forty-two feet in length and weighed close to eight metric tons. By far the largest carnivore in her environment, Jen is, simply put, priceless. But we will attempt to put a price upon her this evening—and the opening bid is—"

The Bear reached up to the top shelf again, and I was getting a bit worried about Lucian's intake when I noticed he plucked the phallic-looking original eighteenth-century decanter-style bottle from the good-stuff shelf, the legendary AsomBroso Reserva Del Porto, instead of the Pappy's. There was only one person I knew of who drank from the thousand-dollar bottle of tequila, and I watched as the Bear walked to the end of the bar and passed the tumbler, which went from patron to patron to where Omar Rhoades, talking on his cell phone, sat at a table by himself with his leg propped up on a stack of beer crates.

I waved, and he gestured back with the expensive liquor and a raised fist, mouthing the words "Save Jen."

"Who will start?" The auctioneer smiled and casually mentioned a figure. "One million, two hundred and fifty thousand?" He pointed at an individual in the audience who raised a paddle. "One million, two hundred and fifty thousand— good evening Mr. Gallmeister, good to have you with us."

I grumbled. "Smithsonian."

Those in close proximity nodded.

The auctioneer quickly pointed again. "One million, three hundred thousand, Mr. Matteson . . ."

"Field Museum, Chicago. I guess they want a pair."

He pointed again, this time to the gallery at the side. "One million, three hundred and fifty thousand."

Ruby arched an eyebrow and asked out of the side of her mouth, "So, who gets the money?"

I leaned against the bar and helped Henry by pulling out a few beers and handing them to the patrons as I turned to my dispatcher/receptionist/moral compass. "Eva and Taylor—the ranch goes to the Cheyenne Conservancy, with Enic having a lifetime interest according to Danny's desires."

"Where are the young lovers?"

"I'd imagine seeing if being rich is going to allow for their relationship. I guess after the video established sole ownership of Jen to the Lone Elk family, they decided to continue giving it a try." I gestured toward the millionaire in the corner. "And Omar decided to not press charges against Enic for shooting him in the leg and the helicopter in the rotors." I sipped my beer. "We're a forgiving folk, here in Wyoming."

"And Randy?"

"Not that forgiving—he goes to the big house in Rawlins. He was the one who convinced Taylor and Jen to run—he's also the one who destroyed the computer in hopes of getting rid of the video of his father at the meetings, and it was his blood at the rock shop."

Ruby shook her head. "But how did he get to the point of killing his own father, Walter? It's a part of this business that we're in that I don't think I'll ever understand."

I nodded my head and drew my face in close to hers in a show of solidarity. "Danny was a drunk for a lot of his life, a charming, funny and entertaining drunk, but a drunk nonetheless. That kind of thing can do things to families that can't ever be repaired. In the long run, Danny sobered up and became a good man, but the damage was already done and Randy just didn't trust him."

We glanced up at the TV as the auctioneer continued taking bids like picking posies. "Three million, two hundred and fifty thousand to Ms. Weisheit."

They all looked at me. "Fernbank Museum in Atlanta."

The auctioneer pointed at another paddle. "Three million, five hundred thousand to Mr. Baumann."

A cheer rose up from the crowd in the bar, but the bidding was off and running again. "Three million, seven hundred and fifty thousand dollars to Mr. Aslanides . . ."

I continued my running commentary. "Iziko Museum in Cape Town."

Lucian shook his head as the bidding continued at a heated pace. "Poor ol' Danny."

"Yep."

"So, who was out there wandering around the place that everybody kept seeing?"

"Maybe Enic . . ." I thought about the warnings I'd received in my dreams from the eyeless man and thumbed the Mallo Cup card in my pocket. *You will stand and see the good, but you will also stand and see the bad—the dead shall rise and the blind will see.* "But then again, maybe not."

There was another roar as Dino-Dave and the Wyoming contingency made their last-gasp effort in obtaining Jen. "Six million, two hundred thousand to Mr. Baumann."

I switched to the bar side but was distracted by two individuals at the end of the counter. I knew their plebian habits and limited income, so I fished two Rainiers out of the cooler and set the beer in front of them. "Who's minding the store?"

Saizarbitoria smiled and held up the pager that connected our 911 system to the carrier. "I've got the rock. We just stopped by to take in the action for a little bit and get a vote." He gestured beside him to his companion.

I glanced at Double Tough and slid down, leaning in to see the newest addition in the available light, stunned that it was an exact replica of the real deal in the other socket. "Good job, troop. Vic would be proud."

There was a tap on my shoulder, and I turned to see Henry, this time holding his cell phone out to me. "You are popular this evening."

There was a resounding booing of displeasure as the bidding continued and the hopes of keeping Jen in Absaroka County were dashed by another bid from the back of the TV house. "Six million, three hundred thousand."

I took the phone and cupped it to my face, knowing full well who it was. "Hey, punk."

"I just got offered a job."

I did my best to sound nonchalant. "Really?"

She sounded alarmingly like her mother. "Nice try."

There was another roar as the crowd began enjoying the Bread and Circus of the overt bidding, figuring that if Jen wasn't coming home to Wyoming, the bidders would have to pay the steepest price.

"It would be hard on Michael's family."

I turned away from the room so that she could hear me. "He said there wasn't any rush."

"I know."

There was another long pause, and I filled it by asking, "How's Vic?"

"Like a rock."

"Good."

"Like a pissed-off rock, but a rock."

The auctioneer continued. "You, sir? Are you bidding?" An individual raised his paddle, and the bids accelerated.

"Anything on Michael?"

"No."

I nodded at the receiver as if she could see me. "Something will break."

"You promise?" I didn't respond, and she changed the subject. "Who won the dinosaur?"

I glanced up at the TV screen and could see the auctioneer still plying his trade at a brisk rate. "The auction is going on right now, but we just went past the High Plains Dinosaur Museum's price ceiling."

"I should let you go."

"No, I don't care who gets the damn thing—I just care about you." I started toward the back. "I'm taking the phone outside where I can talk." I pushed through the heavy door and stepped out into the cool of the night, walked past the parked vehicles, and stopped under a dawn-to-dusk light where a few Miller moths danced overhead, the asphalt of the lot still glistening from the just-departed shower. "Are you going to take the job?"

There was a pause. "I don't know."

Taking the plunge, I spoke with all my heart. "I wish you would."

"What did you say, Dad?"

I took my time forming the words. "I know I don't have any place in making this decision, but I wish you and Lola were closer."

"I'd have to live in Cheyenne."

"Maybe your boss would let you come home on weekends."

There was a very long pause. "Did you have something to do with this?"

"No."

"Daddy?"

"I didn't, I swear. I know better than to try and choreograph your life." There were more cheers from the crowd inside, and I was sure the price for Jen was skyrocketing. "Why don't you think about it."

"I will."

"I love you, no matter what you do. You know that, right?"

"I do." Her voice choked up. "I have to go."

"Tell Lola I said good night."

"I will."

I hung up and raised my head as a few strangers who'd only been here for the spectacle trundled out of the bar and headed for their vehicles. I caught Bob Barnes, just as he began backing out. "How much?"

He looked at me, confused and a bit surprised, but then finally shook his head. "Nine point three million." He snorted. "Who's got that kind of money, Walt?"

I smiled. "Not us."

"That's for sure."

"Who got her?"

"I don't know, some guy with a funny name, from the Middle East, I think."

I was disappointed, thinking of Jen gracing an entryway, but at least the Lone Elk family would be partially compensated for the loss of Danny—if that kind of loss can be compensated for. I patted Bob's arm and sent him on his way. "Drive safe."

He nodded and waved, and I turned to walk back into the bar, pulling the Mallo Cup card out and studying it, thinking about the giant Crow Indian who had been haunting me. Maybe the visitations were over and wherever Virgil White Buffalo was, he was at peace—but I doubted it.

I stopped when I heard a sound, something strange coming from the back of the parking lot. Out of simple curiosity, I set off in that direction.

I looked around the corner of the black Conquest Knight XV and saw a man tossing pea gravel at a sign that read No PARKING. His aim was unerring, and I watched as he leaned on the front fender and continued a conversation on his cell phone while periodically pinging the metal sign.

As I walked around the outrageously expensive vehicle, I glanced at the tan leather interior as the George Armstrong Custer look-alike finished his conversation with "Sure, I can have the money transferred immediately." Looking a little embarrassed, he pressed the disconnect button and glanced at me as he unhooked his cane from the side mirror and adjusted his 100X beaver fur hat. "Finally, a nice night."

"Yep." I gestured toward the cane. "How's your leg?"

He shrugged. "Well, I'm doing some physical therapy." He threw another tiny stone at the sign, once again hitting it dead center. "When I was growing up, I was a pretty good Little League pitcher. I remember my old man teaching me." He thought back. "I was pitching and he was catching and then he stopped and asked me what I was throwing at and I told him I was throwing at him." The big game hunter turned to look at me. "He said that just him wasn't good enough and that I needed to throw at the third snap-button on his shirt."

I smiled at him. "Omar, did you just buy Jen for the High Plains Dinosaur Museum?"

"After that, I started getting a lot better." He threw another stone at the sign, the metallic noise still ringing in the silence of the partially empty parking lot as he responded with a roguish grin and raised a fist. "Save Jen."

Craig Johnson's twelfth novel featuring Sheriff Walt Longmire will be available from Viking in fall 2016.

Read on for the first chapter of . . .

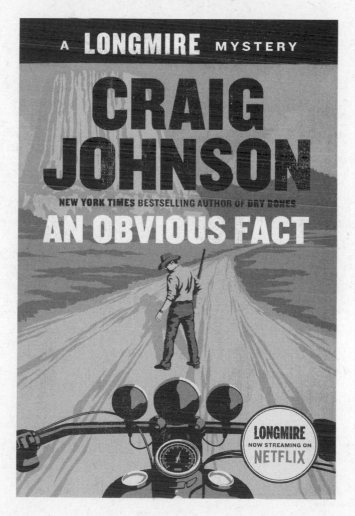

A LONGMIRE MYSTERY

CRAIG JOHNSON

NEW YORK TIMES BESTSELLING AUTHOR OF DRY BONES

AN OBVIOUS FACT

LONGMIRE NOW STREAMING ON NETFLIX

1

I tried to think how many times I'd kneeled down on asphalt to read the signs, but I knew this was the first time I'd done it in Hulett. Located in the northeast corner of the Wyoming Black Hills, the town is best known for being the home of Devils Tower.

I looked at the macadam blend, the stones shining in the mix that was still wet from the early morning rain, and sighed. With the advent of antilock brakes, it was hard enough to properly estimate the speed of a vehicle involved in a traffic accident, never mind in the rain.

"Do you see anything?"

I nudged my hat further back on my head and turned to look at the large Indian leaning against the door of Lola, his Baltic blue '59 Thunderbird and my granddaughter's name-sake. "How about you come over here and take a look for yourself?"

Henry Standing Bear didn't move and continued to study the large book in his hands. "I am on vacation."

I was kneeling at the apex of a sweeping curve on state route 24 where the road veered off toward *Matha Thipla*, the Cheyenne name for the first United States National Monument, so declared by Teddy Roosevelt in 1906.

"There is traffic coming."

I didn't hear anything, but that didn't mean he wasn't right, so I walked to the edge of the road and watched as a phalanx of motorcyclists came around the corner and descended toward us like a flock of disgruntled magpies.

They slowed—not for me, I wasn't in uniform—but because of the corpuscle-red Indian motorcycle with the modified KTM extended rear-axle dirt bike that roosted on the flatbed trailer behind the Thunderbird.

The leather-clad cyclists tooted their horns and gave a collected thumbs-up to the Cheyenne Nation as he leaned there, looking as if he were negotiating a treaty, with his muscled arms folded over his chest, the first volume of Leslie S. Klinger's *New Annotated Sherlock Holmes* in one hand.

"You could have waved back."

He shook his head. "That would not fit with the tourist's stereotypical vision of the stoic, yet noble, savage."

I glanced at the book. "Is that mine?"

"Yes, I took it from your shelves. I did not think you would mind if I borrowed it."

I glanced back at Devils Tower crowding the horizon. The geologic area around the megalith is not of the same composition as the tower itself, and the belief is that about fifty to sixty million years ago, during the Paleogene period, an igneous intrusion forced its way up through the local sedimentary stone, some saying it was an ancient volcano, some saying it was an laccolith, an uncovered bulge that never made it to the surface. "You know how it got its name, right?"

"Yours or ours?"

I ignored him and started back toward the T-bird. "When

Colonel Richard Irving Dodge led an expedition back in 1875, his interpreter got it wrong and referred to it as Bad God's Tower, which then became Devils Tower, without the apostrophe as per the geographic standard." I opened Lola's passenger door and eased in.

The Bear climbed into the driver's seat and studied me.

I reached back and stroked Dog's head. "You don't care."

"About what?"

"The apostrophe."

He hit the ignition on the big bird. "I care that a delegation of my people attempted to have the name restored to Bear Lodge National Historic Landmark, but your U.S. representative killed it. 'The name change will harm the tourist trade and bring economic hardship to area communities.'"

I knew the man he was talking about, and I had to admit that his nasal imitation was spot on. "But as an expert, what's your feeling on the apostrophe?"

He grunted and placed the book between us. "'There is nothing more deceptive than an obvious fact.'" Pulling the vintage convertible into gear, he patted the book. "Sherlock Holmes."

"Did you borrow all three volumes?"

He pulled onto the vacant road. "Yes."

"Oh brother."

It took a while to drive the nine miles into Hulett—eighteen minutes to be exact—because thirty miles an hour was as fast as Henry Standing Bear was willing to drive Lola (the car), especially while towing Lucie (the motorcycle), and Rosalie (the bike).

The Bear liked giving vehicles women's names.

We skipped Hulett's main street to avoid the fifty thousand or so motorcycles parked on both sides of the road. The town's population of just around four hundred multiplies under the August sun as bikers from around the world arrive for the nearby Sturgis Motorcycle Rally, which pulls in close to a million bikers each year.

Held in the town of the same name just across the border in neighboring South Dakota, the rally lasts a week. On the Wednesday of that week, Hulett throws what they call the Ham 'N Jam, offering free music and a thousand pounds of pork, three hundred pounds of beans, and two hundred pounds of chips; they also celebrate something they call No Panties Wednesday, though nothing in the official literature mentions the missing undergarments.

Our destination was the Ponderosa Bar and the Rally in the Alley, which was handy because the gravel back street was the only place where there was a parking spot large enough for the car and the trailer. Henry eased the Thunderbird through the crowd and parked behind a tent set up to sell T-shirts, patches, do-rags, and other souvenirs.

"Today's Monday, right?"

"All day."

I glanced around at the hundreds of people milling about. "And the actual rally doesn't start until Wednesday?"

"My thought exactly."

"Do you think you should put the top up?"

He shut his door and looked at the very blue sky. "Why? I do not think it is going to rain again this morning."

I shrugged and glanced at Dog, the hundred-and-fifty-pound security system. "Stay. And don't bite anybody."

A woman in a provocative leather outfit, a lot of hair, and a multitude of rose tattoos paused as she passed us. "Is he mean?"

"Absolutely." As I said this, he reached his bucket head over the side door and licked her shoulder with his wide tongue. "Well, almost absolutely." She smiled a lopsided smile, which revealed a missing tooth, and continued on down the road. I looked at Dog. "Just so you know, you could get a disease."

He didn't seem to care and just sat there wagging at me.

Moving to the trailer, I watched as the Bear used a chamois cloth to remove what dust had collected on the Indian motorcycle.

"Why do people ride these contraptions, anyway?"

He checked the tie-down straps and stood. "Freedom."

"Freedom to be an organ donor." I glanced up and down the crowded alley. "T.E. Lawrence died on a motorcycle. You know what I make of that?"

"He should not have left Arabia?" Henry climbed over the railing and stood next to me. "Where are we supposed to meet him?"

"Here." I looked around. "But I don't see him."

The Cheyenne Nation took a step and glanced down the alley, choked with bikers of every stripe, and plucked the *Annotated Sherlock* from the fender rail where he had left it. "Maybe he was called away."

"The only police officer assigned to a fifty-thousand-biker rally?" I smiled. "Maybe."

He carefully placed the book under his arm. "There is always the Hulett City Police Department." He glanced around. "If I were a police department, where would I be?"

"At 123 Hill Street, right off Main as 24 makes the turn going north."

"Far?"

"Almost a block."

He started off, intuitively in the correct direction. "The game is afoot."

I shook my head and followed as we made our way, taking in the sights, sounds, and smells that are Ham 'N Jam week. "Doesn't smell too bad, but maybe it's because I'm hungry."

He nodded and smiled at two lithesome beauties in halter tops as they grinned at him.

"What happened to your Native stoicism?"

"Well, anything can be taken to excess."

The crowd in front of Capt'n Ron's Rodeo Bar on the corner was spilling onto the street in joyous celebration of the open container law, which allowed alcoholic beverages to be consumed in the open air during rally week. The party was in full swing, the sounds of the Allman Brothers' "The Shape I'm In" drifting through the swinging saloon doors.

I looked back at the Bear. "Two of the Allman Brothers died on motorcycles—what do you make of that?"

"That if you are an Allman Brother you should not ride a motorcycle."

I sidestepped a short, round individual who was wearing a Viking helmet and drinking from a red plastic cup, but Henry got cut off.

"How you doin', Chief?"

The Cheyenne Nation half smiled the paper-cut grin he reserved for just these situations. "I am not a chief. I am Henry Standing Bear, Heads Man of the Dog Soldier Society, Bear Clan." He leaned in over the man, the bulk of him filling the sidewalk. "And who are you?"

The Viking didn't move, probably because he couldn't. "Umm . . . Eddy."

The Bear extended his hand. "Good to meet you, Eddy. The next time we see each other, I hope you remember to address me properly." They shook, and Henry left Eddy the Viking there, utterly dumbstruck—not that I think it took much.

"Oh, this is going to be an interesting two days."

We rounded the corner, the crowd thinned out, and we stood in front of the Hulett Police Department office, located next to what looked to be a fifteen-ton military vehicle.

The Cheyenne Nation rested a fist on his hip and stared at the white monstrosity. "What is that?"

I shook my head and pushed open the Hulett Police Department door. It was a small office as police offices go, with a counter and two desks on the other side. An older, smallish man sat at one them with his hat over his face. He started when I closed the door, but the hat didn't move. "By God, before you say anything, whoever you are, there better be a bleedin' body lying in the street before you wake me all the way up."

"You haven't been all the way woke up since I met you."

He slipped the hat off and looked at me. "How the hell are you, Walt Long-Arm-of-the-Law?"

I spread my palms. "Vacationing."

He stood and placed the straw hat on his head. "In lovely Hulett, Wyoming?" He walked over and, making a face, shook my hand. "During Ham 'N Jam?" He glanced at the Cheyenne Nation and then extended the same hand to him. "Henry Standing Bear—you come over here to show all these lawyers, dentists, and accountants what a real outlaw looks like?"

Henry shook. "How are you, Nutter Butter?"

William Nutter had been the chief of police in Hulett for as far back as anyone could remember. A tough individual with a mind of his own, he kept the town running smoothly; if the man had an enemy in the world, I didn't have an idea who that might be.

"Ready to retire and even more so after this last weekend."

I nodded and threw a thumb over my shoulder. "What, in the name of all that's holy, is that behemoth sitting out there?"

He smiled. "An MRAP, stands for Mine-Resistant Ambush Protected. We got a bunch of that Patriot Act money that's still around and some funding from a local citizen, name of Bob Nance. He wrote up all the paperwork for us. Hell, the federal government's got twelve thousand of the things—we grabbed one before the ban."

"Your town has less than four hundred people in it."

He gestured toward the overcrowded street. "Not today, it doesn't."

Henry parted the venetian blinds and peered at the thing. "What are you going to do with it?"

Nutter shrugged. "I don't know—we've got to figure out how to start it first." His eyes played around the littered room. "I got the manual around here somewhere, if you guys want to give it a try."

"It's very white."

"It was used by the United Nations."

"What does it weigh?"

"About fifteen tons."

"And how many miles to the gallon does it get?"

"I don't know, maybe three." He leaned on the counter and tugged at his hat like he was saddling up. "We're not allowed to use any town or county money to maintenance the thing, so either Bob needs to come up with some more funding or what it's going to end up being is a big, white lawn ornament." He smiled as Henry continued to stare at the massive vehicle. "She's a beauty, though, isn't she?"

I scrubbed a hand over my face and changed the subject to the one at hand. "So, you want to tell us about the incident this last weekend?"

He shook his head. "No, I'd rather you talk to the investigating officer, who I assume is the one who called you?"

"He did." I studied Nutter, taking in the accumulation of lines on his face, more than I'd remembered from last time.

He moved toward a radio console and, holding up a finger toward us, picked up one of the old-style desk mics. "Woof, woof—hey, Deputy Dog, where are you?"

There was a pause, and then a voice I recognized came over the speaker. "Please don't call me that."

Nutter immediately barked into the mic. "Woof, woof, woof! Where are you? The Lone Ranger and Tonto are here for a powwow."

There was another pause. "I'm down here in front of the Pondo doing a sobriety test on a guy who thinks riding drunk is the same as stumbling down the sidewalk." There was a voice in the background and more conversation before he came back on. "I'm right here on Main Street—how did I miss them?"

"We came in and parked in the alley."

Nutter relayed the message and then sent us on our way back to the Ponderosa Café and Bar. As we closed the door, he called out, "Don't forget to ask Deputy Dog how he got his name."

"It was stupid."

"It usually is." I leaned back in my chair, sipped my coffee, and studied the former Gillette patrolman and Campbell County deputy, Corbin Dougherty.

"Our K9 guy was a little weird."

"They usually are."

He sighed. "The dog companies were sending us all these samples—you know, shock collars and stuff? So the K9 guy gets to wondering how bad the shock is."

The Cheyenne Nation, who had been gazing out the window, turned back to look at the deputy. "What did he ever do to you?"

He shrugged. "His dog bit me. I mean, he's the K9 guy, so he should have control over his dog, right?" Corbin looked around the packed café and lowered his voice. "I told him he should try one on— you know, get a feeling for the things before he put them on his dog."

"No."

"Yes." He glanced around again. "So, we're in the day room, and this idiot puts the dog collar on. I don't mean just held it there; I mean he buckled the thing on around his neck. So, then he starts barking, real low, like 'woof.'"

I peered at him through the fingers covering my face. "Barking?"

"Honest to God—I guess he figured since it was a *dog* shock collar . . ."

"Let me guess what happened."

"Nothing at first, but he kept barking louder and finally it kicked in, and you've never seen anything like it. I mean, the things have these little prongs on the inside that are supposed to work through the insulation of the dog's fur, but this was bare skin on this idiot's neck."

I tried to keep from laughing, but it was hard. "Then what?"

"It flipped him back over the table and put him on the floor. Honest, it was like he was struck by lightning—like a Taser, only way worse. Well, every time the thing shocks him he yells, so it shocks him again."

"What did you do?"

Corbin paused as a waitress arrived and set our breakfasts in front of us. He watched her go and then continued. "What do you mean what did we do? Nothing. Everybody hates the son of a bitch; that damn dog of his has bitten all of us. So, he's flopping around on the floor, screaming and getting lit up like a Christmas tree, and we've all got our cell phones out taking video."

Henry nodded. "The brotherhood of blue."

Corbin sipped his coffee. "So, anyway, one of the other officers posted the thing on YouTube, and it went viral. The *Trib* did a story, and Sandy Sandberg needed a fall guy; I was the one with least seniority."

"So, here you are in Hulett."

"You weren't hiring."

I sipped my own coffee. "I'm always hiring."

The young deputy forked a strawberry. "Besides, it's nice over here, and I met a girl in Sundance."

The Bear and I looked at each other. "There is always a girl."

I remembered the pit bull we'd dropped on the young man last winter. "She like your dog, Deputy?"

He smiled. "More than me."

We started eating in earnest, and the conversation died down. Corbin, the healthiest of us, finished his oatmeal and fruit and straightened his paper placemat before introducing the subject of why we were there. "I hope you don't mind me calling, but I figured after you'd helped out with that mess in Campbell County . . ."

I leaned back in the booth. "This star for hire."

He looked up, a little panicked. "I can't pay you anything, Walt."

"That was a joke."

"Oh." He gathered his napkin from his lap. "Did you stop on your way in and look at the accident site?"

"We did, but it was wet and kind of hard to tell what had happened."

Dougherty glanced around at the crowded café again and whispered, "There was a lot of blood."

"Rain must've washed it away."

He nodded. "Yeah, I mean they had him stabilized down at County Memorial in Sundance, but they moved him to Rapid City. Too small a hospital to keep him here."

"He?"

"The victim—last name Torres, twenty-two years of age, out of Tucson, Arizona. He's got a bunch of priors, mostly drugs along with a few domestics, and an aggravated assault and weapons charge."

"Had he been drinking?"

Corbin shrugged. "A little, according to the doctors, but nothing too bad."

"Current condition?"

"Assorted, along with a whopper of a traumatic brain injury. B-way—" He looked up at me. "That's what they call him, B-way—has got a diffuse axonal injury where the nerve cells are stretched and sheared inside the skull. He was out for six hours and then came to momentarily, but he was acting strange. He's pretty messed up."

"Anybody ask him about the accident when he regained consciousness?"

"I did. I tried to get a statement from him, but he wasn't capable of coherent thought, never mind speech."

"Think he will be?"

Dougherty shook his head. "I really don't know—neither do the doctors, I think. They put him back in an induced coma."

I nodded and then glanced at Henry, who continued to gaze out the windows. "You file a report with DCI's Accident Investigation?"

"I did, and a guy named Novo is coming up tomorrow."

The Bear finally joined the conversation. "Mike Novo?"

"Yeah—you know him?"

Henry smiled. "He is the motorcycle expert in Cheyenne."

I watched Corbin for a moment. "So, what happened?"

"We got a call from Julie, a local girl who was working one of the tents up here part time. She was headed home when she saw a guy and a motorcycle lying on the side of the road."

"I'm going to need to speak with her."

He nodded. "It was about one in the morning on Saturday night, and with the traffic we get around Sturgis, it must've just happened. I got there just as the EMTs did, and they scooped him up and took him to Sundance. Herb Robinson, who owns the wrecker service, came and got the bike but then hauled it over to the Rapid City Police Department impound yard. I guess Robinson had past problems with bikers who liberate their bikes without paying, and the Rapid cops are the only ones with a fenced yard."

"What do you think happened?"

The patrolman pushed his empty oatmeal bowl away and rested his elbows on the table. "I think somebody hit him."

"Passing him? Rear-ended . . . ?"

"On purpose." He stared at me. "The bike was hit on the side, hard, and forced into the ditch. There's a culvert out there near the turnoff to the Tower—"

"Yep, we saw it when we stopped."

"Right." There was a pause. "What do you think?"

"I think you can jump to conclusions in these situations; there are just too many possibilities. Maybe it was a deer, the other driver was drunk, the kid was on his cell phone. . . ."

Corbin crossed his arms. "He did have a cell phone."

"Was it out?"

"His brains were out. . . . Everything was out."

I gave him another second. "I'll need to check the phone."

"Sure."

Leaning back in my chair, I listened to it squeal and finished my coffee. "So . . . why call us?"

"I guess this kid is a big deal with the Tre Tre Nomads, a motorcycle gang out of the Southwest, and things just got really weird really fast."

"How do you mean?"

"Members of the club were in Sundance already for the rally and strong-armed their way into seeing the kid at the Medical Center, but then he was transferred to Rapid City Regional and I guess they wouldn't let them in the Intensive Care unit. When I got back up here on Sunday, they were waiting for me at the police station."

"What'd they want?"

"They wanted to know who did it, who hit B-way." He shook his head and swirled the coffee left in his cup. "They said there was no way that he'd just had an accident, and they wanted a name." He leaned in. "I checked, and you know what? They're right. He's never had a traffic accident—everything else under the sun but not even a speeding ticket."

"Well, maybe they're just worried about the kid."

"No, it's more than that. I'm staying at one of the little cabins the city provides on the north end of town, and when I got through on patrol yesterday, one of them was waiting for me there."

"Okay."

"Big guy, kind of the enforcer, I guess."

"Alone?"

"Yeah."

"Okay."

"Wanted to know where we were on all this, what we were doing about it, and I told him that we were doing the best we could, but with the rally we didn't have the manpower to do a thorough investigation without help from DCI, but that they would be here pretty quick."

"And was he satisfied with that?"

"Not really." He studied me. "Can I ask you a question?"

"Shoot."

"What's the one percent mean?" He shoved his empty cup away. "When the enforcer, the strong-arm guy, said I better find out who did it, he said I better or I was going to meet the real one percent."

I nodded, allowing the information to surface in my memory. "The Hollister riot in '47. It was just a little after World War II, and they had this motorcycle rally in California in this little town. A lot more bikers showed up than they had anticipated."

"And there were riots?"

"Not really, but there were a lot of drunk bikers and racing in the streets. Things got out of hand. Hollister had only a nine-man police department, and they panicked and threatened to use tear gas and it got in all the newspapers." Somebody squeezed in near our table as I tried to remember the wording. "I think it was the American Motorcycle Association that came out and said the trouble was caused by the one percent deviants . . ."

". . . that tarnish the public image of both motorcycles and motorcyclists." I looked up to see a man in a leather vest, jeans, and motorcycle boots. "And that the other ninety-nine percent of motorcyclists are good, decent, law-abiding citizens." He slipped off his Oakley sunglasses and smiled down at Dougherty through a prodigious mustache and goatee. "The AMA came out later and said they never made the statement, but that's bullshit."

I picked up my coffee cup, studied the dregs, and then him, noting the do-rag under his reversed ball cap, his numerous earrings, and enough tattoos to print up a crew of merchant marines. "Hi."

He reluctantly averted his eyes from Corbin to me. "Hi."

"Were you there?"

He looked confused. "Huh?"

"Hollister."

He breathed a laugh. "No, bud, before my time. You?"

"Before mine, too."

He nodded. "Excuse me, but you mind if I continue my conversation with Officer Dougherty here?"

"Yep, I do. We're eating our breakfast, and we don't like being disturbed. Now, if you've got something you'd like to discuss, we'll be through with our meal here in a few minutes and will meet you out front."

He stared at me for a good long time, but I picked up my water glass and just kept drinking as he simmered. "Who the fuck are you?"

I finally set my glass down and stood, my size taking him a little by surprise. He was big—not quite as big as me—but he was younger, probably in his late thirties and built like a strong safety.

His hand dropped to the side toward the small of his back, at which point the Cheyenne Nation also stood, that move immediately getting his attention. As an aging offensive tackle, I was just as glad to have my running back with me.

I leaned in. "How 'bout we make our introductions outside?"

He hard-eyed Henry for a moment and then looked back at me, curving the corners of his mouth underneath his mustache. "I'll see you out front, bud."

I watched him leave, and we sat back down. I smiled at Corbin. "That him—the Enforcer?"

"Yeah, that's him."

We sat there for a while longer, but it seemed as if the conversation had fled the room, so I stood again. "What do you say we go out front?"

Corbin shook his head. "I think I'll change careers—fireman is looking good."

I grabbed his shoulder. "C'mon, Deputy Dog."

All eyes were on us as we exited the packed restaurant, and I noticed a few people were quickly vacating the area in front of the Ponderosa Café. I pushed the door open, and as we stepped onto the sidewalk, about a dozen bikers of all shapes and sizes immediately surrounded the three of us.

The Enforcer was seated on a chromed-out bike, a kind of turquoise in color, his legs crossed with a wrist hanging over one of the grips on his handlebars. "Welcome to my office."

"Nice view."

He shrugged as the others stepped back, letting him make his play. He was the alpha, and if he could handle us on his own, he would.

"Now, how can we help you?"

He pointed past me to Dougherty. "I need to talk to him."

"Why? Who are you?"

He stepped around the front of his motorcycle, came in

close, and extended his hand. "Brady Post. I guess you could say I'm the spokesman for the Tre Tre Nomads." I took the hand; he tried the old trick of grabbing my fingers, but I slipped the meat of my palm in and gripped him back. My old boss, Lucian Connally, had the strongest grip I'd ever felt, but he'd never been able to break me, so I wasn't concerned as Post began applying pressure. I gave just enough back so that we stayed even. His eyes were a deep blue, almost cobalt, and as he brought himself up close to me, I was surprised that he smelled like Old Spice aftershave. "Who are you?"

"Walt Longmire."

A PENGUIN READERS GUIDE TO

DRY BONES

Craig Johnson

"It was difficult to imagine anything that could kill the undisputed seven-ton queen of her time, but life had a way perhaps even then of humbling all of us" (**DRY BONES**, p. 117).

An Introduction to *Dry Bones*, by Craig Johnson

Veteran lawman Walt Longmire has tackled his share of cold cases, but even he's stumped when it comes to figuring out who owns the remains of a sixty-five-million-year-old Tyrannosaurus Rex named Jen. The good sheriff is a mite distracted by the imminent arrival of his daughter, Cady, who's bringing his five-month-old granddaughter, Lola, on her inaugural visit to Absaroka County. When a more recently deceased body emerges to complicate Jen's case, however, Walt is thrust into the center of a political maelstrom.

The specimen in question is only partially excavated, but Dave Baumann, the director of the High Plains Dinosaur Museum, is confident that Jen will prove to be the largest T. Rex found to date. He's also certain that Jen legally belongs to the museum. The fossil was found on private property owned by Danny Lone Elk, and Dave insists he paid the Cheyenne rancher thirty-seven thousand dollars cash for the rights. Unfortunately, Danny will never be able to corroborate Dave's claim.

Omar Rhoades is fly-fishing at a local reservoir when Walt and Undersheriff Vic Moretti notice him chucking rocks into the water. On closer inspection, he's trying to keep the snapping turtles away from Danny Lone Elk's body. Omar tells them, "Danny and his brother Enic protect them ... they're sacred to the Crow and the Northern Cheyenne" (p. 7). In turn, the turtles have already eaten the eyes out of their former benefactor's head.

3

Walt should be hunting down a Pack N Play for Lola's visit, but instead he's trying to figure out why a recovering alcoholic like Danny was toting around a flask of high-grade rye whiskey and a bottle of dubious medications from "a doctor in Hardin named, of all things, Free Bird" (p. 27). A visit to Danny's home does nothing to clarify the situation. Danny's son, Randy Lone Elk, has yet to learn of his father's death, but he does know that thirty-seven thousand dollars is a paltry sum to pay for a skeleton worth at least eight million.

Before Walt can blink, two more groups—the Federal Bureau of Investigations and "Fuckin-Big-Indian[s]" (p. 39)—descend upon his office, contesting the museum's claim. Walt's reluctant to tell Vic, but just before Danny died, he dreamt about a man with no eyes, who warned: "*the dead shall rise and the blind will see*" (p. 11). He'd experienced visions before, but was Danny trying to send him a message?

As Walt tries to untangle the knots binding the dead man to "the Hope Diamond of fossils" (p. 35), Cady and Lola arrive, followed closely by a devastating call from the Philadelphia Police Department. While Vic takes charge of Cady and Lola, Walt turns to Omar, Henry Standing Bear, and former Sheriff Lucian Connally for help when Jen's namesake disappears into the wilderness.

Deeply atmospheric and populated by the series' most beloved characters, *Dry Bones* features everything fans adore as Walt undertakes a politically explosive case while simultaneously grappling with personal tragedy and an unresolved threat from the past.

An Interview with Craig Johnson

1. **Is Jen the T-Rex based on a real paleontological discovery?**

   Oh, yes. I found out that pretty much every T-rex in all the major museums around the world are from Wyoming and a product of the dinosaur wars between Cope and Marsh, the two individuals responsible for the modern science of paleontology. They were in a horrible competition with each other and used the results of their digs to sell to these museums to finance their continued work. But the story of Sue, one of the largest, most intact T-rexes from over in South Dakota, was the seminal discovery with a conflict involving a rancher, the tribe, the federal government, and the paleontologists who discovered her.

2. **You write a lot about the conflict between Native Americans and the claims of those who arrived in the Wyoming area later. What do you think the U.S. government could do to improve the current state of affairs?**

   Probably stop using Indian issues as political footballs and further help the tribes in conserving the artifacts that have been stolen from them over the years.

3. **In *Dry Bones*, you juxtapose the stories of Cady's five-month-old daughter, Lola, and a sixty-five-million-year-old T-Rex. What inspired you to pair them?**

   Actually, much of this novel is about family and the relationships among families, whatever the species. We have a nine-year-old granddaughter and she sometimes acts like a terrible lizard. . . . Just kidding.

4. **Is it true that if a Native American corpse is missing its eyes, it's doomed to wander for eternity?**
The beliefs and customs concerning the afterlife differ from tribe to tribe, but the ones I represent are those from the Crow and Northern Cheyenne. This particular belief stems from the Cheyenne.

5. **Do you feel guilty about poisoning a beloved character like Lucian Connally?**
No, actually I think Walt feels like poisoning him periodically. . . . I think it's important to place the characters in situations that are perilous, especially when they insist on doing those things themselves. It's a part of the character arc, and sometimes they don't make it. Fortunately, this time Lucian did.

6. **Please tell us that the Conquest Knight XV is real, and also that dried buffalo dung isn't actually being marketed as a medicine.**
The Conquest Knight XV is real and you can order one up for the paltry sum of $800k. Chump change. As for the buffalo chips, unfortunately, dubious, non-Native individuals out there are marketing the stuff as medicinal.

7. **Henry Standing Bear feels that it's time for Lola to receive her Cheyenne name, but Walt thinks it's too early. When is it traditional for a child to be given a Cheyenne name? Do you have one?**
You can receive a name within the Northern Cheyenne tribe at birth, but Walt feels they should wait so that Lola understands the gravity and importance of the act. Yep, I received a name, *Ah-choo-sis*, or Tip of the Arrow.

8. **Do you see Longmire and company returning to Philly to seek vengeance? If not, where might Walt be heading next?**
The trouble with seeking vengeance is that life gets in the way and you are confronted with other obstacles before you can move ahead with your plans. There are other things the characters are going to have to

take care of first. In the next book, *The Highwayman*, Walt and Henry are called away to the Wind River Canyon to assist an old friend who appears to be, well . . . haunted.

9. **Over the course of writing the Longmire novels, which character—besides Walt himself—has surprised you the most?**
Both Henry and Vic, who tend to lead the novels in very different directions, but are a constant source of surprises.

10. **Are you enjoying the way the *Longmire* television series is unfolding?**
I am, it's like two separate but equal universes, and since Netflix has picked us up for season 4 and now 5, we've added a lot of content and continuity to the show.

Suggested Questions for Discussion

1. Almost overnight, the phrase "Save Jen" becomes a rallying cry throughout Absaroka County. What does Jen mean to local residents, including those who have no financial stake in her future? How can something like a sixty-five-million-year-old fossil bring a community together in a way that more mundane issues such as road repairs cannot?

2. Did your feelings about who rightfully owned Jen change over the course of the novel? Why or why not?

3. Vic doesn't speak Lola's name, but refers to her only as "the baby." Do you—like Walt—feel this is a result of her inability to have a child of her own? If given the chance, what kind of a mother might Vic be?

4. Henry Standing Bear says that Walt and five-month-old Lola have similar personalities. Is it possible to discern someone's personality that early in life?

5. In Walt's dream at the beginning of chapter four, Virgil White Buffalo wipes away Walt's tear and says, *"Good—we can use the humanity"* (p. 70). What might he mean?

6. Joseph Free Bird is a shyster who peddles useless and perhaps harmful drugs for profit. Should businesses like his be more regulated? Or does it behoove the buyer to beware?

7. Despite his alcoholism, Danny became a successful rancher after leaving the reservation. Based on what you've read about his character, what do you think fueled his success?

8. In what way does Craig Johnson use Jen as a metaphor for the novel's larger story?

9. Spoiler Alert: Don't read further if you don't want to know whodunit!

10. After Michael Moretti's death, would it be in Cady and Lola's best interests to return to Wyoming near Walt? Or should they remain in Philadelphia, where her mother-in-law can assist with caregiving?

11. Would Vic really kill Michael's murderer if she got the chance? How is Vic's desire for revenge fuelled by her complicated feelings toward Michael and Cady's marriage?

12. Do you think Tomas Bidart arranged Michael's death? Whether or not he did, do you agree with Walt's decision not to find Bidart?

13. Do you know someone who was raised by an alcoholic? If so, do you find Randy's actions comprehensible—if not justified—by Danny's years of alcoholism?

CRAIG JOHNSON is the author of *Dry Bones* and the eleven earlier books in his *New York Times* bestselling *Longmire* Mystery series, the basis for the Netflix original series Longmire. Johnson lives in Ucross, Wyoming, population twenty-five.

To access Penguin Readers Guides online,
visit the Penguin Group (USA) Web site at www.penguin.com.

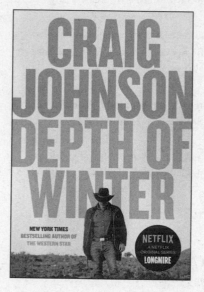
 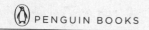